AUGUSTUS

Son of Caesar

Richard Foreman

First published 2015 by Endeavour Press Ltd.

This edition published in 2018 by Sharpe Books.

Dedicated to Anthony Foreman

Table of Contents

1.

"Three's company, four would have been a crowd. I'm glad Marcellus is away on business," Octavius whispered to his friend, Marcus Agrippa. Octavia – Octavius' sister – had left the room to check that all was running smoothly in the kitchen.

"What's wrong with him?" Agrippa – muscular, good hearted and good humoured – asked whilst mopping up the remainder of his squid in mushroom sauce with a slice of freshly baked bread.

"He loves himself far more than anyone else does in this world – and the next. He over-dresses and underwhelms. Every time he opens his mouth and speaks I find myself wanting to open my mouth too – and yawn. Marcellus –"

Agrippa darted his eyes towards the door behind him and he heard the rustle of his sister's silk stola. Octavius swiftly altered the course of his conversation.

"– is away, inspecting a potential business interest in Perusia."

In truth Marcus Marcellus was inspecting the wife of his potential business partner in Perusia. Although he would be losing sleep this evening, it would be due to courting his new mistress rather than regretting missing the company of his young brother-in-law.

Octavia entered the triclinium carrying a plate with a further slice or two of bread for Agrippa. Even standing apart, as opposed to next to each other as they were now, one could discern a strong resemblance between brother and sister. They shared the same fair complexion and hair, fine features, the same expressive (but also at times unreadable) eyes. Neither possessed an overly gregarious manner yet they were charming and memorable in any company. Agrippa could not help but notice the bond between them. Octavius cherished and respected his sister more than any other woman.

This was their second evening in Rome. It was perhaps the first time Agrippa had seen his friend wholly relax and be himself – after a seemingly non-stop round of visits and visitors – since entering the city. The cheers had been plentiful and people had come out to greet the new Caesar and the pandemonium had continued since.

"You will be pleased to know that Marcellus is often away on business so you may wish to come to dinner again. I am well aware that you would rather stomach my food than the company of my husband." There was as much good humour as censure in the remark. The playfulness in Octavia's expression – and her wit – briefly reminded Agrippa of Caecilia, his intended. They had recently met – and fallen in love – at Cicero's country estate in Puteoli. What with Caecilia being the daughter of the republican-minded Atticus – and Agrippa being the lieutenant of a Caesar – the two lovers were prudently keeping their relationship a secret.

"So, Marcus, what do you think of my sister here?" Octavius remarked whilst fondly and mischievously gazing up at his blushing sibling. "We shared much when we were young. It's only fair that we share a certain amount of awkwardness and embarrassment now."

"She is charming, witty and beautiful – to the point where I have my doubts that she could be related to you."

Octavius laughed in reply whilst shrewdly examining the look that Octavia and Agrippa exchanged. He sensed warmth, but no heat, between the pair. He would ask Agrippa how attracted he was to his sister in private. As Caesar had offered his daughter Julia to Pompey, to strengthen the alliance between them, so too Octavius (ever conscious of his great-uncle's stratagems) could utilise Octavia one day in a similar regard. Also, he wanted to see his sister and best friend happy. A union between them could furnish such happiness.

The trio continued with their meal as servants first entered with a course of spiced turbot on a bed of cucumber and rocket, and then roasted pork in onion gravy. Octavius ate little and watered down his wine more than his friend. But then it was mathematically impossible not to dilute his wine any less than Agrippa, who cordially complimented his hostess on every dish and vintage.

"So tell me Marcus, are you betrothed yet?" Octavia asked, thinking that such was his appetite he needed a woman in the kitchen as much as his bed. As Agrippa was caught with a mouth full of honey-glazed crackling Octavius replied for him: "Marcus is married to my cause."

"In that case you should make sure that you have an affair," Octavia playfully replied.

"Was that a proposal?" Octavius retorted.

"Gaius, you are lucky that Marcellus isn't here," Octavia, with slightly less playfulness infusing her tone, answered back whilst crimsoning, unable to look Agrippa in the eye.

"It could be you who proves to be the lucky one sister," Octavius remarked, suggestively raising his eyebrow, "but I do indeed consider it a piece of good fortune that Marcellus is away."

There was more mirth than malice in his comment but nevertheless Octavia's mask slipped a little and she seemed hurt by her brother's jibe. Akin to her sibling though she recovered her composure quickly.

"You must forgive my brother, Marcus. Ever since he stopped begging me to help him with his homework he feels he can say anything without recourse. But, although he thinks little of my husband, he constantly writes to me and speaks highly of you. And we both know how seldom he speaks highly of anyone."

"If you speak highly of everyone then the compliment is diminished," Octavius somewhat sententiously asserted. There was a pause then as both he and Agrippa remembered Cleanthes, the original author of the saying. Cleanthes, Octavius' satirical and sagacious personal tutor, had died whilst their party was attacked by hired assassins as they ventured along the Appian Way towards Rome. The pair remembered the legionaries Roscius and Tiro Casca who had also perished, protecting Octavius, in the skirmish. The two friends fleetingly shared a look, their faces exhibiting sorrow and attempted consolation. A little confused as to the import of the strange moment between her guests Octavia changed the subject.

"Now, although I can no longer help you with your homework brother, is there anything I can do? What are your plans?"

"I will claim my inheritance," the young Caesar stated, simply and sternly. Witnessing how taken aback his sister was by his reply Octavius smiled and flippantly added, "How else will I be able to afford to keep mother in shoes?"

A short pause ensued, before Octavia responded: "You cannot afford to make too many enemies."

"I can if I befriend the legions. And I will need my inheritance to do so. I heard today how, before Caesar's body was even cold, Antony visited Calpurnia. Taking advantage of her frail state he secured Julius' papers and treasury. But he will not take advantage of me."

Agrippa frowned, recalling his visit to Caesar's house that afternoon. It was not just the lack of a retinue missing from the former dictator's house which had made the property seem empty – even the acoustics made the house seem like a mausoleum. Octavius described Calpurnia as being the shadow of the woman she once was. Her nerves were frayed from grief as well as the stress of Caesar's creditors calling on her. Octavius instructed his aunt to now direct all the money-lenders to him, to answer for the debts.

Aside from his debts the only thing which Octavius had inherited from Caesar that afternoon was a servant. Calpurnia introduced the aged Jew, Joseph, to Octavius. A large head bobbed up and down on a scrawny body. There was more hair sprouting from his ears and nostrils than his scalp. Hopefully his head housed more sense than teeth. When Calpurnia exited Octavius had interviewed the servant, who had served both Julius and his father before him.

"So, Joseph, tell me – why I should take you on?" Octavius had asked whilst sitting on a large chair behind the ornate cedar wood desk of the former dictator. The elderly Jew had squinted and raised his eyes as if looking up to his brain for inspiration on how he should respond. Yet there had also been a humorous glint in his aspect as he answered.

"Well, if my hand doesn't shake too much and cut your throat, I am a skilled barber. I shaved your great-uncle most mornings."

"Our fellow here either has a sense of earnestness, or humour, Marcus, wouldn't you say?"

"Indeed. And do you have anything else to offer?" Agrippa had asked, amused and somewhat intrigued by the wizened Jew.

"I can offer you my prayers. Your enemies pray to the same gods as you. As such you may receive equal good fortune from them. Your enemies do not pray to my God however – so I may tip the balance of divine favour."

Octavius laughed.

"Caesar never mentioned your peculiar humour to me Joseph but he did say how you were one of the most honest and loyal men he had ever known."

"I fear I had little competition. Most of the men Caesar knew were politicians."

Agrippa recalled the comment and smiled inwardly. He would report the encounter in his letter to Caecilia later in the evening. He loved sharing his day with her in a letter – and longed to share her bed.

"You still have the option of returning to Apollonia. Mother has enough shoes already. You can return to your studies – live a quiet but contented life," Octavia argued.

Her words echoed those spoken by Cleanthes, shortly before he died. Octavius gently shook his head and grimly replied (quoting a line from an old play that resonated for him): "I am in blood – stepp'd in so far, that, should I wade no more, returning were as tedious as go o'er."

2.

Morning. The camp of the Fourth Legion, just outside of Asculum.

A watery mist poured itself over the rows of tents. The smell of wet grass and steaming porridge hung in the air. Familiar sounds accompanied familiar smells: the clanging of pots and pans and tamp of marching caligae. Antony stood in the principia by the sacellum, the shrine which held the legion's eagle. He was conscious of holding the meeting in the presence of the sacred totem. He would employ any device necessary to help stir loyalty and secure support. He had deliberately left a half-eaten centurion's breakfast, of cooked meats and cheese, on the table. He wished to convey that, at heart, he was still one of them.

Sunlight began to drift into the tent, as did the cadre of senior officers Antony had arranged to meet. He told himself again that he was here to bargain – not beg. He smiled and nodded but would wait for all six men to enter before he spoke.

First was Cephas Pollux. Caesar had once joked that such was his hard-headedness that he need not wear a helmet into battle. Although usually as garrulous as a Spartan it would perhaps be this ardent Caesarian who would speak for the group. His rank and experience merited seniority.

Next came Gratian Bibulus, limping a little from where the damp air was cramping up an old knee injury. There were fewer superstitious men in a devoutly superstitious army. After each battle he would order his cohort to dilute their wine with blood and toast their fallen comrades. He also abstained from sex until he earned the pleasure through the killing of an enemy.

Felix Calvinus followed. His nickname was Paris due to his good looks and way with women. Enobarbus had informed Antony of

15

his taste for gambling, as well as women. Providing the price was right, Calvinus' loyalty could be bought, Antony surmised.

Upon his heels entered Manius Sura. His nickname was Patroclus, such was his way with men. As he grew older his lovers grew younger. Drink appeared to be a vice too. The Etruscan's nose was as red as the clay soil of his homeland.

Aulus Milo's bulkiness nigh on blocked out the light as he entered the tent. A blacksmith's son from Ravenna, his immaculately maintained armour and weapons were a testament to his former mentor. Tiro Casca had taken the recruit under his wing upon first joining the army – and Antony thought how Milo would run him through in a second if he knew that he was behind the attack on Octavius which had led to his Casca's demise.

Matius Varro was last to enter. Like Enobarbus, Varro was as much a scholar as a soldier. His manner and education bespoke of a moneyed and privileged background yet Antony was unaware of his family and Varro's life before the army. Although studious and somewhat introverted Matius was a good officer – and when he had a drink inside him he could be gregarious and entertaining. Many a time had Antony been there when Varro had enthralled half a cohort by reciting Homer around the campfire – or composing satirical epigrams about comrades or politicians. Varro had always intrigued Antony a little – perhaps now more than ever. For just as Matius' past was a blank page Antony could not be rightly sure where his loyalties would lie in the future either. Varro had served under Caesar yet one often found him reading tracts by the likes of Cato or Brutus.

Antony stood with his hand resting on the golden pommel of his long cavalry sword. Tanned, scarred, stubble-dusted faces stared back at him. The figures were a marriage of honour and savagery.

"Gentlemen, welcome. Stand at ease. I may wear a toga more than a uniform nowadays but I am still as much your friend and comrade as I am your consul," Antony warmly expressed, borrowing his opening from a speech which Caesar had once given to potentially mutinous officers. He approached the soldiers, smiling and clasping them heartily by the forearm in a Roman handshake.

"Cephas, how are you? I trust you have had time to visit your wife, or at least your mistress? It has been a long time – too long. Much has changed."

"But not for the better," the centurion gruffly replied, recalling the loss of Caesar.

"No, Caesar's death casts a shadow over us still. You are right," Antony enjoined, whilst inwardly seething at the officer's impudence. He retained his composure and gracious manner, however, to work his way down the line.

"Bibulus, the last time I saw you we were in that brothel in Pisa. It was a shame that snowstorm kept us there an extra night, eh? ... Screwed any of my former mistresses lately, Calvinus? ... Sura, I have with me an amphora of your favourite vintage ... Milo, I was sorry to hear about Tiro Casca. I know you were close. He was an old friend to me too ... Varro, you are looking well. Enobarbus sends his regards."

Antony then beckoned for his attendants to serve some wine and food. Once the servants departed Antony formally opened proceedings.

"You know why I am here. You can either refute these rumours or confirm them – and then what will be will be. It has come to my attention that a number of officers and wish to declare their loyalty to Octavius." Sternness displaced warmth in the consul's tone.

As the officers had discussed beforehand, Pollux would speak for them.

"Permission to speak freely, sir."

"Granted."

"It is not our desire to choose between you and Octavius – but rather we wish to serve you both. The legions want you to become allies, not opponents. Only by operating together will we be strong enough to defeat the Senate's forces and avenge Caesar's murder."

"Are you somehow saying that I should treat this boy as my equal, that we should hold joint command?" Antony replied, ire and bewilderment firing his aspect and flaring his nostrils. "He's just a fucking boy, with about as much noble blood as a Gaulish drab. He has spent more time potty training than he has training to be a soldier."

Antony's hands gripped the pommel of his sword even tighter but, despite his rush of blood, the weapon remained in its scabbard. Although brave enough to fight any man, Antony was smart enough to realise he could not defeat every man. In contrast to Antony's fury and bombast the deputation of officers remained calm. Antony increasingly sympathised with the philosophy of Pompey and Caesar, that it was the army, rather than the Senate, who ultimately decided the fate of Rome. He currently needed the legions more than the legions needed him.

"I apologise my friends. But be wary of the boy. He'll fill your ears with promises rather than your purses with gold – whilst I will make good my word and grant every man an additional one hundred denarii who serves under my banner. You will be rewarded accordingly too."

"Octavius has promised five hundred denarii to every man."

"He is but a child, playing with pretend money. Your men can be spending my bonus within a fortnight. They may find it more difficult to cash in mere promises."

"The first payment from Caesar has already arrived, with a letter from Oppius to say that more will follow. And Oppius' word is as good as any bond I warrant," Aulus Milo announced in his rough, rural accent.

The light dimmed outside and Antony could hear the faint splatter of rain against the tent. The offer – and its apparent acceptance – filled his breast with rage and astonishment and he shook his head in disappointment.

"Have you become mercenaries rather than centurions – willing, like some harlot, to be purchased by the highest bidder? Has the rainy season washed away your honour? Does this eagle behind me mean nothing to you? You should be ashamed to look upon it."

All, aside from Pollux, could not look Antony, or the gleaming eagle, in the eye. They lowered their heads in shame though their resolve to side with Octavius (or better still encourage the two Caesarians to join together in a coalition) remained the same.

"If you match the boy's offer then we will reconsider. Know though that our actions are not solely motivated by money. If we declare for you we would also want to defeat Decimus Brutus for being Caesar's assassin, as well as for being your enemy. Cassius Longinus and Marcus Brutus should meet the same fate."

Although a flabby stomach hung over his belt beneath his breastplate Antony still possessed an imposing physique. His bulging biceps tensed, as did his face in a sneer, as he approached the senior officer.

"You seem to have forgotten your basic training Pollux. A general gives orders to his army – the army does not command its general. I came here today to make peace with you all but it seems you wish to declare war."

A pregnant pause ensued. Sweat trickled down Pollux's brow. He could smell the cheese and salted ham on Antony's breath as he stood and snorted in front of him. Pollux and Milo, akin to Antony, gripped their swords. The pair had formed a pact beforehand that they would defend each other if things should turn nasty. Both men were devoted to Caesar and resented Antony for making peace with Caesar's assassins. Finally Sura spoke and eased the tension.

19

"We should not give the libertores the satisfaction of having us fight among ourselves. We all stood together at Alesia and Pharsalus. We should all stand together now."

"Aye, we should draw breath before we draw any swords," Calvinus enjoined, fraternally placing his hands on the shoulders of Antony and Pollux. "All of us here have carried the legionary's shovel but let us not dig a hole for ourselves by becoming so entrenched in our positions that conflict becomes sovereign over a will to compromise and conciliate."

"Antony, if any legions declare for Octavius then know that being for him does not mean that we are against you. We urge you to return to Rome though and embrace the young Caesar. The gods, as well as the legions, would smile on such a union," Bibulus, raising a hand to the heavens, declaimed.

Embrace him? I'll crush him – Antony sneeringly thought to himself but nevertheless smiled and eased the confrontational atmosphere.

"Who am I to argue with you, or indeed the gods, Bibulus? Sura, you are as wise as you are valorous. We should not fight amongst ourselves. Come, let us not waste this time together or this fine vintage."

Matius Varro observed the scene in silence, half amused and half worried.

Playing the host again Antony filled his guests' cups. The rain drummed harder on the roof of the principia. A low gurgle of thunder sounded in the background.

"Let us raise a toast, rather than our voices. Let us drink to peace between friends and war upon our enemies," Antony cordially announced whilst inwardly judging which of his former friends might prove to be his future enemy.

3.

Dear Cicero,

Antony returned to Rome today. Agrippa and I watched him enter from the Servian Wall. Such was the size of the army that accompanied him – it must have numbered around five thousand – Agrippa wondered whether Hannibal and Alexander had come back from the dead and allied against the consul. Although it should be noted that Antony pronounced the force to be his "personal bodyguard" rather than an army.

Rome seems a living, breathing mosaic (fragmented, but the whole appears cohesive) – a marriage of circadian appetites and divine inspiration. I find myself longing for the quietude of the countryside sometimes, though I know if I was so located I might then yearn for the diversions of Rome. Streets drip with wealth or conversely poverty. I try to remain anonymous but when recognised the populace offer their condolences and support. Coins are thrust into my hands (which I give back) and I receive dinner invitations from strangers, whether walking through the Subura or Forum.

Invitations from senators have been conspicuous by their absence though. If you know of anyone who can hold their drink as well as a conversation I would be grateful for an introduction. Unlike Aulus Hirtius I will leave enough food for their breakfast the next day too.

Thank you for your previous letter and the copy of Demosthenes which accompanied it. Which, to your mind, is his best speech? I shall take note and read it with added interest.

In reply to your letter I share your surprise – and contempt – at the open corruption which made Lepidus Pontifex Maximus. Antony appears to be dishing out favours to all and sundry yet he is far from in credit with everyone – the populares and optimates alike – as a result. At least the Vestal Virgins are likely to want to keep their virtue in his presence. Ironically however Lepidus is the only man whom his wife remains virginal towards.

I look forward to you returning to Rome. I would welcome your counsel and company.

Gaius Octavius Caesar

Cicero sometimes smirked, sometimes grunted and sometimes furrowed his already wrinkled brow at reading and re-reading Octavius' letter. The aged statesman sat at his desk, his back to the open window. Outside pink blossom coloured and scented a well-kept garden. Flowers craned their heads towards a glistering sun, gently fanned by a spring breeze. Bees thrummed and birds performed their trill songs and courtship dances.

Cicero's secretary, Tiro, sat at an adjacent desk and diligently ploughed through a variety of correspondence.

"Tiro, read this. It's from our baby Caesar," Cicero remarked, handing over the letter. "I will de-code his shorthand for you. He first reminds me of Antony's martial intentions and strength – as if I need reminding of such a thing," he uttered and sighed, briefly slumping in his chair a little before regaining his vigour and train of thought. "The sight of five thousand troops attending upon Antony does not blind me to his own recruitment campaign. The Fourth Legion will probably declare for Octavius. Money and promises are also being offered, through Oppius and Balbus, to other Caesarian forces and retired veterans. But our young friend fails to mention this in his gossipy missive. But the truth is we must turn a blind eye to his illegal recruitment of a private army – for every soldier who declares for Octavius will be one less man standing in Antony's ranks.

"Again we find ourselves employing the arts of politicking and rhetoric but ultimately we will need to remember simple arithmetic.

We must count up who will command the most legions. Antony commands six in Macedonia, three in Campania. As he commands Lepidus, so too might he command his legions. Antony will look to sequester the legions posted in Gaul but Decimus Brutus will not hand over a single pack mule from his forces there. Hirtius and Pansa will command the forces loyal to the Republic although we need to squeeze more money out of the optimates to maintain their loyalty. Blood from a stone is a phrase that comes to mind though Tiro. Why is it that our best men have so often proved to be the worst men over the years?" Again Cicero sighed but again he mustered himself as he witnessed Tiro's reactions whilst reading the letter. "And how arrogant does our young friend think he is, flaunting his modesty so? He says he has tried to remain anonymous – aye, about as much as Antony has tried to remain celibate. There is not a street corner in Rome where he has not acted out the role of the disinherited orphan who is only trying to do right by his father and the people. Yet, though the mob may have fallen for his act, the political classes are snubbing him – hence his plea for me to grant him some introductions. In order not to snub him myself I shall send a few letters of introduction – but to those Caesarian senators who he already knows and possesses the support of."

Tiro wryly smiled at the wily statesman's cunning and Cicero permitted himself a chuckle, pleased as he was by his own stratagem.

"This is just like old times Tiro, no? Again we are trying to steer a politic course between Scylla and Charybdis. Again we seem to be stuck in the middle."

"You should judge it as akin to being centre stage," Tiro answered, fondly gazing at his master – and then popping a brackish olive into his mouth.

"You know how to both flatter and ridicule me better than I can myself old friend. But let us not fool ourselves, Rome is where one sees the action and garners applause. I can but wait in the wings for now. Antony is too powerful at present. I cannot risk him arresting me, or worse. Anything new to report?"

"Despite the enmity in his letter Octavius has requested to meet Antony. Doubtless he will be asking for his inheritance."

"The most he will get from that meeting is an insincere promise of a part payment."

"Agrippa also disclosed in a letter to the young Salvidienus that it is Octavius' intention to approach his cousins for support, Pinarius and Pedius, who were also benefactors in Caesar's will."

"The old Salvidienus has been quite a font of information."

"The likelihood is that he has passed the same information on to Antony. He is hedging his bets."

"Everybody has to stand somewhere though when the fighting begins. In the same way that the father intercepts his son's mail let us try to intercept the father's. We may be able to use Salvidienus to feed Antony false information."

Tiro handed the letter back and echoed Octavius by asking, "Which is, to your mind, Demosthenes' best speech?"

"His longest one. When I was a young advocate someone once asked me which speech by Hortensius I preferred. With my sense of humour overruling my sense of judgement I replied 'the shortest one'. But I miss my old rival. I remember attending a lavish party he once arranged for his fellow advocates at his country villa. After dinner he had his musicians play and – as if by magic – all manner of woodland creatures ventured out from the forest. Of course our host had trained them to do so by having the animals equate the music with being fed. But it was quite a sight.

"Believe it or not I found myself missing Caesar the other day too. Julius may have been a tyrant, thief and butcher but one could never have accused him of being boring. Cluvius, a banker friend, left this property to both Caesar and I. I purchased Julius' share at a more than reasonable price. When he visited he used to lounge in the exact same spot where Octavius decided to sit in the garden. I was going to tell the boy but I did not want to encourage him in any conceit that he is his great-uncle re-cast. Yet he is as impressive as Julius – but in different ways. If I had not met him for myself I would now be saying that the heir is but a puppet of Balbus. But our baby Caesar is his own man, for good or ill. I am told he lives quite modestly, despite his wealth. Perhaps I could be an Aristotle to his Alexander. However, although I may flirt with Octavius know that I am still married to Brutus and his cause Tiro. For all of the olive branches that Octavius offers with one hand I am worried that he clasps a knife in the other. As you know my friend, I am not one for being superstitious – unless there is a full moon," the satirical statesman said with a wink. But his features then dropped, the light vanished from his eyes. "But I had a strong presentiment the other evening that somehow Octavius will be the death of me."

4.

"Don't think, just do," Quintus, the young Roman officer, whispered to himself as he crouched on the mountainside, waiting for the signal to attack the oncoming wagon train (carrying a cache of arms, bound for Antony's forces in Macedonia). Quintus thought how diametrically opposed this new mantra was to that of his father's, "Think before you act," who had often expounded on his theme whilst walking his son to Orbilius' lauded college in Rome. Quintus hoped that the gods would forgive him for choosing the advice of his centurion over his tax-collector father during his first engagement.

A sweaty palm clasped a zealously sharpened gladius. Dusk was a dull red, akin to the colour of his dusty leather breastplate. Despite the drop in temperature his helmet still felt like an oven, with his head the guinea fowl inside it. His hand shook a little as he opened his canteen and took another swig of water. A craggy-faced legionary beside him offered an encouraging wink and smile. Sometimes he thought it was the legionaries who commanded him, rather than he them.

Again he listened intently – more intently than he ever did during his lectures in Athens. It was whilst studying at the Academy that his now general, Marcus Brutus, had recruited him. Initially the auspicious senator, now more renowned for murdering Caesar than for his philosophical writings, had lectured at the institution. But his tenure was a mere cover whilst Brutus recruited the brightest and the best for his cause. Boredom and a yearning for adventure had motivated Quintus more than a belief in the Republican cause. Brutus' noble character had inspired the student, rather than his politics. He felt sure that should Cassius Longinus or Mark Antony have attempted to recruit him then he would be still holding a stylus rather than a sword.

The sound of the distant shushing sea and the wind sighing through the pass was increasingly accompanied by the approaching clang of metal, as well as the carping of gulls. Brutus, remembering his Polybius, had adopted a tactic of Hannibal's. The plan was to attack the enemy with a small mobile force and then withdraw. The enemy would then give chase – and be ambushed. There would be little room for manoeuvre or retreat inside the killing zone.

The general, riding a handsome grey charger, with a brace of arrows protruding from his shield, gave the signal to attack. The hounds were finally let off the leash.

Battle yells curdled the air. An avalanche of men and metal poured down the mountainside. Roman soldiers appeared out from behind trees and boulders, as if from nowhere – like spirits from the underworld. Most of the enemy were Greek and no match for Roman drills and brawn. Pilums and arrows zipped through the air. Horses whinnied. Men screamed. Dust was kicked up from the track and mountain, forming a gritty mist.

Quintus' speed fuelled momentum and surprise as he attacked a youth who appeared little older than himself. Bearing down upon him the pock-marked enemy held up his shield in anticipation of Quintus' sword crashing against it – but at the last moment the Roman officer changed his angle of attack and stabbed rather than slashed. The slim blade slid between the enemy's ribs. Quintus stabbed again – and again. The enemy fell, blood gurgling from his mouth and covering the Roman's sword as if it were sheathed in a red scabbard. Quintus had been swifter than him, more deliberate. He appreciated even more what the quartermaster had said, quoting some veteran legionary called Tiro Casca – "There are the quick and the dead." Adrenaline and a desire to prove himself and not to let his comrades down spurred Quintus on to find his next combatant. Brutus ordered a decurion to take his cavalry troop and prevent any wagons from escaping.

Resistance melted like snow on a bakery chimney. The enemy were swiftly outnumbered and outfought, caught in a murderous vice. It was a slaughter rather than a battle. The tang of blood replaced that of the salt in the air. Although exhilarated, from surviving and proving his mettle, Quintus did not share the blood-lust of his comrades. He killed a couple of the wounded men out of pity, rather than cruelty, and offered up a brief prayer in silence to both of them. Brutus allowed his men to dispossess the enemy of any of their valuables but forbade any acts of torture. Night descended and made the blood appear brown upon the grass.

*

Embers still glowed from the previous night's fires as the chariot of the dawn rode across a soft blue sky. A few veterans still drunkenly caroused and finished off their jugs of acetum but most in the camp were sleeping off the celebrations. The victors had raised their cups to Brutus, Mars, Cassius, the Republic, Fortune, Bacchus – and then Brutus again.

Quintus had excused himself from the celebrations halfway through the evening. Tiredness, rather than triumphalism, had got the better of him. Yet he awoke early and took advantage of the relative quiet of the camp to sit in the shade of a cypress tree and compose a letter to his father. He recounted a little of the skirmish – suggesting that his education was not wholly going to waste, for *"I felt that Euclid and Pythagoras were on my shoulder in the melee, as the gods had once protected the heroes of Homer; their instruction helped me predict the trajectory of the missiles fired at us."* On finishing the letter Quintus possessed a fancy to compose a poem as he gazed on the encampment – and then stared out across the towering mountains and eternal sea.

"Dread kings rule over their own,

28

But over those kings is the rule of Jove,
Famed for the Giant's defeat,
Governing all by the lift of his brow."

The young officer pensively closed his eyes and soaked up the birdsong and massaging beams of the sun. Nature accepted him, both as a worshipper and its herald. *The world may be at war but let me be at peace.* Upon opening his eyes after his repose the youth picked up his copy of Pindar and read.

"I wish more of my officers would bury their head in a book rather than in between the legs of Greek slave girls."

Quintus immediately recognised the voice – and swiftly commenced to stand to attention before his general.

"At ease. You have little desire to stand and I have a desire to sit."

Brutus' tone was amiable but weary. The dark circles around his eyes – Quintus fancied that they could serve as archery targets – bespoke of a lack of sleep. The general briefly took in his junior officer before sitting down. He had a pleasant, friendly face and was short of stature. The uniform still didn't quite fit right. Conditioning had shed the youth of his puppy fat though he was still tubbier than the rest of the recruits from the Academy. He owned a wry sense of humour and appreciated logic, although he would not become its slave. His tutors had spoken highly of him and he had won prizes for his verses.

Brutus sat down next to Quintus on the grass.

"Was yesterday your first time in battle?"

"Yes, although I suffered many a beating under Orbillus, if that was any preparation," Quintus drily replied, making reference to the revered tutor.

"Why did he beat you? Were you an unruly pupil?"

"No. He beat myself and others because he enjoyed it, sadly. The lecturers at the Academy, however, desired to bend their charges

29

over their desks for different reasons. My friend Publius preferred the Greek attitude to discipline, as opposed to the Roman. When in Athens, he used to say."

"It seems little has changed since my days there," Brutus replied, more disapproving than wistful. Julius, whilst Servilia was his mistress, had paid for Brutus to study in Greece. He had proven to be one of the Academy's finest students yet often whilst attending lectures he would daydream and yearn to be riding with Caesar on his latest campaign.

"And did you kill for the first time?"

"Yes," Quintus replied, with more grief than pride in his expression.

Brutus couldn't help but feel an affinity for the virtuous student and placed a hand on his shoulder in consolation.

"I thank you for your service, as does Rome. You fought well and survived. If the gods haven't blessed you already may they do so now. But to die for one's country is also a sweet and glorious thing. Would you die for the cause of the Republic?" the commander asked, his dark eyes boring into the soul of his young officer.

"I would prefer to live for it," Quintus answered, unable to share Brutus' fervour.

"You do not have faith in the Republic?"

"Permission to speak freely, sir?"

"Granted."

"The only thing I have faith in is my scepticism."

Brutus' tanned, leathery face cracked into a crooked smile. He had been similarly intellectually precocious in his youth. Perhaps he would promote the candid young officer to his personal staff.

"But you should have faith. There are more things on heaven and earth than are dreamt of in your philosophy, Horace."

5

Lucius Oppius sat up in bed, combating his dehydration from the wine the night before by downing a large cup of water. Battle-scars lined his torso like some half-finished map. His body was taut, a catapult waiting to be fired. His expression was stern. Oppius had witnessed too much barbarity to think much of people. Civilization was but a poultice over the wound of man. Yet in the face of such misanthropy he still valued honour, duty and friendship as if they were rocks he could cling to during life's storm – and he considered the army to be a home to those virtues far more than the Forum. He had served as Octavius' bodyguard for over two years now, having been personally ordered to do so by Caesar. At first the centurion had deemed the task to be a dull chore. His desire was to serve under Caesar on his campaigns and earn promotion and booty, not babysit his bookish nephew. But Oppius, over these past few weeks, had started to understand just what Julius had seen in his heir – his steeliness and acumen. And what had once been a chore was now becoming an honour.

The mission of accompanying Octavius on his perilous journey from Apollonia to Rome had also afforded Oppius the opportunity to further mentor Agrippa. The centurion could scarce believe how the youth had managed to possess such an advanced appreciation of tactics and strategy with little formal training. Yet diligence and an attention to detail were alloyed to Agrippa's natural abilities. Whilst attached to the legion in Macedonia Agrippa had been conscious of learning the duties of the quartermaster and engineer, as well as the decurion. Two weeks into serving with the legion Agrippa had spent half a day with a cobbler – and the other half training up a cohort, teaching them how to repair their own boots when on campaign. Old enough to be his father, Oppius would have been proud to call Agrippa his son.

They were remarkable young men taken on their own but together they were greater than the sum of their parts, Oppius judged. Yet even together Antony could prove too powerful and wily for them. If the consul was smart he would grant Octavius at least a portion of his inheritance during their meeting later today – lest he lose sympathy with a number of Caesarians. Oppius hoped that he could somehow facilitate an alliance between Octavius and Antony but he feared that battle was as good as lost.

The officer rose and dressed quietly, careful not to disturb the raven-tressed woman strewn next to him on the bed. Her milky flesh appeared almost translucent in the pale sunlight. He partly did not wish to wake her because she was sleeping so peaceably but mainly he wished to avoid the awkwardness that would arise from him not remembering her name. He knew she was the wife of a libertore though. Oppius smiled, remembering his own crude joke to Agrippa the night before. "I am going to pump her – for information." The joke was worthy of his former comrade and friend, Roscius. Unfortunately she had been bereft of intelligence, though not of passion.

*

Joseph removed the hot towel from around his young master's head and then rubbed an ointment, of his own concoction, into his freshly shaven face. Octavius had been uncommonly quiet this morning, with Joseph rightly judging that his master had things on his mind – namely his imminent meeting with the consul.

"Thank you, Joseph. May I ask, what did Julius say in regards to Mark Antony, when he was sat before you in the chair?"

The old Jew scrunched up his face and closed his eyes as if he were a librarian trying to recall where a certain scroll resided in his stacks. Finally he spoke.

"Caesar believed that Antony was a better lieutenant than he was general. Caesar encouraged Antony to take on more responsibility but then often regretted his decision to do so. He once told me how he felt sorry for Antony – whilst Caesar had Marius as a mentor and influence growing up Antony was too easily led astray by the wastrel Clodius. Antony's dissolute ways had eroded his potential. He opened wine at an age when he should've opened up his books. Such were his self-destructive appetites Caesar worried that, if Antony obtained an appetite for power (or worse obtained power itself), then it would not just be himself he would destroy."

"Your memory is still as sharp as your razor Joseph, thank you."

"You have your appointment with Antony today?"

"I do indeed. I much prefer to sound out the judgement of my barber, than that of the augurs, as to how things will transpire."

"I'm cheaper than an augur too. Alas though, I would not wish to judge either way as to the outcome of the meeting. Ignorance will have to serve for wisdom. Yet I will duly say a pray for you."

"Do you think that will help?" Octavius remarked, quizzically raising his eyebrow.

"If it doesn't help, it cannot do any harm," Joseph warmly replied. "Next to God we are nothing. But to God we are everything. That's not from my good book, but yours. Cicero."

"I am grateful to you for your prayers and advice. You could well put all the astrologers, quacks and augurs in Rome out of business."

"I hope not. They may consequently take to being a barber – and put me out of business."

*

Domitius Enobarbus scowled and sighed after reading the report, which was tantamount to Antony's intelligent and disciplined lieutenant losing all of his composure. One of his agents had informed him that the wealthy banker Rabirius was now backing

Octavius. Enobarbus recalled a maxim of Caesar's: *It matters not how much you're worth – but rather how much you can borrow.*

The steam from the hot bathing chamber poured out into the reception room and increased his irritability as he waited for Antony to get dressed after his morning workout. Since returning from Campania Antony had started to condition his body again. "It's time I started to resemble the statues of me which have been commissioned. If I am to promote myself as a descendant of Hercules then it is best that I don't possess the figure of Hirtius," Antony had joked. Fencing, wrestling and athletics had replaced the lunchtime bouts of drinking and whoring though the evenings were still filled with revelries and entertainment. Yesternight, amongst the various festivities, a dwarf had climbed in and out of an elephant's mouth – and a Persian prostitute had swallowed a snake.

Antony was running late but tardiness was the least of the faults which Enobarbus forgave his commander for. In some ways, unconsciously or not, Enobarbus acted as a counterpoint to Antony. When the consul started to lose himself in his vices his lieutenant would soberly remind him of his duties (or perform those duties for him). Similarly, whenever Antony was in a rage or gloom Enobarbus would remind him of his good fortune and accomplishments.

The consul finally appeared. His short, black hair was glossier for being damp still. Flecks of grey around the temples gave him a distinguished rather than aged air. The sun had varnished an already healthy complexion. His muscular arms, glazed in massage oil, which had cradled more mistresses than even Archimedes could number, could also crush the ribs of a man as if cracking a walnut. His chest was broad, as was the smile that he wore on seeing his friend.

"Morning Domitius. Anything to report? Or should I say any good news to report?" Antony remarked whilst heartily clasping his lieutenant's arm.

"The policy of including former centurions on juries has gone down well with veterans and the officer class, if not some of the old families in the Senate. But you can't please all the people all of the time. Also, Cleopatra pledges her support to your cause. Unfortunately she doesn't pledge any gold."

Antony grinned on hearing the Egyptian queen's name. He was sorry that he had not had the opportunity to say goodbye before she fled the city after Caesar's murder. Rome's loss was Alexandria's gain, he mused.

"On a different note I've unfortunately just received news that Postumus Rabirius is providing financial support for Octavius – and is granting him a substantial line of credit."

"Pah," Antony replied with a dismissive wave of his hand, "Rabirius is doubtless doing so from greed rather than love. And Octavius needs to borrow money, for he'll get none from me. We are due to meet the pretentious stripling now, aren't we? I think we should leave the boy sweating at the gate for an hour or two. With any luck the pup will be without his sunhat and, feeling faint, will want to return home."

*

The muggy humidity sapped Oppius' strength and fired his impatience at the same time. The centurion, Octavius and Agrippa – along with a handful of attendants and bodyguards – stood outside the gates to Pompey's gardens, which Caesar had gifted to Antony after the civil war. Again Oppius ordered one of Antony's men to inform the consul that "Caesar" was waiting.

Octavius was calm, imperious. He drank another cup of water before biting down on a sharp, juicy apple with visible pleasure.

"He is being blatantly disrespectful," Oppius gruffly remarked.

"It is his dignitas that he is tarnishing, not ours. Besides, I have more time on my side than he," Octavius replied.

"And perhaps it's fear, rather than rudeness, which detains him," Agrippa added.

Pink clouds turned to grey and fomented in the sky, like a smack of jellyfish clustering together. A sudden breeze animated the wind chimes in the fruit trees which resided just behind the garden walls. Their silvery sound was briefly drowned out by the clang of the iron gates finally opening.

"The consul will see you now."

It had been agreed beforehand that only Oppius and Agrippa would accompany Caesar and attend the meeting.

Even in the increasingly dull light the vitality and colours of Pompey's gardens shone through. Octavius noticed a small herb garden – laden with mint, thyme, basil and celery seed – that rivalled Cleanthes' back in Apollonia. Octavius' step-father, Marcus Phillipus, might have similarly coveted the small attractive pond in the garden, filled with his beloved koi carp. Light and shadow mottled the marble pathways and manicured lawns as trellis work, garlanded with myrtle and ivy, hung above large sections of the grounds. Flowers erupted out of rich black soil, dazzling and perfuming the air: roses, violets, amaranths. Bees giddily swirled and then dived into the various blooms, rummaging and mining pollen. Numerous statues welcomed visitors with open arms. Agrippa recognised Alexander (commissioned by Pompey), Odysseus (commissioned by Caesar) and Priapus (commissioned by Antony).

The trio were led to the centre of the garden where they encountered an elaborate fountain – and Antony. The consul was accompanied by Domitius Enobarbus and a handful of burly lictors.

"My lad, it's good to see you. Lucius, I thank you for your service to Julius' nephew. We should share news – and a jug of Massic – soon. You must be the young Agrippa."

An effusive Antony warmly greeted his guests. Octavius thrust out his hand before the consul had a chance to embrace him.

"My sincerest apologies for keeping you waiting but I have been engaged in some pressing affairs of state. And I'm sure you will agree that Rome must come first. Allow me to introduce you to my friend and general secretary, Domitius Enobarbus."

Domitius nodded to the party. He surveyed the young Caesar. His demeanour was polite and relaxed but Enobarbus couldn't help noticing how his bright, piercing eyes took everything in – observing, collating and judging. His appearance was smart but not ostentatious. Whilst Domitius assessed Octavius Agrippa noted Antony's secretary. Balbus had instructed Agrippa to do so, arguing that it would perhaps be through his lieutenant that they would either make war, or peace, with Antony. "Better to deal with Enobarbus that Antony's hot-headed and cold-bloodied brother, Lucius. Or his shrill, ambitious wife, Fulvia." The secretary was neither tall nor short, broad nor slim. His features were neither overly handsome nor unpleasant. His dress was neither gaudy nor commonplace. Agrippa deemed that the secretary could have been anyone – and indeed Domitius was often content for people to consider him a no one. It was his brief to know more about others than they knew about him. "He prefers to observe rather than be observed," Balbus had remarked, admiring the modesty and intelligence of Antony's lieutenant, thinking himself lucky that his employer was devoid of such similar subtle virtues.

"You look well. You have even grown a little I think. Julius was forever fretting about your health, knowing how frail you were as a child – which, after all, was not that long ago."

Octavius offered a perfunctory smile before responding in earnest. "I thank you for your thoughts in regards to the state of my health but as we both know this visit is concerned with the state of my finances. It is my understanding that, after Caesar's death, you secured his estate. I thank you for that service but I have come to Rome to collect my inheritance – and subsequently honour the rest of Caesar's bequests in his will."

There was equanimity in his tone, galvanised by an uncommon resoluteness. Antony transformed a grimace into a smile and replied: "I admire your verve and idealism in wishing to honour Caesar's bequests but you are inexperienced in business and the ways of the world. When I took control of Julius' estate, in the name of the Senate, it soon became apparent that one could not easily separate what belonged to Caesar and what belonged to the state. I dare say that not even Julius himself could unpick the Gordian Knot he had created in his finances. I am doing you a favour by absolving you of your responsibilities in honouring Caesar's promises – else both Rome and you would suffer bankruptcy."

Again the young Caesar smiled. His manner was confident and composed. "It may prove difficult but that does not make it impossible to render unto Caesar what's Caesar's – and to render unto the state what belongs to it. What we can surely agree on to begin with is that the treasury does not belong to you."

Antony moved closer to the arrogant adolescent and his mask of charm began to slip. A sneer replaced his smile and he lowered his voice menacingly. He towered over the youth and spoke down to him. "You may well wear Caesar's belt but do not pretend to dress yourself in his authority. You should be grateful that I have even deigned to see you. Believe it or not I mean well towards you for you are Caesar's great-nephew. But do not take my goodwill and generosity for granted, boy."

The statesman's spittle flecked his face and Octavius could smell the wine on his breath but he flinched not and calmly replied, "Again, you are mistaken somewhat. I am Caesar's son. I would have you read the will, as well as Plautus when he writes that 'he means well is useless unless he does well'. The whole of Rome and Caesar's faction knows what I am entitled to. If you will not listen to me, you may then listen to us."

Enobarbus could sense that Antony was losing his composure and the argument – the one being almost inexplicably bound to the other. Things were not going according to plan. Antony had envisioned Octavius leaving their meeting grateful – for some feigned goodwill and promises of assistance. Failing that, he had remarked to his secretary that he may well intimidate the youth into compliancy or work the brat up into such a tantrum that he would exhibit a lack of dignity and authority. Perhaps he would make him beg. Yet it was the young Caesar who was retaining his dignity and authority. Enobarbus observed fonts of perspiration forming on Antony's temples. Antony had grabbed the pommel of his cavalry sword, a sure signal that he was getting frustrated, and angry.

"I *am* Rome, for all intents and purposes," Antony answered back – this time shouting. The pair of finches on the trellis-work above darted away in fear at the booming voice. "How dare you come here and yap at me like some spoiled pup. Do you not know who you're talking to? I am your consul!"

Antony pointed at himself upon expounding this before stabbing his finger into the chest of his callow antagonist. Yet Octavius, just in his cause and confident of outwitting the brutish statesman, stood steadfast and continued to goad his opponent with a wry smile on his face and amiability still lacing his tone, like poison.

"Dignity does not consist in possessing honours, but in deserving them," Octavius drily asserted, quoting Aristotle. Enobarbus couldn't help but be impressed by the young Caesar's wit and courage (although he knew well that stupidity often resided on the reverse of the coin where courage was minted).

"You impudent little bastard. It seems you think you have an answer for everything. Well perhaps *my* answer is to just cut you out of the will," Antony spat out, baring his teeth and clasping his sword even more firmly. Before his blade had a chance to see sunlight though, Oppius was by Octavius' side, his gladius half unsheathed. Antony gazed at the centurion, fury and astonishment animating his countenance.

"You would draw your weapon against me, Lucius? We shared more on one campaign than you will share in a lifetime serving this whelp."

"You have my sympathies Antony, but Caesar has my sword," Oppius dutifully replied.

Enobarbus instructed the lictors to stand down and sheath their weapons. He wished to douse the flames of conflict, not stoke them.

"You have my sympathies too, Lucius, if you are to side with a boy who owes everything to his name," Antony exclaimed, pursing his lips and dismissively shaking his head at the fresh-faced youth.

"You owe everything to that name too. The gift of this arbour is a testament to that," Octavius calmly replied.

"Caesar loved me more than you," Antony said, raising his voice again.

"We could argue that point until these gardens grow into a forest. What you can certainly boast about is that you loved Caesar's murderers more than me, such was your willingness to make peace with them after his death." Again Octavius' tone was measured and his face betrayed a hint of being amused by Antony, rather than fearful of him.

"I'd be even more willing to make peace with the man who slays the upstart before me. You have made an enemy today. Your friends have made an enemy of me too," Antony remarked, glowering at Oppius and Agrippa. "No more talk. Talk is cheap. It's probably all you can afford. The only money you'll get from me is that which I pay to you for the ferryman. This meeting is over."

6.

Dear Atticus,

Good news (how paradoxical it seems to put those two words together, especially of late). The meeting between Antony and Octavius was a wonderful disaster. Aeneas and Dido had a happier ending. The bad blood between them thickened. Octavius' demands to be granted his inheritance fell on deaf ears. Antony's pride, which has helped him rise so high, may prove to be his downfall. I even heard a rumour that swords were drawn – though unfortunately no blood was spilled. But the Caesarian faction has officially split rather than united.

Yet Octavius remains undaunted, indeed he seems to have been inspired by the setback and has campaigned even more vigorously. To half the people he encounters he pleads poverty, citing Antony's refusal to hand over Julius' estate. He plays the victim and the dutiful son. Everything he does is done "in the name of Caesar and the people". It's a tedious and fraudulent mandate of course – but it's also effective. There was an incident at the Festival of Ceres. Octavius asked that Caesar's golden chair, which was bestowed upon him by the Senate, be put on display. Antony refused. Yet my agents report that Octavius worked the crowd and turned defeat into victory. Antony came out of the incident looking unfair and petty. It seems that Antony views the boy as a mere gadfly. I believe, however, that he is underestimating Octavius. Let him.

To the remaining half of the people he encounters – soldiers, merchants and officials – Octavius promises riches and rewards. He is speculating to accumulate, using money he has borrowed to buy more support. At present Octavius is planning to host a season of gladiatorial games to honour his father (to his credit he is also paying for a number of theatrical productions of Plautus and

42

Sophocles). The Senate is still rightly wary of the boy but the people are taking him to their hearts. As we know though, the mob can be more changeable than the weather, or a woman.

Octavius seeks my counsel and claims he is devoted to me. We regularly exchange letters containing both personal and political matters. He has a mind and wit of someone older than his tender years. I can see why Julius chose him as his heir. Yet he still has much to learn. He believes that he is recruiting me to his cause, but I am recruiting him to mine.

The bad news is that Antony is actively recruiting too. He is using the resources of the Republic against the Republic. Even taking into account those centurions and legions loyal to our cause – and those who have been bought by Octavius – Antony still holds the upper hand. Decimus Brutus has again written to me, stating that he will not hand over his province of Cisalpine Gaul to a drunk and a tyrant. What Antony will not be able to win through force of character he may be able to win through force of arms, however.

I have heard that Antony will soon be travelling to Brundisium, to gain the support of the legions there. During his absence I will return to Rome, in order to try and gain the support of the Senate. Once his tenure as consul is up we must declare Antony an enemy of the state and denude him of his legions, though a peaceful solution seems about as likely as Antony remaining faithful to Fulvia.

I will take Caecilia with me to the capital. She has been urging me to do so now for some time. Do not worry my friend, I will duly keep her away from any rakes or fortune hunting suitors.

I will write again soon. Although I am confident of investing in Brutus politically, I want to ask your advice in regards to investing in some prospective financial opportunities.

Cicero

43

One of the lamps flickered as the midnight oil began to burn out. The young Caesar sat in his study, fighting off a yearning to sleep. He was keen to finish off his correspondence, even if it meant writing in the half-light. Octavius remembered how his uncle had often worked late into the night, a freshly sharpened stylus furiously working its way across wax tablet after wax tablet. "I'll rest enough once I am dead," Caesar had said to his great-nephew. "Deeds and words can live on though ... I will also live on through you."

Octavius, for personal and public reasons, wanted to live up to Julius' expectations and reputation. Still the boy wanted his great-uncle – father – to be proud of him. He would only rest once his enemies were dead.

He decided not to water down the wine, hoping that its sour taste might jolt him back into life. His body ached and he could still smell perfume on his skin. *Aemilia.* She had been another wife of another senator. Since coming to Rome a veritable banquet of women had been laid out before him – daughters, courtesans, slave girls and wives. *It would be foolish to eat just one dish.* Octavius enjoyed kissing compliments and poetry into their ears. Seducing them, or letting them seduce him. He pictured again the way Aemilia's red silk dress had fallen from her slender body, as she deftly unclasped the sapphire brooch pinned to her right hip. *A gift which unwrapped itself.* Aemilia had sighed and whispered the name "Caesar" over and over again as he took her, standing up, in the room next to where his guests were having dinner. Women were a wealth of gossip as well as pleasure and Octavius encouraged pillow talk. Julius had seduced women for similar reasons. Women were a source of intelligence (well, some of them were). Aemilia had been predictably indiscreet and Octavius learned of her husband's enmity towards Antony. It was not even beyond the realms of possibility that the ambitious senator had instructed his wife to bed Caesar's heir in order to communicate whose side he was on. His bed would never have to be cold again.

As well as taking various lovers Octavius had also enjoyed, or in some instances endured, a procession of visitors paying their respects. His mother and step-father had recently written to him, pledging their support again. Balbus, his great-uncle's secretary, provided a wealth of advice and contacts. His sister loved him unconditionally, despite knowing most of his faults. Agrippa and Oppius were seldom far away and would give their lives to protect him. Yet Octavius had never felt more alone than he did now. He was a tiny pebble among millions of others on a vast beach, before an even vaster ocean. He missed Caesar and Cleanthes. There was an ache in the pit of his stomach, like a hunger. Was it fear, guilt, grief or ambition? *Why can't I be as indifferent to life as life is towards me?* Cicero would understand him. The young student was in awe of the statesman's wisdom, writing and achievements. He admired his good humour too in the face of an ignorant, or malevolent, world.

Julius had possessed the same good humour. He knew how to balance a sense of pleasure with a sense of duty. Sex had been a means for him to further his political ambitions but sex had also been a means of forgetting about politics. When Octavius made love he wasn't making war. His enemies were as numerous as his lovers although he wryly thought to himself how some of his lovers may well become enemies as he neither returned their messages nor love. *There is no need to unwrap a gift more than once.* Cleanthes, his former philosophy tutor, wouldn't have approved of his behaviour, Octavius mused. He would have advised him to take Aristotle to bed with him, rather than an Aemilia, each night. Just before Cleanthes had been killed he had urged his student to return to Apollonia and complete his studies. "Everyone thinks he will become master of Rome. But everyone becomes its slave." There

45

had been a time when it was the youth's greatest desire to win the approval of his enigmatic teacher. But his greatest desire now was to avenge Cleanthes' – and Caesar's – deaths.

Octavius sighed. There was no turning back now. In crossing the Ionian Sea, as he journeyed to Italy from Apollonia, he had crossed his Rubicon.

Octavius sharpened his stylus and worked on through the night.

7

The balmy evening air blew through the windows of the tavern, diluting the pungent smells of wine and garum. As late as it was the night was still young for most of the patrons of *The Bunch of Grapes*. Greasy-haired whores draped themselves over wealthy-looking customers and laughed at their jokes, even if they couldn't quite hear what was being said over the general din of inequity. Wine was continually sloshed into cups by overworked serving girls. Various stains mottled the cracked, tiled floor. Cheers and curses erupted in one corner where a group of sailors played dice, with varying degrees of skill and luck. Bronze oil lamps, strewn with cobwebs, hung from the damp-ridden ceiling.

The three centurions sat around the table in the far corner, dressed as civilians. Oppius remained impassive on hearing the news from Pollux that a number of their friends and fellow officers had decided to side with Antony.

"Calvinus said that he owed Antony his loyalty, having shared many an amphora of wine and mistresses with him over the years. But it was more about money. For once Antony paid someone else's gambling debts, as opposed to his own ... Bibulus was instructed by an augur to serve Antony. Who could foresee that? Antony made Sura an offer he couldn't refuse – putting him in charge of recruiting young men ... Despite repeated offers, financial or otherwise, at least Matius Varro refused Antony's advances. Yet he has also declined ours. He will remain neutral, for now. Matius said that, instead of Antony or Octavius, we should consider that war is our enemy. Perhaps the bookish bastard is right ... But the friend of my enemy *is* my enemy. After Caesar's assassination Antony shouldn't have made peace with Cassius and the rest of the murdering dogs. I fought beside Decimus Brutus at

Alesia, he even saved my life that day. But I'll now fight against him, without mercy, for killing Caesar."

Aulus Milo nodded his head and occasionally grunted in agreement as he listened to his friend and worked his way through a second plate of pork chops. His face was a picture of concentration, from trying to follow what Oppius and Pollux were saying and from trying to work out how best to extract all the meat from the bones left on his plate.

Oppius was disappointed, more than surprised, at the news that so many Caesarians were deciding to join the ranks of Antony's burgeoning army. The consul was beginning to offer the same amount of gold as Octavius – and Antony was by far the more prudent option. They were betting on the favourite to win the race. The centurion would not consider his former comrades enemies, yet. But should they take up arms against Octavius...

Oppius' brow creased as he remembered the previous civil war, between Caesar and Pompey. Caesar had triumphed but there were few other winners. On the night when Caesar crossed the Rubicon Oppius' friend, Marcus Fabius, had died. He had been murdered by Flavius Laco, Pompey's agent. Oppius in turn killed Laco at the battle of Pharsalus. The civil war between Octavius and Antony – or Antony and the Senate, or Brutus and Octavius – had yet to commence in earnest but already Oppius had lost Roscius and Tiro Casca. Something had died inside of him with their deaths – as something inside of him had died when his lover, Livia, had betrayed him at Alesia. How much fight was left in him? *Too much blood has been spilled.* The soldier had given his word to Julius Caesar, however, that he would protect his great-nephew. Antony had recently written a letter to Oppius, promising him various rewards should he switch over to the consul's side and abandon the young Caesar. Antony was the safer bet but Oppius would keep his word. He recalled something Caesar had once said: *I love the name of honour, more than I fear death.*

The centurion was distracted from his grim thoughts by the arrival of an ageing, but still buxom, whore. She stood before Aulus Milo, showing off her gap-toothed smile. The neckline of her dress revealed her two virtues to the grinning soldier. Her face was caked with make-up. She had been a beauty once – under Sulla's reign – Oppius mused.

"Seems like you've had a good meal there. Ready for your dessert? I'm Diana," the woman said, winking.

"And I'm all yours," Aulus replied.

"Are you a sailor?"

"No, a soldier. But I'm not about to put up a fight if you wish to win my heart."

"It's not your heart that I'm interested in," the woman said, with an even more suggestive expression.

After the whore led Aulus off upstairs to a private room Oppius and Pollux resumed their conversation.

"Antony will be sending out the likes of Sura and Bibulus to recruit veterans and fresh meat alike, both in the towns and countryside. We need to get to these men before our rivals."

"Agreed," Oppius said, thinking how much his old friend Roscius would have been an asset in working the taverns and recruiting men. "I'll need you to take charge of recruitment. Have Aulus and others find us some legionaries. I have a list of potential officers from Balbus we should approach too. They served Julius loyally. Here's hoping that they will serve Octavius."

"He's young. And an unknown quantity," Pollux said, voicing the opinion of thousands of doubters.

"His money is good and so is his character. He's a Caesar."

"Will that be enough?"

"It'll have to be."

"And how are you fixed for men? Do you need me to find anyone to replace Roscius and Tiro Casca, to guard Octavius?"

"I sent a message off to an old friend as soon as I knew we would be coming to Rome. I'm hopeful he'll respond."

"Have you heard anything more about who could have been behind the ambush on the road to Rome? Tiro Casca was like a father to our friend upstairs. Aulus is as keen as anyone to avenge his death."

Oppius shook his head in reply. Unfortunately the name of Caesar attracted as many enemies as allies.

*

Tattoos covered the sailor's brawny arms and bull neck. Carbo Vedius' face was as brown and weathered as an old wine skin. The ups and downs of the rolling seas he sailed upon mirrored his fortunes at the gambling tables. He had nearly lost all of his money towards the beginning of the evening – and had bullied a shipmate into lending him some coins to keep him in the game – but fortune's wheel turned and Vedius won a number of games in a row. He cleaned out a few of his fellow dice players around the table. He often patted the purse which hung on his belt, enjoying the sound of the coins clinking together. Not wishing to waste his run of good luck Vedius worked his way around the tavern in order to find new players to join the game.

Oppius was now sitting on his own. Pollux and Aulus had gone home. The centurion was finishing off his last cup of wine and about to retrieve some money to pay the bill when the sailor approached him.

"Fancy a game of dice, friend? The wine will be on me."

"No thanks. I'm about to leave."

The navvy's disappointment manifested itself into resentment. The bully was not one to take no for an answer.

"Are you army?" Vedius asked, taking in the man's build and short haircut. "I thought that you boys never ran away from a challenge. Do you not fancy your chances? Have you not made your offerings to Fortuna and Victoria today?"

"The only good fortune I'd ask for now is for you to move along," Oppius said flatly. He was in no mood to suffer the drunken sailor's company or sarcastic comments. Although the centurion wasn't superstitious himself he knew many a soldier who offered up prayers to Fortuna and Victoria before they went into battle. Roscius had sometimes done so – and Oppius didn't look kindly on the man standing before him, sneering at his dead friend's religious beliefs.

Vedius didn't look kindly on the soldier in return. From Britain to Brundisium there was, at best, tension between the army and navy. At worst there was an inexplicable but tangible hostility between soldiers and sailors. Each service thought the other looked down on them (which often they did). Many a legionary and sailor traded blows in taverns across the provinces.

"You army think you're so special. You think that you're the guardians of Rome but really you're its scourge. For a few extra coins that Caesar gave out you marched on Italy and the capital. And you're all about to offer your services again to the highest bidder, whether it be Antony, the Senate or Brutus and Cassius. Meanwhile our taxes will continue to go on buying your jugs of acetum and paying for your whores."

As the navvy was finishing his short speech he was joined by two bleary-eyed shipmates. The first man, who stood to Vedius' right, wore a tunic which was as stained as the floor. His face was leathery, his expression permanently pinched. Drink fuelled his emotions, whether he was feeling a sense of triumph or antagonism. The second man, to the left of Vedius, wore a cloak over his tunic – which hid the dagger tucked into his belt. His face

51

was as flat and square as the stern of a ship. Both men were willing and able to back up their friend should any trouble arise – and given their shipmate's volatile temper trouble was often a safe bet.

Oppius calmly stood up and surveyed the three men and his surroundings.

"Are you coming back to join the game Carbo?" the first man asked. He believed that their luck was in for the night.

"Not just yet. I thought I might have some sport with this dumb soldier first. I had come over to teach him a lesson in playing dice but now I think we should teach him a lesson in respect."

Malice gleamed in the dicer's eyes. The centurion noticed the sailor's hand begin to curl itself up into a fist. The second man also slid his hand beneath his cloak and reached for his dagger.

The trio intended to have their fun and then return to the gaming tables. Three against one were good – and familiar – odds.

But their luck was about to run out.

Oppius quickly grabbed his wine cup from the table and threw its contents into Vedius' eyes – which temporarily took the man out of the fight. The soldier, a veteran of various tavern brawls over the years, then smashed the clay cup into the face of the sailor who was reaching for his knife beneath his cloak. Blood gushed out from his broken nose before he fell to the ground. The first sailor's expression became even more pinched with anger as he stepped closer and aimed a punch at Oppius. At the last moment, before connecting, the centurion bent his head down – and his opponent's fist struck the top of his forehead, fracturing a couple of bones in his hand. Oppius made his punch count as his hardened knuckles swung through the air and struck the sailor's chin.

By now half the tavern was scrambling to move away from the fight, fearing that the violence might spread. The rest of the patrons were wide-eyed and sucked in the scene. A couple of spectators even let out a few cheers whilst others winced at the sight of blood and sound of snapping bones.

As Oppius knocked the first sailor out – adding another stain to the floor – Vedius retrieved the long-bladed knife from his prostrate friend. He could still smell the wine on his face – and drip down his chin – but he could see clearly. The navvy stood before the soldier, swishing his weapon in the air; he grin-cum-snarled, believing that the dagger gave him the upper hand.

I'm going to cut the bastard open. And enjoy it.

But the smile fell from the sailor's face as soon as Oppius picked up the stool he had been sitting on.

"You should have just moved on," the soldier said.

Vedius' eyes widened in wariness. He was expecting his opponent to swing the wooden stool – and was confident of avoiding the attack – but Oppius quickly jabbed the chair forward catching the sailor squarely in the chest. A winded Vedius stumbled backwards and fell to the ground. Oppius felt a surge of fiery hatred as he stood over his enemy. The thought coursed through him that he should smash the stool down on the sailor's head – not caring if the blow killed him or not. There would be one less bully in the world. One less Flavius Laco. He needed to be taught a lesson. Oppius' nostrils were flared and his eyes were ablaze as if he was on the battlefield once more. But the moment passed and he breathed out. Vedius flinched as the soldier bent over him but rather than attack the sailor again Oppius merely unhooked his purse from his belt and tossed it to the distraught-looking landlord.

"Here, this should pay for any damage."

The small crowd duly parted as the stone-faced stranger walked out the door and disappeared into the now cold night.

Carbo Vedius remained on the floor and groaned. Defeated. He felt like there was a marble slab on his chest and he was unable to get up. Yet fear was already giving way to malice and he vowed that he would track the soldier down and kill him.

Blood begets blood.

8.

Octavius woke shortly after first light, dressed and retreated into his study. The humid air throbbed through the open shutters. The window looked out across a verdant garden, vibrant with life and colour. Flowers – violets, lilies, oleanders – perfumed the air. The sound of birdsong and a trickling fountain also thrilled through the window. Pristine sunlight gleamed off the white Carrara sculptures which Octavius had recently bought and installed in the garden – statues of Aeneas, Apollo, Caesar, Janus and Nemesis, the god of vengeance. The garden – and the property as a whole – projected a sense of taste rather than ostentatiousness. The house had once belonged to the general Lucullus.

The former philosophy student had already started to buy books – and Calpurnia, Caesar's widow, kindly gifted him several titles from her husband's library that she thought he might want to bequeath to his great-nephew. Volumes of Polybius and Aristotle made the shelves bow. Bronze busts of Caesar and Alexander the Great sat on either side of the large cedar wood desk, angled so as to face where Octavius sat. Various styli and wax tablets rested in front of him, ready for his attention. Maps covered the walls of the room – of Italy, Macedonia and Gaul – and marks, denoting allies and enemies, covered the maps. A wide-brimmed sunhat also hung on the wall by the door which led out to the garden for when Octavius would sometimes sit and each his lunch outside.

The first ten letters he wrote were to loyal supporters of Caesar – merchants and officers who had made their fortunes under the dictator's rule. "My first duty is to avenge Caesar's death and support those who supported my father." Octavius also reiterated that he would honour his father's promises in regards to government contracts the dictator had signed with the merchants.

He then went on to compose a dozen letters to various senators that Balbus said might be sympathetic towards him. "Although they may not be quite for you yet Octavius, they will be most definitely be against Antony." Octavius tried to reassure the senators of his noble intentions. "My first duty, my only concern, is to secure my inheritance and carry out Caesar's bequests to the people of Rome … My loyalty is to Rome and the Senate, as opposed to its current consul."

Octavius surprised himself by how easily the lies came. He smiled hollowly to himself as he thought about how he had spent years – and Caesar had spent a small fortune – being schooled in ethics and moral philosophy. But Octavius was now schooling himself in the subject of politics in a fraction of the time – and one of the first lessons he had learned was that the dictates of a moral life and a political career were at odds with one another.

Joseph entered. The aged Jew now shuffled more than walked. Joseph had served with Julius Caesar – and his father before him. Caesar had often taken Joseph on campaign with him as a source of wit and wisdom.

"Morning Joseph. No matter how hard I try you always seem to wake before me. You're almost too dutiful," Octavius remarked. He had quickly grown fond of the dry-witted old man and, like Julius before him, Octavius gave Joseph licence to speak his mind behind closed doors (even if he couldn't always tell how much the Jew was being ironic or not).

"Duty has little to do with it, master. I just try to leave the house before my wife stirs." Joseph's wife was a source of regular amusement, or anxiety, in his conversation.

"I'm sure your wife cannot be as burdensome as you sometimes make out. Despite you painting her as a harridan I'm tempted to ask to meet her."

Joseph gently shook his head and puffed out his cheek in a sigh, perishing the thought. "Be careful what you wish for is all I can say. She will either make your life a misery or, worse, you may be impressed by her and take her into your service ... And if I see my wife throughout the day, as well as at night, then my life will be made a misery. Or should I say even more of a misery? I couldn't help but note a piece of graffiti the other day: 'Why do Jewish husbands die five years before their wives?' it asked. 'Because they want to!' was the sage reply."

Octavius broke into laughter. His face softened to reveal the nineteen year old behind the marble-like mask.

"Perhaps I should desist from meeting with your wife then. I think I'm more frightened than curious now anyway. What with Antony, half the Senate and Brutus already against me she could prove to be one intimidating opponent too many."

Joseph thought it was a shame that Marcus Brutus was an enemy of his new master. He had encountered the principled aristocrat many times over the years. Julius had treated him like a son, even when his affair with Brutus' mother, the formidable Servilia, had ended. As soon as the battle of Pharsalus had been decided it had been Brutus whom Caesar had sought out. To make sure he was safe. To forgive him. In another life Octavius and Brutus could have been friends, allies. Both were bookish. Both possessed a strain of pride, or rather stubbornness. Caesar had seen something in the pair of them also – ambition married to abilities. But even more than Antony or Cassius Octavius wanted to see the praetor dead. "Brutus drew first blood but I'll spill the last of it."

Agrippa entered the room with a broad smile plastered across his face. Joseph believed the expression was borne from seeing his friend in good humour but Agrippa had just received a message from Caecilia to say that she would soon be accompanying Cicero on a visit to Rome. Although he would hide the news from everyone he couldn't disguise his happiness. Octavius' loyal lieutenant had woken up before the dawn so, by first light, he was practising his archery. There was due to be a tournament during the games Octavius was arranging, in honour of Caesar. The prize was a sapphire-encrusted bow, made out of gold. His intention was to sell the trophy in order to buy Caecilia something special. He wanted to prove himself worthy of her – and her wealthy father. *Money marries money.*

"You seem to have a spring in your step and glow about you this morning Marcus. Did you finally take my advice and visit the actress Valeria? On second thoughts an encounter with her leaves a man bow-legged and exhausted, as opposed to one having a spring in one's step."

"I thought you wanted me to make war, not love," Agrippa replied. The young soldier had fought off the actresses' advances the night before in order to remain faithful to Caecilia.

"I'm not such a tyrant that I will not permit you the odd evening off, to have some fun. But despair not. If you have missed out on the appetiser, or dessert, of Valeria the main course will be served tonight," Octavius said, referring to the party he was due to host. "I've invited every eligible daughter, widow and wife in Rome. For all of their high-born manners we may consider them to be low-hanging fruit. You shall have your pick of them, after me of course."

Instead of looking forward to the party that evening and grinning accordingly Agrippa pictured Caecilia, the contours of her figure and smile. He admired her immensely. She was as much privately, as openly, amused by things. Her sense of humour was playful but never malicious. Agrippa read over and drank in the fragrance of her letters each evening before sleeping, brushing his lips against her words. He longed to feel her body slot next to his, have the light in her eyes shine upon him again.

She's coming to Rome. I'll see her soon.

But could they ever be together? She was the daughter of a wealthy aristocrat, he was the son of a humble freedman. He may as well try to pluck a star from the sky as think he could marry someone so high-born. Caecilia had assured Agrippa that she would win her father over or else he would risk losing his daughter. Atticus wanted to see Caecilia married but he also wanted her to be happy with her choice of husband too. Caecilia told Agrippa about the parties she had attended over the past couple of years – and the would-be suitors paraded in front of her that she had to endure. "They were more like peacocks, boars or serpents than men. Rather than a party I sometimes felt like I was visiting a menagerie … No, I will not wait forever for my father, as much as I now believe love to be eternal … Fate is more powerful than ill luck or party politics. I have been re-reading Plautus and Terence of late. Happy endings are not just the province of plays and literature."

"Of course," Agrippa said, in answer to Octavius. "I wouldn't want to come between a host and his guests." He was smiling as much at the thought of Caecilia as at his friend's increasingly priapic ways.

"Caesar must be Caesar," Octavius replied whilst shrugging his shoulders and making a face, jokingly quoting one of his great-uncle's phrases.

*

Agrippa left to fit in another bout of archery practise, after Octavius told him that Mutilus Bulla would be entering the tournament. Not only was Bulla, a veteran of Pompey's Ninth Legion, considered the finest archer in the army but he was also loyal to the optimate cause. "If he wins then it is likely that Bulla will claim his victory in the name of the Senate or worse dedicate his triumph to Brutus and Cassius. Unfortunately sport is never just sport where politics is involved. Oppius says he has a plan to combat the threat of Bulla but the desired outcome will be to have my lieutenant claim victory, in honour of Caesar."

Octavius sat in his chair, leaned back and closed his eyes as Joseph rubbed a number of oils into the young man's freshly shaven face. Octavius sighed in pleasure. He mused on his new found wealth and influence. He was the son of Caesar.

Life is good ... But is this the good life?

Octavius told himself that he would trade his new villa, all the nights with the desirable women and all his power to have his great-uncle back with him. Not just for himself but for the good of Rome. Caesar was worth a thousand self-serving, fractious senators. If he were alive now there would be peace.

And if Caesar were alive now I would doubtless be back in Apollonia, discussing philosophy with Cleanthes. My only worry would be how I could sneak Briseis into my room at night ... I would be taking orders from my mother rather than giving them out to statesmen and centurions alike.

Octavius had long lost count of the number of times people had described him as "sweet" and "kind" whilst growing up. *But few will now describe me as such – and they will have good reason for judging me cold and ambitious.*

"Tell me Joseph, do you think that Caesar had any regrets? Did he speak of any?"

Joseph briefly paused in his duties before replying. He could have claimed to have known Caesar more than most. But the manservant knew him enough to admit that he barely knew him at all in some respects. His life was too colourful, his traits too numerous, to frame in one simple portrait. Caesar, right up to the very end, still possessed the capacity to surprise Joseph – be it through an act of compassion or cruelty.

"Julius mourned Julia. He once confessed that she was his greatest achievement and that she was the author of her character

60

for the most part, so his achievement could barely be described as such. She was a remarkable woman. She even turned Pompey into a good man. Well, good-*ish*. Her death changed everything for Caesar, personally and politically. But as to regrets? Caesar spent too much of his time looking forward to stare backwards. Cicero once dared to ask him if he regretted causing a civil war. Caesar replied that he didn't, because he had won."

Joseph took in the reaction on the heir's face as he spoke but, even more so than his old master, Octavius was unreadable.

9.

Candlelight gleamed off polished silver hairpins, gold necklaces and decorative brooches. Most of the men wore simple tunics apart from certain traditionalists and senators of rank who wore togas (the woollen material of which proved uncomfortable in the summer heat). The women added colour to the party by wearing expensively dyed dresses, made from imported silk. Scantily-clad young servant boys and girls weaved their way through the esteemed crowd in the large triclinium carrying Samian ware and silver trays of food: oysters on a bed of rocket, sweetened asparagus tips, spiced sausages, cheeses from as many regions as Rome had conquered … Servants also kept cups filled-up with the finest wines – Caeres, Tiburtinum and Falernian – whilst others provided bowls of perfumed water and towels for guests to use to wipe their hands.

Oily-haired aristocrats puffed out their chests in self-importance and peered over the shoulders of the people they were talking to in hope of spotting someone more interesting and distinguished to make contact with. They feasted their eyes on various female guests on show at the party. Some of the women turned their noses up and looked haughtily in reply at their advances, some gazed back demurely.

Laughter and conversation proliferated around the house, along with the aromas of fine food and wines and the smell of rose petals and musky perfumes. Octavius had opened up his garden and entire house – save for his bedroom and study – for people to occupy and enjoy. Guests greeted each other, smiling widely or formally nodding. Others gave fellow invitees looks like daggers and snubbed political opponents or people they considered below them in rank. As well as political and business ties the room was a web of personal relationships too, involving extra-marital affairs – past and present. Infidelity in Rome was like Chinese silk – always in fashion. And at the centre of the web, nodding with approval in the middle of the triclinium, stood the man who had organised the gathering – Cornelius Balbus.

The Spanish fixer and financier could be as cold as he was charming, depending on the circumstances. He had once served as a secretary and political agent to Pompey, before aligning himself with Caesar. It was more than just rumour that Balbus had been the architect of the triumvirate between Caesar, Pompey and Crassus. Cato reported that Balbus had been "the oil, or poison, which had lubricated the wheels of the nefarious agreement." Despite his greying hair and burgeoning wrinkles there was still a sense of strength and virility in the Spaniard's tanned countenance. His normally hard, hawkish eyes softened and emitted a playful amiability for the party. He warmly welcomed guests and smiled at those the most whom he knew the darkest secrets about.

Cicero had warned Octavius about employing the agent.

"Everyone owes Cornelius Balbus a favour – especially his enemies. He is always in credit with people and always willing to keep them in his debt. Balbus will work for you for as long as it serves his own interests. The financier is as trustworthy as a Carthaginian and as principled as a jackal. Cornelius probably made more money out of Julius than Julius made himself. He knows where all the bodies are buried because, often, he put them in the ground himself."

Yet Cicero failed to dissuade Octavius from forming an alliance with Balbus. Oppius said that he could trust the Spaniard – and that Balbus "only backed winners." In return for his support Balbus asked of Octavius that which he had asked of Julius – that he could one day become Rome's first foreign-born consul. He was also not averse to helping Octavius bring the men who had murdered his friend and former employer to justice. Caesar was worth a thousand libertores and had granted ordinary Romans more freedoms in six months than the aristocracy had given them in six centuries. Balbus recalled a comment he had overheard from Brutus one evening, as he spoke to Caesar: "Tradition must be observed. I would die before seeing a foreigner serve as a consul of Rome."

I would see you dead, you treacherous and hypocritical bastard, before I'm even nominated.

After introducing Octavius to several key guests at the party – and securing promises of political and financial support from others – Balbus decided to collect his thoughts and take some air in the garden. He exhaled, sighing with relief. The party was going well. Guests were having a good time. Octavius was being a gracious and entertaining host.

He's being Caesar-like.

Balbus' eyes narrowed and sucked in the scene. A line of red mullet sizzled on the grill. A wild boar, stuffed with a suckling pig, turned upon a spit. Merchants and senators were mixing business with pleasure, sharing salacious gossip and state secrets. Balbus smiled to himself as he spotted Senator Piso continually swivelling his head, making sure that his wife and his mistress didn't meet. Balbus also noticed how the predatory Senator Sabinus couldn't take his eyes off one of the fresh-faced serving boys. Balbus would give the youth to the influential statesman as a gift, in return for throwing a dinner party for Octavius and inviting several people who were wavering in their support for Antony. Other familiar faces came into view – young aristocrats keen on borrowing money, and those who were already in his debt, who would ask him for more time and credit in repaying their loans. He would duly give them the money they wanted. *But money always comes at a price.* Yet Balbus also needed to hunt the big beasts at the party who had little need of capital. They were, like him, bankers rather than beggars. Balbus needed to sell the idea to them that Antony was the past and Octavius the future – a future they should invest in. And in return they would one day be granted a praetorship, or consulship. Any donations to Octavius' campaign fund would be paid back tenfold through government subsidies, mining contracts or the power to collect taxes, in the name of the state. Or he would entice them with titles and honours. Yet tonight it was all about the guests enjoying themselves. Balbus had selected this evening for the party as, although absent from the city, Brutus had arranged some games for the next day to try and win back personal and political support. But people would now be too tired or hung-over to support Brutus' event – or, as Oppius' had remarked, they'd be "too fucked" to attend the games tomorrow.

In the background the Spaniard could hear the sound of wooden swords clacking against each other as a number of gladiators put on an exhibition of their skills in the far corner of the garden. Blushing, or lusty-eyed women, would be taking in their oiled torsos. The men would be placing bets on the bouts. Servants continued to fill their cups. A few of the courtesans, who Balbus had shipped over especially from Athens, draped themselves over certain influential senators and laughed at their jokes.

It'll be a late night for everyone. All is going according to plan.

"You must be pleased Cornelius. It seems that the best of Roman society is here this evening. You have Senator Aetius over there in the corner, displaying his predilection for oysters. When he gets home he will show his predilection for pre-pubescent girls, no doubt. I see you have invited representatives from some of our great patrician families. You are keeping your friends close and your enemies closer it seems. If you spot them holding their noses up in the air it's not because they're trying to smell the flowers or food – it's because they're looking down on their fellow guests. Ah, and there's Senator Valerius' wife. It wouldn't be a wine-sodden party without her. The woman's let more gladiators in than the gate-keepers at the arena. And is that Flavius Laetus? I can't remember, is he due in court this time for taking a bribe or receiving one? It's difficult to keep up. Yes, you have assembled quite a cast list. You must be proud. You have a full house, which may explain why the best brothels in town are most likely empty tonight," Cicero wryly remarked as he approached the Spaniard. The latter had taken great pleasure over the years in using his position of influence to deny Cicero access to Caesar when he petitioned to see him. In return Cicero called Balbus 'a glorified secretary', among other things, and tried to turn opinion against the outsider and foreigner whenever the opportunity arose. Although the two men were in some ways rivals there existed a mutual respect – and even admiration – between them. Political opposition did not spill over into (too much) personal enmity. Despite of their opposition to one another over the years they enjoyed their bouts of verbal sparring. Both men could be sarcastic and cryptic. They left as much unsaid as said. Both knew the extent of each other's influence and intelligence networks. Both knew not to underestimate one another – and both knew that, to combat Antony, they might have to work together.

"Yes. It's also difficult to keep up with how many of them you have defended as an advocate in the past, or will do in the future. But, Marcus, how are you? Thank you for coming. Octavius will be especially pleased too that you could make it. Can I get you a drink?"

"No thank you. I wish to keep a clear head. I also need to wake early tomorrow, in order to attend the games being put on by Brutus. You are probably unaware of them, else you would not have arranged this party for the night before."

Cicero was also keen to return home to work on a series of speeches he was composing, to denigrate Antony and declare him an enemy of the state.

"Indeed. Accidents will happen. I wish Brutus' games every success of course. But as much as you are always up for a fight I didn't think that the spectacle of gladiatorial combat was your thing."

"I thought that I would show my face and support. Similar to my being here tonight. It's always better to make friends than enemies. It seems I am but one dull star in the firmament however. There are more senators present than attended the last vote in the Forum. Perhaps the Senate should look to hire your caterers to improve attendance rates. Although our revered consul is conspicuous by his absence, I see."

"Octavius would have, of course, invited Antony – as you say, one should make friends not enemies – but he's currently out of the capital if you didn't already know. Few will be mourning his absence, however, I suspect. Tonight is about Octavius. People like to worship the rising, more than the setting, sun."

"Nothing can come of your campaign, Cornelius. He's too young. You're playing with fire and I don't want the boy or Rome to be engulfed in the flames," Cicero said, shaking his head in disagreement with Balbus. The playfulness departed from his voice, to be replaced by hardened seriousness – and a sense of dire warning. Rome needed to break its cycle of violence.

Balbus merely raised his eyebrow in response to Cicero's blunt words. The statesman had seldom been so direct with him before and it gave the politic strategist brief pause.

"They also said that Alexander the Great was too young, when he came to power."

"A somewhat ambitious comparison. Have you been drinking?" the dry-witted philosopher replied. Cicero's playful tone returned, as if it had never gone away.

"No. I like to keep a clear head too. It's my job to make sure other peoples' glasses are filled. But perhaps you're right and Alexander is indeed the wrong comparison. Rather Octavius should be mentioned in the same breath as Caesar. As ever I'm grateful for your counsel Marcus."

*

Octavius' arm ached from all the handshaking and he felt like the fixed smile upon his face must be resembling a rictus. He had lost count of the number of fatuous compliments he'd received, most common among which was, "Julius would be proud of you."

Women were presented to him as well as distinguished guests. Mothers introduced their unwed daughters with all the subtlety of tavern bawds. Occasionally he would share a look with Agrippa or Oppius and roll his eyes. Octavius chose to be amused and intrigued by the scene – performances – before him. *Politics is a game.* He recalled a comment by Caesar: *You can be victorious and become the First Man of Rome – or the other way to win is to just not take part.*

"This is a beautiful painting. Did you commission it yourself?" The aristocratic woman's voice was clear and sharp, like glass. Octavius took in a short gasp of breath as the young woman came into view. She wore a silk stola, dyed light purple, which clung to her lithe body. He could see the present beneath the wrapping. She could have been aged between fifteen and twenty. She turned more heads than even the host did but Octavius was willing to forgive her. She held herself like an elegant flower – surrounded by weeds. Her figure was slender – strength intertwined with elegance. Her light brown hair was bound tight and styled in a bun. There didn't seem to be a strand out of place. Gently arching eyebrows and intelligent, almond-shaped eyes sat over high cheekbones and a classically sculptured face. There was a coldness to her beauty, which only fired Octavius' heart – or loins – even more.

"I did," he answered, turning towards the fresco depicting Aeneas' escape from Troy, carrying his father Anchises on his shoulders as the city burned. Two years ago the bookish youth had promised himself that he would one day attempt to write an epic poem, charting Aeneas' odyssey from his homeland to Italy and the founding of Rome.

"Did you do so because of a love of Homer or because you wish to project the idea of yourself as a dutiful son to Caesar?" the enigmatic woman said with a satirical smile on her lips.

"Both," Octavius said, wishing to honour a direct question with an honest answer. "The painting is not just the work of one artist, however. Light is the load where many share the toil," he added, quoting Homer.

The captivating aristocratic woman had approached the host of the party out of curiosity. She had once been introduced to Caesar, after she had read his books and studied his career. She thought his pride and self-belief justified. If Caesar hadn't come along then the gods would have had to invent him. People – whether they be a senatorial elite or unwashed mob – have the habit of creating chaos from order. People need something, or someone, to believe in. Caesar gave people hope, martial glory and prosperity. He should have been made king or at least been called Emperor. But what of his great-nephew? There were some, from fellow patrician families, who were dismissive of Caesar's heir – citing his youth and less than noble lineage. Yet she had also overheard conversations in which senators and soldiers had been impressed by Octavius, he was wise beyond his years. So far she had given him some credit for being well-versed in Homer. But the shallow lust in his eyes failed to thaw her out.

69

Does he just want me for that one, predictable thing? Is he just like all the rest? Does he think that I would be flattered to be another cheap conquest? I intend to be a wife, not a mistress. Why do men think that women should either behave like decorative, vestal virgins or role-playing harlots?

"You have me at a disadvantage. May I ask your name?"

I like having people at a disadvantage. "You can ask the question but I'm not sure I should answer. I wouldn't want to one day end up on some proscription list," the woman said, her sense of humour dryer than the paint on the fresco.

Octavius let out a burst of laughter. His aspect softened – he was starting to like the woman and her black wit, rather than just lusting after her.

"I warrant that I would put myself on any list before such beauty," Octavius half-jokingly and half-nobly replied. "I couldn't promise the same for your husband however," he added, noticing the wedding band on the woman's finger.

It was now time for the usually haughty-looking woman to laugh – and the sound was more joyous and musical for Octavius than the flute playing from an adjoining room. Her round, normally pouting mouth bloomed into a smile. In becoming rounder her face also became prettier too, Octavius judged. As much as the imperious beauty could be privately amused by things she so seldom laughed out loud nowadays. Her husband may have had a sense of decency but he lacked a sense of humour.

"Allow me to keep my name a secret for a while longer. If I remain something of a mystery you may then remember me for longer. I dare say you will be introduced to plenty of hopeful – and hopeless – women this evening who will be keen to give you their name and anything else that Caesar's heir asks for." There was now a flirtatious as well as satirical light in the young woman's aspect as she spoke.

"I will remember you. In youth and beauty, wisdom is but rare," Octavius remarked, quoting Homer.

*

I'd rather be in a shield wall than line up and be introduced to some of these simpering senators … Politicians are the scum of the earth.

Lucius Oppius did his best to smile rather than growl. The centurion employed the tactic of trying to drink himself into having a good time – although unfortunately he had developed too great a tolerance to wine over the years. Oppius spotted the wife of Senator Valerius across the room and downed another cup of Falernian. She was his mission for the evening, according to Balbus.

"Sabina has a fondness for soldiers and gladiators. She will open up to you, in more ways than one … Try to gauge from her which side her husband is on, aside from his own."

Oppius made eye contact with her. She smiled, not even coyly, in reply.

I've accepted worse missions. The best years of her life are behind her. But perhaps mine are too.

*

The wind rustled through the leaves of the fruit trees Agrippa and Caecilia were concealed behind and her silk dress rustled against his tunic. Agrippa kissed her, tenderly then hungrily, as he breathed in her perfume. Caecilia sighed. At first her body went limp in his arms but then it grew taut in desire. She ran her hands over his muscular shoulders, back and arms – storing up the sensations for when he would be absent again. She arched her back and stretched out her entire, enthralled body – tilting her head so that he could kiss her upon the neck. Her body had stretched itself out in a similar fashion before, when she woke from dreaming about him.

Agrippa had just finished speaking to Oppius at the party. He had stood alone for a few moments, wistfully thinking about her. The

71

image in his mind's eye was then suddenly, almost miraculously, fleshed out before him as Caecilia appeared through a small group of ogling merchants and priests. She was a vision of loveliness. Her features and soul glowed. She was a young woman in love. His mouth was comically agape. Diamond droplet earrings hung down, along with her golden blonde ringlets, but he was more captivated by her gem-like eyes, sparkling with good humour and devotion.

The two guests had smiled at one another, sharing a private joke. As much as their hearts raced and yearned to unleash themselves, likes horses champing at the bit at the beginning of a chariot race, the two seeming strangers had politely spoken to each other.

"I'm surprised to find you on your own. I thought that a young man like you would be aiming to charm a young woman at such a gathering," Caecilia had remarked, her tone and smile playful. Agrippa noticed how her complexion had become even more sun-kissed since last seeing her. Her dress accentuated her hour-glass figure, which he wanted to wrap his arms around.

"I am just waiting for the right woman to come along."

"So tell me more about this woman. You never know, I may well encounter her at some point and be able to introduce you both."

"She's the kind of woman who would let me take her by the hand and lead her out into the garden. Once there we would hide behind a tree, where she would let me whisper sweet nothings in her ear. I'd tell her how much each line of every letter she wrote meant to me, when I read them at night."

"She sounds almost too good to be true. But the problem might be that she would start kissing you before you had a chance to speak."

"Well that's a risk I'd be willing to take, for the right woman."

Moonbeams poured through the branches above them and danced in the light of her diamond earrings and pleated, sky-blue stola. The couple sat on a bench. Caecilia rested her head on his shoulder, their fingers laced together. A thoughtfulness had now ousted their joy and passion.

"Do you remember when we first met?" Caecilia asked, tucking her legs up beneath her on the bench.

"Of course," Agrippa answered. He had probably thought about the moment every day since their afternoon together at Cicero's villa in Puteoli. Her vivacious blue eyes had shone in the sultry heat. Her pink lips had curled upwards into a smile. White, silk slippers had poked out from a shimmering summer dress. She hadn't worn any make-up because she didn't need too. *She looked beautiful because she is beautiful.* Agrippa had been sketching the valley he was overlooking at the time and inserting the designs of an aqueduct into his drawing.

"I know I teased you at the time but thinking about it on the journey here – and seeing the capital today – Rome needs more fresh water, to drink and cultivate its crops. As a soldier you will be asked to go to war at some point. But you are and can be so much more than just a soldier. Promise me, Marcus, that you will always build more than you destroy. Save more lives than you take. Do more good than ill each day."

"I will," Agrippa promised, kissing her on the brow and squeezing her hand.

"I'm not sure how long I will be able to stay in Rome. My father may summon me back home. I don't want to lose you." Tears glistened in her eyes as she spoke. A mournfulness was about to oust the happiness that had recently sung in her heart.

"You won't. Why would I want to lose someone who has promised to introduce me to the right woman?" Agrippa slyly joked.

Caecilia laughed-cum-sobbed and affectionately rapped him across the arm.

"I love you, so much," she said.

73

"I know. I love you too. I don't want you worrying about loving and losing me. I remember another promise from when we first met. *I'll wait for you.* And if I fall behind, wait for me. But I am worried that we may have gone missing from the party for too long. Cicero may be looking for you and he wouldn't want to find you in the arms of his prospective enemy. Instead he may want to introduce you to a prospective husband."

Agrippa also felt uneasy about failing in his duty to support Octavius at the party. Balbus had given him a list of names to introduce himself to and win over to their cause.

"It should be fine. He's probably far too busy talking about himself to mention my name. I'm fond of him though. But let us just stay a while longer here. Let Rome be Rome. I want this moment to last," the young woman said.

Agrippa smiled, nodded and wrapped his arm around her, pulling her even closer, as the birdsong in the trees serenaded them.

*

Wine and gossip continued to fuel the party. The smell of spices and roasted pork and guinea fowl wafted into the house and enticed more guests outside. Courtesans sat across laps and nuzzled their patrons before discreetly leading them away for the evening. Balbus had paid good money for them to show certain senators a good time. Various guests concluded that Octavius was a generous host and he would be equally generous towards his supporters if ever he served in office.

Balbus approached Cicero again, carrying a bowl of oats sweetened with honey – after Cicero had mentioned that the food at the party was too rich for his stomach. He placed the bowl on a small bronze table next to the revered statesman.

"I made it myself, would you believe?" Balbus said.

"I would, if it contained poison. But I know that's not your style Cornelius. Your counsel may be poisonous but not your cuisine.

Besides, by my calculations, I'm worth more to you alive than dead."

Balbus nodded, smirked and appreciated Caesar's comment about his erstwhile opponent. "Cicero may not share my politics but there are few men who I would rather share a conversation with. His influence may have diminished but his wit is still as sharp and piercing as a ballista bolt."

"I read one of your books the other day. You were your normal, engaging and erudite self but I thought that you were far too forgiving of the gods. For as much as we might argue that the gods made us in their own image I believe that in some ways the opposite is true – and we have made the gods in our image. Which is why I think that the gods can sometimes be too cruel or petty," Balbus said, deftly plucking a fig from a serving girl's tray as she walked by.

"You may well be right but even if my words didn't persuade you of anything you should look to the virtues of reason and your divine spark to light the way forward. I hope – or I may even say that I pray – that you still possess some faith and devotion in regards to the gods."

A short scream and then guffaw sounded out in the garden as a lustful senator squeezed the breasts of one of the courtesans. The distraction was but momentary and was quickly swallowed up by the general revelry. Balbus and Cicero continued their conversation, as did others.

"I'm not altogether sure that I have the time, let alone will, to worship your deities at the moment. My faith and devotion are all invested in turning Octavius into a god. But do not underestimate how much faith and devotion Octavius has in you, Marcus. I sometimes think he considers you a god. If so, what would you ask of him?"

"That he becomes a good man," the philosopher replied.

"I would posit that he is already a good man, certainly in the context of the company presently surrounding him at this party. The question is can he remain so? Especially once this city and its sins get their teeth into him. Politics is a game played by good actors rather than good men, wouldn't you agree? And the most successful are the ones who believe in their act. But you know even more than I do about how Roman politics work – or don't work. Besides, I should be absenting myself from the party soon. I have a long day tomorrow, helping Octavius distribute bread and money to the people."

No doubt at the same time as when Brutus' games are due to start. "Perhaps I have underestimated just how much of a good, selfless man you are too, Cornelius," Cicero replied, sarcastically.

"Octavius isn't your enemy. We both know that Antony is the greater threat to Rome and all those things which you hold dear, including your own life. If ever Octavius comes knocking and asks for your help, answer him. Similarly, if you come knocking Octavius will answer your call. I give you my word." Balbus dropped the glibness and irony from his voice, and wore a look of grave sincerity.

Aye, but unfortunately there are harlots here who I trust the word of more.

*

Octavius abandoned his guests and took a turn around the torch-lit garden with the woman who had caught his eye and curiosity. Occasionally they were interrupted by people who wanted to introduce themselves to the host. Sometimes the woman felt irritated at having her time with Octavius disturbed, but she also felt twinges of pride and flattery that Caesar's heir was choosing to spend time with her over others – and that senators considered her of importance for accompanying him. He picked a flower for her and put it in her hair and she thought there was still a boyish sweetness beneath his manly arrogance. They spoke a little of poetry and philosophy but more so the woman came alive at having the opportunity to talk about politics. All too often in the past her father and husband had been dismissive of her opinions when she had tried to join the conversation about matters of state and the personalities of leading politicians. They asked her to leave the room. It was "unnatural" for a woman to concern herself with such topics, her mother had told her. So she learned to think for herself and hide the extent of her education (and not just because she disagreed with her husband and family's opposition to Caesar). Yet Octavius seemed genuinely interested in what she had to say and she felt she could, in some ways, be herself with him without putting on an act.

"Cicero's idea of politics and government should be re-classified as history. His ideal of harmonising the classes is out of tune with the world ... Rome needs one strong voice to guide it, instead of a directionless din of squabbling consuls, self-interested factions and a mob which looks to either beg or bully. Caesar's death was a tragedy for us all."

Octavius grew attracted to her intellect as well as her sharply beautiful features.

"When they murdered Caesar they killed part of me, but at the same time they gave birth to something else," Octavius declared, staring at a marble statue of his dictator father as he spoke. *They gave birth to a monster, one which will not be sated until it kills everyone involved in killing you. Blood for blood. Justice.*

The woman gazed at Caesar's heir, captivated by his power and potency. Her husband was, like Cicero, too mired in an old, stagnant world. He had never satisfied her sexually, though that was not why she had married him. But Octavius was different. Forbidden fruit. *If only I had met him a year ago, before Tiberius. But, a year ago, he would not have been a Caesar.*

77

The woman stood next to Octavius and admired the statue. He breathed in her perfume, took in the lustre of her jewels and her flawless, pearl-like skin in the lambent moonlight. Her demure glance was met by his amorous gaze. He clasped her responsive hand and pulled her even closer.

"What do you want?" he asked, hoping that she would reply "him".

I want to be the First Woman of Rome. "I want everyone I love to be happy," she said, trying to cool her ardour. Keep control. She wanted convey a selfless, virtuous side. Most men found ambition in a woman to be unattractive or unnatural. She wanted him to see her as more than a mistress. She was worth loving as well as bedding. *Be strong. He will want you more if you deny him.*

The same birdsong serenading Agrippa and Caecilia could be heard in the background. The sultry evening air warmed their skin, glazing it with a film of perspiration. Octavius moved closer – his lips were about to brush against hers – but she pulled away.

"No, I'm sorry. I can't. I cannot give you my heart, nor that thing which most men value even more. But I will now give you my name."

"What is it?" Octavius asked, his voice and features imbued with understanding and affection still. He felt disappointed at her not giving herself to him but he wasn't angry or resentful. He would rather keep her as a friend than lose her as a lover. He wanted to see her again.

"Livia."

10.

Brutus dedicated his games to Apollo – but more so they were dedicated to himself. He needed to raise his prestige. If the people wouldn't give their love freely then he would need to buy it, Cassius had argued in a letter to his fellow libertore. Brutus needed his name to be synonymous with duty rather than treachery. One of his agents had arranged for a number of people in the crowd to chant out his name and call for the praetor's return to Rome. Brutus had at first baulked at stooping to such cheap, political tricks but Cassius persuaded him.

"A noble politician is still a politician," Balbus drily remarked after finding out about Brutus' intentions. "It seems that people can still try to stage manage a performance even when their lead actor is absent."

The crowd was under half of what Brutus' representative had hoped for as he announced the commencement of the games. A number of senators and aristocrats who had promised to attend were absent, lying in bed with either sore heads or a high-class prostitute (or "actress", as some called themselves). The master of ceremonies for the event creased his brow and scratched his head, wondering where the mob were. Questions were finally answered when, as paid supporters began to cheer Brutus' name, they were shouted down by a rival mob (arranged by Balbus) which declared the games' patron a murderer and traitor. *All is fair in love and politics*. Fighting broke out between the two partisan groups and the crowd dispersed. The games went ahead but were, in the words of Agrippa, "about as well attended as an orgy involving lepers".

*

The games which Octavius would arrange, in honour of his father, Julius Caesar, would be another story. Much of the funding for the games came from Octavius' step-father, Marcus Phillipus. The money, generated from the sale of various properties, was freely given rather than asked for.

"You're a good investment," Phillipus remarked.

Octavius was temporarily lost for words. There were tears in his eyes as he embraced his step-father and told him that, more than Julius Caesar, he considered Phillipus to be his father.

"You are the most decent and honourable man I've ever known … I'm proud to call myself your son."

"I'm proud of the both of you," Atia then tearfully declared.

"I'd be happy for you to be proud of me less mother, if it meant that I wouldn't have to worry about you dehydrating from crying too much," Octavius fondly joked.

The games would last for ten days. There would be a feast of gladiatorial bouts. Balbus poached the best of the fighters that were due to take part in Brutus' games to fight for Octavius. Oppius called in a favour and the legendary Decimus Baculus agreed to appear in an exhibition bout with the centurion himself – the *Sword of Rome*. Men would battle beasts and beasts would battle beasts too. "The white sand will turn red with blood," an advertisement boasted. Admission would be free. Influential senators and supporters would be given the best seats and Balbus had arranged for some of Rome's best actresses and dancers to sit with them. In return for their services the actresses and dancers were given parts in the theatrical shows that Octavius also put on.

Despite their busy schedules Octavius, Balbus and Oppius had all found the time to take part in the auditions process.

*

The crowd – filled with soldiers, tradesmen, Jews, hangers-on, merchants, mothers – squinted in the light of the blazing summer sun and shielded their hands over their eyes as they looked up at the platform in the Forum which Octavius stood on. The smell of garum and freshly baked bread hung in the air from food venders. Octavius wore a look of imperious calm on his face, though his heart was racing and he felt his fair skin begin to burn in the stinging heat. Beads of sweat formed on his brow and he willed them not to fall into his eyes. He wore a simple white tunic, similar to that of what many in the crowd were wearing. He wanted to appear to be one of them. He gazed out, taking in the sea of people, as if he were a captain about to address his crew. Men, women and children stared up at him expectantly. Some even had an expression of wonder on their countenances. For a moment Octavius was tempted to laugh at the scene. The gods seemed to be playing a joke on him or Rome, that the populace would place their fate in the hands of a nineteen year old boy. Several months ago he was spending his days reading philosophy, dreading fencing bouts or being coddled by his mother.

You're a long way from Apollonia now.

As well as amusement, however, Octavius felt a sense of duty towards the people before him. Like Caesar he wanted to be above them but with them – do right by them and make Rome even greater. Earlier in the day Octavius had unveiled a new statue of Caesar in the Forum, of Caesar as a young man. Balbus had commissioned the statue, instructing the sculptor to make sure there was a slight resemblance between the youthful Caesar and Octavius.

A trumpet sounded, calling for silence and the audience's attention. Octavius had given a number of pre-arranged and spontaneous speeches in the capital over the past month but never to so large a crowd. Yet he had confidence in himself. He was no longer a day-dreaming philosophy student. *I am a Caesar … Make him proud.* His voice carried further than it used to. He was learning when to speak plainly and when to colour the air with rhetoric and hyperbole. He was learning how to read an audience

81

as if he were deciphering a poem. He was learning when to be pious, satirical, conservative or radical. "Know how to be all things to all men," Caesar had once counselled him, "but be no man's slave."

Out of the corner of his eye Balbus gave him a nod of encouragement. Octavius took a deep breath and began.

"These games are not in my honour. Should Caesar still be with us he would posit that these games should not honour him either. Rather these games are in your honour. Our wise friend and statesman Cicero would argue that we all carry within us a divine spark, one which can light the way and lead us to wisdom and glory. Equally, I see before me a multitude of good souls each possessing the light of Rome inside them and the divine virtues which this city has the power to inspire in us all: courage, liberty and duty."

Heads bobbed up and down and nodded in agreement in the crowd. Chests swelled with pride.

"To be born Roman is to have won the lottery of life. Caesar knew this and by bequeathing much of his estate to Rome he wanted to share his winnings with you. And I see it as my duty, both as his son and as a fellow Roman, to make good on his promise. His legacy should be fulfilled. The money is no longer Caesar's. Nor is the money mine. And it doesn't belong to our consul. The wealth of Caesar belongs to you. Mark Antony is not the law. The law is the law."

As if on cue a few shouts of support could be heard in the crowd from some of Caesar's veterans who Oppius and Balbus had invited. Soldiers who had once bellowed out orders on the parade ground or in battle could easily make themselves heard in the Forum. A few in the crowd also thrust their hands up in the air as if grabbing invisible coins.

"I am trying to honour my name. At the same time Mark Antony is dishonouring his as he uses your money to fund a personal army – though I am not sure if he is recruiting an army of soldiers or an army of vintners and actresses."

Laughter succeeded indignation.

Rome wants bread and comedy.

"As much as Antony has tried to silence me I still have a voice, attuned to yours. As much as some of you may have already heard me speak I have listened to you twice as much as I have spoken. I have heard your calls to establish a legion of vigils in the city, paid for by rich landlords, to put out fires in the poorer districts of the city... I have seen how some senators own a dozen different litters whilst children are shoeless... I have heard your worries about overcrowding and unemployment. Immigration, rather than curing all our ills (especially those of the rich who enjoy cheap labour), can cause more problems than it solves... Rome for Romans... Jobs should go to the deserving – not just the privileged... I promise to fulfil Caesar's mission and retrieve Rome's lost standards from our enemies in the east... And I promise to build a network of aqueducts across the capital and the empire; as much as we may wish it to be so Rome cannot live on wine alone... And these are not empty or unfunded promises I offer up to you today. To pay for these projects I will petition the tribunes and senate, in Caesar's name and my own, to instigate a "Villa Tax" on our most affluent citizens... I believe in the institutions of the family and marriage ... Rome is great but we can be greater still. More prosperous, freer."

During the night before, as Octavius composed his speech, Balbus had counselled that the less power one has the more one can promise the people. "False promises are food and drink to those who are in opposition. Promise them the world and when you get into power blame your enemies for being unable to keep your promises." Although Octavius had nodded in receipt of the wily agent's advice he had made a vow to himself that he would honour his promises.

Rome is a city of bricks. I will leave it as one made of marble.

"As a Caesar it is my intention to be a servant of Rome, not its ruler. My father is doing more for Rome from the grave than his killers are doing whilst they live. Cassius and Brutus have guiltily run away. They are now embezzling taxes and monies meant for Rome in order to recruit an army which, no doubt in the name of freedom, will try to enslave Rome. I hope that my father will approve of these games. As much as Caesar liked to enjoy himself he wanted others to enjoy themselves too. We are both remembering him and saying goodbye to him today."

Octavius looked out in front of him, hoping to see a throng of faces nodding in agreement and devotion. But instead he witnessed eyes widen and jaws drop. The sound of a hundred gasps created one long hissing sound which drowned out the wind. Fingers were raised and pointed up at the sky behind Octavius – at the chariot of fire.

The sight of the comet streaming its way across the serene blue sky burned itself into the eyes – and souls – of everyone in the crowd. Even the pickpockets throughout the square looked up, amazed. And the entire city too, from the Subura to the Palatine, turned its head as one to the once in a lifetime spectacle. People clutched the sleeves of those standing next to them, whether they were friends or strangers, and pointed at the comet and asked, out loud or to themselves, what was the meaning of it all? Octavius was also not immune from a sense of wonder and speculation. He was dumbstruck – but not for long. Augurs would likely interpret that the comet presaged doom. Doom made the augurs money, and made the people hang on their words even more. Octavius had no intention, however, of letting a cloud hang over his games and

84

blacken his moment in the sun. He would set the agenda before others had a chance to.

"And see the sign. Caesar is saying goodbye to us. The gods are calling their own back to them. His soul is ascending upon the wings of our devotion. Caesar and the gods are giving us their blessing…"

Cheers and chants here went up – and not just voiced by those in the crowd who had fought under Caesar or were paid to give their support.

"Caesar… Caesar…"

The sunlight began to warm rather than sting Octavius' skin as he bathed in the crowd's adoration. Balbus would later congratulate Octavius on his speech and improvisation – "It was divine inspiration". Although Octavius laughed at the cynical agent's joke he considered that perhaps the gods were on his side. The odds were too great, impossible, that the comet should appear at that exact moment. *Am I the son of fate as well as Caesar?* A couple of glasses of wine further fuelled his sense of superstition that night.

The gods may not have even been heralding Caesar – but me.

By morning a polished bronze star had been placed on the new statue of Caesar in the Forum. Graffiti also sprung up around Rome, proclaiming that Caesar was a god.

"Let the games begin."

11.

Dusk.

The flames devoured Marcus Brutus' letter but they couldn't burn the contents from his thoughts. The news from Rome was dire. Brutus cursed Balbus for ruining his games. *Snake. For just once it would be nice if you had a taste of your own medicine – or poison.* Brutus poured himself another cup of undiluted wine, as sour as his mood, and gulped it down. Sometimes the drink dulled the ache but sometimes it enflamed his misery and ire. He also cursed Caesar, who seemed to haunt his thoughts more now that he was dead than when he had been alive. His intention had been to save the Republic, not be exiled from it.

Are you punishing me from the afterlife?

Brutus also cursed Octavius – at the same time as cursing himself for underestimating the boy. Cicero had claimed in a recent letter that he would be able to guide Octavius.

Cicero probably thought that he guided me too, when I was young. Caesar and Cato probably thought the same as well. But I was my own man. I am guided by principles, not personalities. But how much is this boy now becoming his own man?

Finally, Brutus cursed his agent underneath his breath. He had suggested the idea of arranging the games and taken his fee – but had failed to deliver. It had all been money which Brutus could ill afford to spend and waste. He would have to ask to borrow funds again. It was unspoken, but explicit, that the merchants and politicians would want favours in return when Brutus won office. He would have to make compromises, his legislature would be mired in corruption from day one. He would not be his own man.

Caesar was his own man.

Horace watched his commander as he paced back and forth by the fireplace and muttered under his breath. His once bright eyes were now red-rimmed. His once strong jaw was rounder. He no longer trimmed his beard. Horace took a mouthful of wine. He was several cups behind Brutus but could still hold his own ("No poems can please for long or live that are written by water drinkers," the would-be poet had recently written in his notebook). He knew better to try and keep up with his commander though. He also knew better than to try and disturb him when he was deep in thought.

The villa they were staying in was built in the crevice of a valley and the chamber let in little light. The room was austere. A rickety desk housed some correspondence and maps. A large jug of wine and an uneaten plate of salted pork and cheese sat on another table. A couple of couches flanked the crackling fireplace.

Brutus had recently dismissed his senior staff but had asked Horace to remain behind after the meeting. The commander enjoyed the young soldier's company and allowed him to speak his mind, even if his thoughts were contrary to his. Caesar had been the same with him, many years ago. The former student was well read and witty. They spoke about literature and history. Crucially Horace also knew when not to speak – when Brutus was in a mood to brood in silence. The poet reminded the praetor of himself as a young man – before his world had started to crumble.

In front of his men the commander still projected authority and a sense of purpose. He was the descendent of the legendary Junius Brutus, saviour of the Republic. He embodied Roman virtues whilst Mark Antony embodied Roman vice. His forces were growing and his army was well provisioned. He was in constant communication with Cassius, Cicero and Decimus Brutus. There was a plan and the gods were on their side.

Yet on nights such as these Horace witnessed a fractured rather than forceful soul. Brutus was less than half the man he used to be.

He felt betrayed by the people of Rome and the gods. He had had right on his side but the new saviour of the Republic had somehow become an enemy of it – a faithful lover spurned. Horace likened him to a mathematician whose formulae and life's work had been proved wrong. He had miscalculated Mark Antony's ambition and abilities. He had also miscalculated the people's love for Caesar, which had been greater than their love for Brutus' ideals. In public Brutus had murdered a dictator but in private Horace saw a man dealing with the sorrow of having murdered a friend. Where some might have considered Brutus weak for wallowing in such guilt, Horace considered him to be human – and all the nobler for it.

"Rome is a white bull, willingly laying its head upon an altar to be slaughtered. And Mark Antony is holding the knife. The Republic is becoming a memory Horace," Brutus remarked, thinking that, as punishment for rejecting him and embracing Antony, the mob should be damned.

"Rome is populated by people, not gods. Its leaders are flawed as much as its citizens, although on balance the former tend to transgress more than the latter. Elections are bought, votes are sold. What one man may call a hero another can call a tyrant," Horace replied philosophically.

"But the Republic was and can be different. It desires laws, not tyrants."

"Laws can prove just as tyrannical as men."

"You would have Rome become lawless then? Anarchy isn't freedom. Your philosophical mind is proficient at questioning things but what we need right now are answers. What would you do to save Rome?"

"I would lower taxes," Horace said undramatically. Brutus was somewhat stunned into silence and did not know if the youth was joking. "The more a man can make from his labour the more content he'll be – and incentivised to work harder. More money should go to his family than thieving bureaucrats. Or worse, officious bureaucrats. And he will use that money more wisely than any senator, I warrant. The state has proved itself over and over again to be inefficient or iniquitous when it comes to managing its finances. Large states are more likely to go to war. If we reduce the size of the state – and allow people to keep more of their money – then the likes of Sulla, Caesar and Antony might be less inclined to play the dictator as the job will not pay so well. Ironically though, by lowering taxes – and I say lower rather than abolish for the state must still function properly – treasury revenues may increase due the rewards of work and more money being ploughed back into the economy rather than pocketed by the political classes and their cronies. Lower taxes and there would be less money to fund a dole system which, in the name of government generosity, enslaves people and keeps them on the bottom rung of society."

"Telling a politician that he is unable to tax would be like telling a drunk he could no longer have a drink," Brutus said, wryly smiling and thinking about his friend's arguments.

"A drunk cannot drink wine if it's not there. And similarly a politician cannot spend money he doesn't have. He would no longer have cause to exist – and would have to find a proper job. And a world containing fewer politicians would be a better world."

Before Brutus could reply he was distracted by the sound of a door creaking open. He betrayed a flicker of frustration, or something worse, at seeing his wife but quickly forced a polite smile.

"Are you coming to bed?" Porcia asked, sheepishly but also somewhat pleadingly. She forced her own smile on seeing Horace. She didn't like the satirical young officer and resented him for the way her husband now seemed to confide in him more than her. She was the daughter of Cato. He was the son of a commoner.

As with her husband Porcia had changed, physically and otherwise, since leaving Rome. Her eyes seemed more deep set, her face more drawn. Brutus and his wife argued behind closed doors but the walls were thin. Porcia missed her friends, the theatre and her home. She didn't like being in the company of soldiers – they were "coarse and vulgar". She couldn't remember the last time she had bought a new dress. She wanted him to appreciate the sacrifices she had made for him.

"Not yet. I've still got some work to do," Brutus replied. The politician did indeed need to catch up on some correspondence, most notably he needed to reply to a letter from Atticus to ask for a further loan, but that was not the reason he decided not to retire for the night. The husband and wife no longer made love. He always tried to climb into bed after his wife had fallen asleep. The thought remained unvoiced but Brutus couldn't quieten the belief that his wife had partly manipulated him into murdering Caesar. Her motive had been that Caesar had been responsible for the death of her father, Cato. The door to the issue was ajar but Brutus refrained from opening it fully. Things were strained between them at present but not completely broken.

I still need her. But I just don't want to be with her right now.

Porcia motioned, as if to respond, but then merely pursed her lips and retreated from the chamber. The sound of the closing door creaking drowned out her sigh. The fire was unable to thaw out the frosty awkwardness in the room.

Rather than Rome you need to save your marriage, Horace thought to himself.

12.

"Think of yourself as an actor. You just have to hit a slightly different mark," Octavius had advised Agrippa the day before the archery tournament.

If I am an actor then there are plenty in the audience who would wish to boo me off stage right now, Agrippa thought to himself as the jeers and abuse directed at him seemed to reach a crescendo. Beads of sweat threaded their way down his dust-laden body. His throat was as dry as dust too. His arm ached as if he had been continually punched there for the past three hours.

The archery competition was being held in a converted theatre. The well-to-do were sitting on cushions on the stone steps surrounding the stage whilst the lower-classes crowded themselves onto the sand-coated area in front of the stage. A central channel ran through the throng where the competitors could shoot their arrows into the targets, which were positioned on the stage.

The afternoon sun throbbed, sometimes charging and sometimes sapping the competitors' strength. The tournament had started early that morning but the ongoing rounds had separated the wheat from the chaff and now only three competitors remained: Agrippa, Mutilus Bulla and one other, whose name Agrippa failed to hear over the cacophonous crowd.

Bulla was the threat. The people cheered his name not because he was the Senate's champion (and he would dedicate his victory to the Republic if he proved triumphant) but rather because most of them had placed a bet on the favourite. Bulla had not let them down in the past and it was likely that he would not let them down now.

Bulla's tanned body was taut with muscle. He was both tall and broad, bull-necked and square-jawed. He wore a light blue tunic inlaid with gold thread. Agrippa couldn't help but notice the archer's necklace too, strewn with polished teeth and small bones. Trophies from previous kills. Poking out through his tunic were two legs which were as thick and sturdy as pillars or tree trunks. His brawny, tattooed arms were only a little narrower than his legs. There was an intimidating solidity to his figure. A flat, brawler's face only added to his fearsome appearance. His large, yew bow was decorated with ivory and gold.

Bulla spoke to Agrippa in the early rounds, while he was taking his shots.

"Good aim, boy. This is your first competition it seems... Rest that arm, it'll grow tired soon and feel like a piece of lead hanging off you shoulder..."

His voice was low and guttural. Agrippa continued to take his shots. He'd suffered worse distractions and insults from fellow soldiers at the camp he had trained with in Macedonia.

He's also too big to get inside your head.

By the third round Bulla was merely grunting, either appreciatively or dismissively, whilst Agrippa fired off his five arrows.

For the final round the distance to the target was extended as fresh wooden boards marked with inner and outer circles were placed at the back of the stage, and the line from which the competitors were asked to shoot from was moved back by ten paces. Bulla grinned as he watched the youth gulp, assessing the new challenge.

"This should now separate the men from the boys, eh?" Bulla declared within earshot of his rivals, coughing up and spitting out phlegm afterwards.

The third man taking part in the final appeared not to hear the cheap taunt. Agrippa looked him over. He was middle-aged, slim but well-conditioned and could often be found wryly smiling at a private joke. His dress neither singled him out as being rich or being poor. His complexion was pale – which led Agrippa to believe that the stranger was visiting from a foreign, colder land, although after overhearing the stranger speak Agrippa couldn't tell his background from his accent. The stranger had been fortunate to be in the final after nearly being knocked out a couple of rounds earlier (save for a brilliant – or lucky – final arrow).

At the very least I'll come second. But second isn't good enough…

Agrippa glanced up at Octavius, who was sitting next to Oppius in the crowd. Agrippa was looking thoughtful whereas Oppius was looking at a busty brunette sitting a couple of rows down from him. Agrippa pictured the look of disappointment on their faces should he not prevail. He sank his chin into his chest. He felt nauseous. Yet his spirits lifted as he imagined the look on Caecilia's face should he present her with the gold, sapphire-encrusted trophy. She was in the crowd, having petitioned Cicero to bring her. Agrippa dared not stare up at the woman he cherished for fear of distracting himself or having his expression betray his heart to Cicero or Octavius. She understood and tried to temper her emotions and reactions too, lest Cicero read something in her profile as he sat next to her.

"If I was looking for gold from a suitor then I could have married someone else years ago," Caecilia had said to Agrippa the previous evening, after he explained that he wanted to win the valuable trophy for her.

"I want to give something to you though."

"You already have – twice," the woman replied, lying next to him on the bed, with a minx-like grin on her face and laughter filling

93

the air. The pair had made love for the first time. Agrippa arranged to rent a clean, well furnished apartment close to where Caecilia was staying with Cicero. He bought a fine vintage, decorated the room with flowers and painted her a picture of the valley where they had first met (this time without including the sketch of an aqueduct).

"I want your first time to be special," Agrippa said, coming up for air after they kissed.

"It is. It's with you."

The virginal girl was nervous at first but then willingly surrendered to the experience and pleasure the second time round; she stretched out her singing body and then held him tight, coiling her legs and arms around his sweat-glazed muscular torso. Agrippa was tender and conscious of not wanting to seem too much of a practised lover for fear of Caecilia getting the wrong idea about his past.

She had sighed, breathlessly and beautifully, as she climaxed. She sighed again now as the master of ceremonies announced Agrippa's name in the list of finalists. Her heart raced and she wanted to briefly catch his eye and communicate her love and support – to combat the majority of the spectators who lacked both for him. The crowd undulated, like a serpent, around the theatre. The smell of cheap wine and sweat wafted in the air. Soldiers and officials began to link arms to prevent the spectators from veering too close to the remaining participants.

"Do you have a preference, my dear, as to who you would like see win?" Cicero asked.

"I hope the best man wins, of course," Caecilia answered, fanning herself in the shimmering heat, hoping to cool her crimsoning face.

"Well I'm not sure who the best *man* may be but the best archer, I am told, is Bulla. He was loyal to Pompey rather than Caesar in the civil war and I'm reliably informed that he intends to spoil Octavius' party and dedicate his prospective victory to the Republic. It used to be that myself and the likes of Hortensius and Cato would give speeches and the mob would listen. Now it appears that monosyllabic archers can do so too. But I suppose it's still preferable to listening the voice of the great unwashed mob itself."

Octavius briefly bit his bottom lip and betrayed his nerves. His anxiety was more for his friend than himself. He would be disappointed but not distraught if Bulla walked off with the trophy.

The crowd cheered when I arrived and they will cheer when I leave. Their chants of "Caesar" were as much for me as Julius, I warrant.

Octavius again scanned below him, where the aristocrats were sitting in the crowd, to see if she had come. But she hadn't. Livia's husband, who had opposed Julius Caesar, was now wary of being seen to support his heir. Other women had been in his bed since the party but Livia had occupied his thoughts.

Agrippa gulped down a cup of water and then poured a second over his head to take the sting out of his sunburnt skin.

The young archer squinted as he tried to make out the target in the distance. He would have to draw his bowstring back even further and judge a new arc of flight.

A boisterous section of the crowd continued to hurl insults at the fresh-faced archer. Some of them had bet half a week's wages on Bulla. A stream of curses came out of their mouths accompanied by a surprising amount of spittle which spotted the sand. A lazy-eyed, gap-toothed member of the throng, not content with hurling abuse, was also tempted to hurl half an apple at the unsuspecting young soldier. His rumbling stomach thought better of it however.

"Take no notice of them lad. They probably have more to lose than you, in terms of the bets they've placed on the competition," the strange-accented archer amiably remarked. "I've just been called, by one particular cretin, both a 'wanker' and a 'eunuch' within the same sentence."

Agrippa smiled, easing his tension. "There are a few betting on us it seems. But the smart money is on Bulla," he remarked.

"Money's neither smart nor foolish. But people are usually the latter. You'll do fine though, lad. You shoot well. Remember to control your breathing and as a result you'll control your aim more. This final round won't be won or lost on the first two arrows, so don't despair if you get off to a bad start. You might now be asking why I'm helping you. It's because if I don't win I'd like you to pick up the trophy. Bulla is a cretin and a bully, who'll prove neither honourable in victory or defeat."

"My name's Marcus Agrippa. What's yours?" the young archer said, offering his hand to the stranger.

"Well, 'Outsider' and 'Lucky Bastard' are two of the more polite names I've been called today."

The cacophonous noise continued to stretch upwards, as if desiring to alert the gods to the tournament.

Octavius caught the eye of Aulus Hirtius as he scanned across the audience. The consul designate gave the young Caesar a nod. Originally Hirtius had aligned himself with Mark Antony after the assassination but Cicero had persuaded him to side with republicans in the senate. Julius had always spoken well of Hirtius. He was a competent commander and more scholarly than most of Caesar's lieutenants. Caesar had entrusted Hirtius with editing and completing his book on the Gallic Wars. As to his Pansa, Hirtius' fellow consul designate, he would follow his friend's lead. Neither Octavius nor Hirtius knew much they could trust the other at present. Or how much they might need each other. They were neither allies nor enemies – yet.

The young Caesar nodded back, respectfully. *Better to build rather than burn bridges.*

"So who do you think will win Lucius? Marcus or Bulla?" Octavius said, finishing off a plate of asparagus tips and turning towards the centurion.

Neither of them.

"I hope that Marcus wins," Oppius replied, his mind preoccupied by the thought of what he might spend his winnings on.

The trio drew lots as to which competitor would shoot first. Agrippa silently cursed his luck when he realised he would be starting the round off. But at least he would be getting things over with quickly and he might be able to put pressure on his fellow competitors by setting down a good score. Hitting the small black circle, which was the diameter of the span of a man's hand, was worth ten points whilst any arrow which hit the larger surrounding red circle on the board scored five points.

As Agrippa stepped up to his mark another wave of jeering hit him like a blast of hot air. Faces were contorted in antagonism and drunkenness. Blackened teeth were bared. A win for Bulla could see a number in the crowd swap their rags for the kind of fine tunics worn by those sitting in the stands. And a loss could mean them not eating or, worse, not drinking for a week. Some even appeared to be scuffling their feet along the ground to try and build up a dust cloud and narrow Bulla's odds on winning. The determined archer allowed the braying crowd to fall into the background though – ignoring the people as wilfully as a politician would.

Sweat soaked his brow and palms. The latter he rubbed against his tunic, to dry them. He tried to control his breathing and slow his quickening heart. Agrippa remembered something Oppius had told him when the tournament was first announced: "Just do the best you can. Winning will be a by-product." To accompany his advice the centurion bought the young archer a new bow and introduced him to the finest fletcher in the capital.

Agrippa breathed out and nocked his first arrow. Such was the expectation in the air that most of the crowd quietened themselves. If only the same could be said for Bulla.

"You've got more chance of hitting puberty than hitting that target boy," the surly archer remarked – and laughed at his own joke. "Remember, there's no pressure. Ha!"

Agrippa's contempt for the oaf fuelled his determination. Pressure had been shooting fire arrows at the pirate ship off the coast of Apollonia. Pressure had been launching arrows into a group of assassins who had ambushed his friends on the road to Rome, killing them before they killed him. He had succeeded then. He could succeed now.

The string cut into his fingers as he drew back the bow, further than he had ever pulled it back. He narrowed his eyes and strangely the target became bigger.

You can do this.

To compensate for the extra distance Agrippa aimed slightly higher – as he pictured the shaft arcing downwards into the centre of the target. He breathed out and in a moment of stillness, just before he believed that his arm might start to wobble from the strain, he fired his first arrow.

There was silence – and then more laughter from Bulla. Cheers from those who had bet on the favourite also reverberated in his ears. The arrow had thumped into the wooden board but outside both circles. Agrippa let out a curse. His blood pumping, in frustration rather than excitement, the archer nocked a second arrow and it zipped through the air – before again landing just outside the target. His face was flush from the heat and shame. He sighed.

You can't do this… You should have let Oppius shoot instead.

98

Agrippa dared not stare up at Octavius or Caecilia. He didn't want to witness the disappointment, or understanding, in their expressions. Yet he pictured Caecilia's face and heard her voice. He gently smiled as he recalled her words from the previous night: "If you win then I know how we should celebrate. But if you somehow lose then I know how to console you too," the woman had said, with a playful light in her eyes.

His smile widened. *You can do this. But if you can't she'll still love you. And Octavius will not think any less of you either.* Instead of cursing Agrippa offered up a couple of prayers to Venus and Pietas – for had he not entered the competition out of a sense of love and duty towards Caecilia and his best friend?

Agrippa filled his lungs with air and determination and nocked his third arrow.

Love and duty. Love and duty.

The shaft struck the board, inside the red circle for five points. A small cheer went up. Further cheers filled the air as the remaining brace of arrows scored five and then ten. The crowd appreciated the adolescent archer's pluck in coming back from such a terrible start. Even Bulla was temporarily lost for words. A portion of the crowd chanted Agrippa's name. The air rippled with applause. He turned and waved. As he did so he took in the looks of devotion and friendship from Caecilia and Octavius. They had both risen to their feet and were clapping.

Bulla shook his head as he stepped up to his mark, in condemnation of the fickle crowd. He snorted rather than breathed as he nocked the custom-made arrow for his custom-made bow. His neck and arms bulged with muscles and veins, like a marble statue of Atlas coming to life. His figure exuded strength as every arrow scored: five, five, ten, five and ten. A special cheer went up when the favourite went into the lead and eclipsed Agrippa's score. As he shot his final arrow and the scorer on the stage made a sign to verify the "ten" Bulla raised his arms in triumph as if he had already won. His chin jutted out in pride and victory. He roared and thumped his chest. The crowd chanted his name and he soaked up the adulation, nodding in approval of their admiration for him.

Many in the crowd began to think about what they would spend their winnings on, believing that Bulla's victory was now a foregone conclusion. The third, non-descript competitor had only made it to the final by accident.

"He's no threat. He's lucky to have even reached the final," Bulla remarked to a friend in the crowd, within earshot of his rival archer.

Agrippa offered up another couple of prayers for the stranger to win. The enigmatic stranger gave Agrippa a reassuring – and conspiratorial – wink as he stepped up to his mark. He seemed impervious to Bulla's words and the multitude of sounds around him. Agrippa noticed a steeliness and level of concentration in his features which had been absent in previous rounds. He examined the shaft and flights on his first arrow before nocking it. He waited a few moments for what little breeze existed to subside. His whole body, rather than just his arm, appeared to adjust itself as he smoothly pulled back the bowstring.

The arrow sang, rather than twanged, as it left the bow.

Ten.

A superior technique more than compensated for Bulla's brute strength. The theatre let out a collective gasp of surprise. In four fluid movements the stranger struck the inner black circle four more times. A few might have wondered if Apollo had taken possession of the mortal. Bulla's jaw, which had recently jutted itself out with pride, dropped to the ground in bewilderment. The only face in the crowd which appeared immune from astonishment was Lucius Oppius', as the centurion knew what his friend and former comrade was capable of. Unbridled applause rang out, even from those who had lost money on the outcome. Some stood dumb however, transfixed by the scarcely believable grouping of arrows housed at the centre of the target. They had been witness to a masterclass, or a miracle. Tavern goers would recount the episode for days. People would proudly say, "I was there".

"The harder you practise the luckier you get," the stranger remarked to a sour-faced Bulla. The expert archer then turned to Agrippa. "In answer to your question earlier lad, the name's Teucer."

*

The friends drank long into the night, celebrating Teucer's triumph – although Agrippa retired early to write a note to Caecilia. As he was awarded the gleaming trophy Teucer (a native of Briton who had served alongside Oppius under Caesar – and whose real name was Adiminus) gave a short speech: "I spent a good part of my life and career fighting for Caesar, from the beaches of Britain to the plains of Pharsalus. As much as he gained personal glory from his campaigns he always fought for what was best for the people of Rome. I would be equally proud to use my bow in the service of his son, Octavius Caesar, who shares his father's courage and generosity."

On hearing Teucer dedicate his victory to Octavius a number of staunch republican senators got up and walked out of the theatre. Mutilus Bulla also decided not to stand on ceremony and left the arena before his rival was awarded the trophy. Witnessing the fearsome scowl on his face the sea of people duly parted to let the defeated archer through. He muttered to himself as he left, arguing that he would have raised his performance if he had known the true extent of his competition. "I've been cheated. A plague on you all." Octavius noted how Hirtius remained behind and still applauded the winning archer.

Octavius invited Teucer (along with Oppius and Agrippa) back to his villa. Wine, women and a victory banquet were laid out before them. The pleasure-loving archer licked his lips at all of them. On seeing the Briton up close Octavius realised that he had met the soldier before, in Rome, many years ago – as he and a fellow soldier named Marcus Fabius had come to his house to deliver a letter from his great-uncle.

"We've both become a Caesar since our last meeting, in some ways. After Pharsalus I went home to lead my tribe in Britain. The weather may be inhospitable there but thankfully my people welcomed me back. I think I also raised their spirits by the wagon load of wine I brought back with me. I'm here to raise some capital again, to take back with me and provide for my tribe, should you have use for my bow. I also wouldn't mind finding out who was behind the attack on you on the road to Rome. Roscius was a good friend. Just say the word and I'll put an arrow between the eyes of the man who hired his killer."

Before reaching the villa Oppius also took Teucer aside, partly to give him his share of the winnings from the bet he had placed on his friend.

"I'm glad you're here," the centurion said with relief and a certain weariness. "The world may have turned upside down but at least I can rely on your aim and friendship. In murdering Caesar they killed any chance of peace, prosperity and stability. Rome is again a prize that's up for grabs, which men will wade through a river of blood to secure. Antony can't be trusted. If Cassius gains power he will add Octavius' name to a proscription list in the blink of an eye. My name would doubtless follow. Hirtius will side with his new optimate friends rather than with the veterans who he fought alongside – and had his life saved by – during Caesar's campaigns."

"Have we picked the right side? As Antony has said, Octavius is just a boy with a name. From what I can gather his forces are fewer than half that of Antony's or the Republic's. The odds are against him," Teucer replied. Although he had praised his former general for his courage and generosity during his speech the Briton was also aware of Caesar's ambition and cruelty. It was just as likely that Octavius could inherit the dictator's vices as well as virtues.

"As you showed today, the favourite doesn't always finish first. And as Julius once said, it's where you are at the end of the race that counts."

13.

The tiled floor was sticky with wine, at least Enobarbus hoped it was just wine. Dice, broken jugs, oyster shells, strophums, half-eaten trays of food and olive stones also littered the floor. It had been quite a party. Most of the lamps had burned out but dawn was stirring. If only the same could be said for the occupants of the chamber. Enobarbus noted Felix Calvinus snoring in one corner, being propped up by a dockside drab. Manius Sura slept in the opposite corner, a serving boy lay curled up by his feet. Antony scarcely needed to have a reason to throw a party but he was celebrating the coming together of some of his friends and retinue who had journeyed from Rome to Brundisium: the lute-player Anaxenor, the dancer Metrodorus and the flautist Xanthus (who, by the looks of him, had performed his party trick of sucking up wine through his flute a few too many times).

Enobarbus pursed his lips in disappointment as he took in his general, slumped over a couch – his tongue hanging out like a dog. Metrodorus lay slumped over him, her usually beguiling face smeared with make-up. Her dress left little to the imagination (not that the dancer couldn't fire a man's imagination regardless).

If less is more she's wearing too much.

Antony's lieutenant didn't regret his decision to pass on the previous night's revelries. He'd had work to catch up on. Enobarbus had spent the evening writing to various supporters and would-be supporters of the consul. Some he offered bribes to, promising positions of influence or lucrative government contracts should they side with Antony. Some he threatened, in a veiled way or otherwise. After every upheaval there were always proscription lists. Gradations of guilt were often linked to property prices. The greater the estate the greater the punishment. Despite having procured the bulk of the treasury and the bulk of Caesar's estate (although Antony argued that they could be classified as being one and the same) his commander still needed more resources. Antony would at least agree with Cicero that "Endless money forms the sinews of war" – though they were unlikely to agree on anything else, Enobarbus thought.

It was an arms race but Antony was confident he was winning. "We have a force that's three times as strong as our rivals and a commander ten times more experienced," the general had boasted to his lieutenant. But, having recently come from Rome, Enobarbus knew that the consul wasn't winning on all fronts. Octavius' games had been a success. Priests and augurs would have envied the way he played on superstitions in regards to the coming of the comet. Politicians must have admired – as well as resented – his capacity to make contrary promises to different groups of people. As well as securing support from Caesar's veterans Octavius was also becoming the housewife's favourite (especially perhaps with those wives whom he slept with). Where the son of Caesar used to command sympathy he now commanded respect.

And with Octavius' star on the rise Enobarbus recognised Antony's popularity wane in the capital as though the two figures stood either side on the scales. Graffiti was beginning to spring up around the city labelling the consul a thief and a tyrant. Some propaganda even accused Antony of being part of the assassination plot to murder Caesar.

The people no longer seemed to believe in him.

But the people change their minds more times than a woman buying shoes.

The most important thing was that Enobarbus still believed in the man who had saved his life at Alesia. The man who had commanded the left wing at the battle of Pharsalus. The First Man of Rome. And his friend.

History will treat him well. History will judge him on what will happen in the future rather than what is happening now. Caesar slaughtered a million barbarians during his campaigns in Gaul but he was hailed a conquering hero.

Should any other man have woken him at such an early hour, with such a hangover, they would have experienced a less jovial Antony compared to the one who had held court the previous evening but the general forgave his lieutenant for disturbing him.

"Morning Domitius," Antony slurred, his bleary eyes cowering from the light. "From the look on your face – and the fact that you've woken me at dawn – I take it it's bad news?"

His voice was rough, his throat dry. His tongue felt furry and fat in his mouth. His brow throbbed. He felt hungry but knew he wouldn't be able to hold down any food. The morning after was always worth paying for the night before though. As Antony untangled himself from Metrodorus, the dancer stirred a little. Her eyes remained closed yet she still smiled dreamily, a reflex action from hearing her patron's voice and smelling his scent.

Antony picked up a large jug of water as if it were no heavier than a cup and gulped down a third of its contents. He put on a silk robe, embroidered with golden thread, which hung upon a throne-like chair. Enobarbus then passed him the letter. It was now Antony's turn to purse his lips as he noticed the seal on the correspondence.

"It's even worse than bad news," the general remarked, as he scanned the message. "She's already on her way."

Fulvia. Even when sober Antony's wife – or just the very thought of her – was capable of giving the consul a headache. The sound of her shrewish voice hammered into him like nails going into a crucifix. In order to maintain his marriage Antony had realised, long ago, that he needed to spend as much time away from his wife as possible. Being on campaign and serving Caesar had provided him with genuine reasons to be absent from Rome (although even when living in the capital Antony would much rather spend his evenings with his mistresses than his wife).

"I'm happy to let you off the leash, as long as you come running when I call your name," Fulvia had once remarked to her husband. She was ambitious for herself – which largely meant being ambitious for Antony. She had been proud to marry the charming, attractive lieutenant of Caesar. He had been the Second Man of Rome, then. She believed that other women envied her or, better still, feared her.

Antony had married Fulvia for her money. She had paid his debts and, even now, her network of bankers, merchants, aristocrats and senators helped cement his powerbase. "I feel like I'll be paying off my debt to her for the rest of my life. I would rather owe the moneylenders," Antony had confessed to his lieutenant one evening. Although Antony wasn't his wife's puppet Fulvia still controlled many of the purse strings. There were still traces of beauty in her sharp features but little softness or femininity in her heart. Satirists derided her and called her a "she-wolf". Her greatest desire was to rule a ruler, govern those who governed. She could be ruthless on a political level and cruel on a personal one. On hearing how Cleopatra often punished servants who displeased her by sticking hairpins into their limbs she imitated the Egyptian queen. The terror on her victim's faces amused her.

"Come Domitius, let us talk outside. There are more pleasant sounds to wake to in the morning than that of Felix snoring."

Antony and his lieutenant walked out onto the first floor balcony of the grand villa. At first the consul winced slightly and shielded his eyes from the rising sun and cloudless blue sky. But then he smiled – his tired countenance becoming handsome again – as he took in the picturesque view. The colonnaded balcony looked out across the crescent-shaped bay of Brundisium. The flower-filled garden of the villa framed the foreground. Petals of amber sunlight and tufts of foam decorated the expansive, shimmering sea. Ships, their sails seemingly puffed out with pride, sailed off over the horizon or skirted along the coast. Many of the ships, Antony thought, would be bringing in supplies for his burgeoning army – or silks and perfumes for his cohort of mistresses. The general had instructed his quartermasters to dictate prices to merchants rather than vice-versa. "Order them to comply, for the good of Rome." When some of the merchants complained that really they were being ordered to do so for the good of Antony the quartermaster's argued that they were now one and the same thing.

The sea breeze took the sting out of the humid air. Birds silently winged their way across his eye-line. He could thankfully no longer hear the snoring from inside. All seemed peaceful. Yet the smile fell from Antony's face when he remembered that Fulvia would be arriving soon. His brief moment of peace shattered like glass (or like a plate – which Fulvia was fond of smashing when she grew angry). She had been better as a mistress than wife, Antony thought. She had been fun-loving and had tried harder to please him back then. Fulvia had clung to him out of devotion when they had first became lovers. Now she held onto his arm as if he were her possession when they attended parties together. Marriage had worked its magic and dissipated any affection or passion they felt for one another. Over the years, during their lovemaking, she had grown colder, unresponsive, he judged. *Soon it'll be like making love to a corpse.* Enobarbus had recently reported to him that his wife had been spending a large amount of time in the company of his brother, Lucius. "They deserve each other, such is their raw selfishness and ambition," Antony had remarked. "Lucius can even fuck her, for all I care. She's so cold he may well contract frostbite. Aye, let him fuck her until his cock falls off."

"Has Fulvia mentioned how long she will be staying for?" Enobarbus asked, thinking that he would move his plans forward to return to Rome. Partly because of the influence the lieutenant held over her husband Fulvia little disguised her resentment for him.

"Even if it's a brief visit she'll be staying for too long," Antony replied, sighing as well as joking. He took in the landscape again and filled his lungs with the warm sea air. "There are worse views in the world, no? It's like a painting or a perfect moment caught in time. Have you ever dreamed of going back to a perfect moment in your life Domitius?"

"I like to think that my best days are ahead of me."

Having been a soldier for nearly half of his life Enobarbus had little desire to return to a time of war. He had experienced enough violence and death for ten lifetimes. Enobarbus saw it as his job now to facilitate peace, either through diplomacy or by helping Antony to a quick and decisive victory.

"Sometimes I wish I was back in Rome, during my youth. With Curio and Clodius. I once arranged a competition with the former, to see which one of us could sleep with as many cousins from just one family. Curio won but I had a fun time in coming second. We would make a wager on almost anything. We once tossed a coin on whether one of Clodius' slaves should live or die after having been caught stealing. I led a carefree life. I slept during the day and my nights were filled with parties and love affairs. I was a slave to my pleasures, or rather I was a master of them. The only burden of choice I experienced involved deciding who I should sleep with each evening. Am I still not, in party, the Antony of old though? Can I ever wholly bury him or the past? People only can gain bad reputations, they can never lose them. Or I was happiest when in Egypt? I married together a life of pleasure and a life of duty and martial glory. The Egyptians understood and loved me. The army

109

also taught me that there was more to life than just wine, women and song. I owe a duty to Rome and its people. Julius saw something in me and at that moment I saw something in myself. Hercules is always lauded for his strength, never his wisdom. Yet you are also right, my friend, why should I not consider that my best days are ahead of me? Why shouldn't I complete Caesar's reforms and carry out his campaign in the east to retrieve the standards which Crassus lost? Or better still I should come out from his shadow and initiate my own reforms and military campaigns – be a slave and master to my own ambitions."

Antony grasped the air as he spoke, in hope and determination. Sometimes Enobarbus thought that his general was a man who didn't know what he wanted and sometimes he thought that Antony wanted everything. Sometimes he seduced, sometimes he wanted to be seduced – either by a woman or a cause.

"We also need to be mindful of the ambitions of others. Initial reports have been confirmed that Brutus has conducted raids against our forces and supplies in Macedonia. He's recruiting an army although he will not be able to mobilise any significant force soon. Cicero has been writing begging letters on his behalf, I believe, looking to raise capital and political support for his former acolyte. Sooner or later we will have to deal with Brutus," Enobarbus remarked. *Soldiers rather than diplomats will ultimately decide the outcome.*

"The self-righteous prig. I agree that Brutus won't abandon his cause. For all of his noble posturing he's just a dog with the bone of republicanism between his teeth. Brutus thinks that he's got right on his side but the gods on are the side of those with the biggest and best legions. Let us deal with him sooner rather than later. I cannot spare the time or men to have a small army chase him around Macedonia at the moment. But I want him dead. Brutus is the figurehead, and once he's gone support for Cassius and the other libertores will scatter to the wind."

"I'll take care of it," Antony's agent stated, having already formed the basis of a plan. Instead of employing mercenaries and arranging an ambush, as he had done in the failed attempt to murder Octavius on his way to Rome, Enobarbus would use subtler means to assassinate the praetor. It would even be the case that Brutus would invite his killer into his own home.

After Enobarbus finished his morning report Antony retired to his bedroom. He would wake at midday and summon Metrodorus – and one of her friends – to his chamber. He still had a day or so to enjoy himself before his wife arrived.

14.

Time passes.

Leaden skies snuffed out the dusk. Summer was receding too. Cicero sat in his study, in his house on the Palatine. *The darkness always returns and dominates.* Tiro entered, stoked the small fire and placed a blanket around his master's shoulders. When the statesman had first taken his secretary on he had felt a certain paternal affection for the bright-minded and hard-working slave (whom he eventually freed) but now Cicero was more like the child and Tiro was the parent. Tiro felt his old master flinch as a raucous shout sounded out from the street outside. Drunks – be they rowdy aristocrats or plebs – were an unwelcome disturbance. The writer, whether drafting a book, speech or correspondence, needed quietude to concentrate. Cicero momentarily yearned to be back at his villa at Puteoli, couched in the bower of nature. Fields and streams didn't expect anything of him or remind him of failure. Rome did. Atticus had recently implored him to leave the capital, return to his country retreat and write history books. Be free of politics. Be free from danger. *But I still have it within me to make history as opposed to just write about it. All these years I've told myself that I've been above the concerns of the world but really I've just been hiding from them too much.*

"Thank you, Tiro. Although I could well be shivering from the prospect of Antony becoming dictator instead of merely consul. Crime and taxes are up, business confidence is down. The state's funds are devoted to building up his army instead of building roads, baths and theatres. Our young men are lining up outside of taverns to be recruited when they should be planting and harvesting crops. Such is Antony's desperation for men that one of his centurions

112

may well even try to recruit you, my friend," Cicero joked, appreciating the renewed glow and warmth from the fire.

"I am not sure how much use I'd be. The only experience I have with a blade is using a letter knife," the sharp-witted secretary replied. "But these are indeed dark times." *Rome is like a drunk, staggering around on top of a cliff. It is just a matter of time before he meets his end. Civil war is imminent as surely as night follows day or corruption follows winning office.*

"But it's always darkest before the dawn. Where there's life there's hope." Cicero remarked, his voice and body more animated. He clasped the younger man's forearm to bolster the secretary's spirits. The statesman proceeded to open a message from one of his agents, who had infiltrated Antony's army camp at Brundisium.

*

Laughter and the intoxicating smell of perfume swirled around the air. Teucer had just told another joke: "'How do you want your haircut?' said the barber to the customer. 'In silence'."

The party – Oppius, Agrippa, Balbus, Teucer, Pollux and Milo – were returning to Rome from their mission in Brundisium. Balbus had arranged for them to spend the evening at the house of one Septimus Vinicius, an old merchant friend of Caesar's. As per Balbus' instructions, which out of love or fear Vinicius followed to the letter, their host laid on some entertainment.

"Did you like that one lad?" Teucer called out to Agrippa. Since the archery competition the Briton had grown fond of the young Roman. He spent many a morning with him, practising. At first Agrippa felt somewhat frustrated and deficient compared the veteran bowman but Teucer then made his day by saying that Agrippa was a more accomplished archer than the Briton had been when he was nineteen.

Agrippa didn't respond, however, as he had already left the celebrations. Teucer put the boy's behaviour down to tiredness but

113

Oppius, noticing that it wasn't the first time that Agrippa had turned down some entertainment, suspected that the normally red-blooded soldier was saving himself for someone special back in the capital. *The lad's either noble or stupid enough to remain faithful to someone.*

The Briton merely shrugged in the face of his friend's absence and duly turned his attention to the lissom girl – Clara – lying next to him on the sofa. Age – and the rigours of her trade – had yet to despoil her beauty. There was still a natural air of joy and hope in her aspect. The soldier didn't know whether to be attracted to her all the more for her freshness or pity her all the more, for time would despoil her in the end. It had done the same for his wife back home, but then again the archer had shrugged his shoulders in the face of that too. Vinicius had spotted Clara in the local market and made an offer that the carpenter's daughter could not afford to refuse. The merchant had said that Clara "had potential." He also promised that she would be "his special girl" – though few remained special for more than a month. Women were, for the merchant, either assets or liabilities. And their value always depreciated over time. It was always a matter of when, rather than if, Vinicius would sell his special girls on.

Clara popped a couple of grapes in her mouth and then leaned over, crushing her lips against the fun-loving soldier's.

I wish she tasted of wine instead of grapes.

"I've never been with a Briton before," Clara said, beaming enthusiastically. There was a disarming mixture of innocence and curiosity in the girl's unaffected voice.

"We are lovers of wine and women. Unfortunately our love for the former can sometimes hinder our ability to please the latter."

Aulus Milo grinned even more widely than the teenage girl as the Nubian courtesan he had picked out straddled him on the sofa opposite to the archer. Her low-cut gown showed the promise of

114

things to come. The girl Teucer was with may have been considered *beautiful* but his whore was *bountiful*. Niobe was a woman of few words, spoken in broken Latin, but that didn't bother the enamoured centurion.

"I love a woman with a huskier voice than me," Milo remarked to Oppius, who was sitting next to him alongside a bronzed, Arab woman entwining her tattooed arms around his neck.

"Aye, but also one who is slimmer and prettier," Oppius replied, as the courtesan proceeded to thrust her tongue into his ear and twist it around for good measure.

"I agree. I should thank you. You promised me gold but you have also given me ebony," Milo declared, running his hands along the Nubian's oiled, strong thighs.

"Shall we go somewhere quiet?" she whispered into his ear, like a kiss.

"Yes, although we may not be quiet for long," the ribald soldier answered and then laughed at his own joke. Niobe led him off to a room upstairs, although he briefly returned to retrieve a jug of wine.

Cephas Pollux also gave thanks to Oppius for convincing him to side with Octavius, given the favourable position he was now in. Pollux sat in a chair in the corner of the room, with a sweet-smelling dancer on his lap, writhing against his groin and flicking her braided hair in his face as she turned her head sideways to the music playing in her mind. A slit in her gauze-like scarlet dress revealed a slender, silken thigh which gleamed in the light of the ornate lamps hanging from the ceiling. As she rhythmically undulated her feline body the dozen or so silver bangles on her arms clinked together. Her jangling reminded Pollux of a dinner bell. *It's time for me to go eat.*

The lust-filled centurion kissed her – hungrily – and then carried her upstairs. She sighed in his arms. She said something in a foreign

115

language which the Roman couldn't understand, yet he knew what she meant. Pollux made sure to pick a room that wasn't situated next to the one that his friend was in. He didn't want to hear Milo through the walls and similarly he didn't want Milo to hear him.

Despite the obvious distraction of the woman's serpentine leg curling its way around his Oppius noticed that Balbus had disappeared for the evening, as well as Agrippa. "It's my job to remain off stage and to just prompt the actors should they forget their lines," the political adviser once confessed to the centurion. "I'm happy to go unnoticed but not unrewarded."

His expression was often as impassive and unreadable as a professional gambler's, Oppius thought. He was forever working out odds, options and outcomes. Perhaps even Balbus was pushing himself too far of late though. His tan couldn't completely mask the rings around his eyes. But the hard work had paid off. Their mission had been a success.

"As much as you might wake up with a sore head in the morning Antony will feel worse," Balbus had remarked to the soldier as they rode back from Brundisium. "Cicero could now be the key to unlocking things. Octavius will meet with him soon, carrying an olive branch in one hand and a sword in the other."

The Arabian courtesan snaked her arm around the centurion and pulled him closer. She flicked out her tongue and teased him with kisses, on all but his lips. The careworn soldier thought of Livia but only briefly. She hummed in pleasure as Oppius slid his hand beneath her finely embroidered dress. The fate of Octavius and Rome soon fell into the background.

"Pleasure is the beginning and end of living happily," Teucer pronounced, quoting Epicurus, after downing another cup of wine (though half dripped down his chin). Clara grinned and nodded in agreement but then stopped his mouth with a kiss. She thought that the Briton talked too much.

116

*

Dear Atticus,

I have just received a report from one of my agents at Brundisium. A lightning bolt has struck, cleaving Antony's forces apart (though he still retains more than half unfortunately). A couple of evenings ago Balbus and Lucius Oppius, along with a number of others, infiltrated Antony's camp. It was a bold move but, as Terence wrote, "Fortune favours the brave." Oppius met with a number of officers and by force of argument, or more likely bribery, the Sword of Rome (a crass title if ever I heard one) cut ties between them and Antony. At the same time Balbus and his agents distributed propaganda throughout the camp. They also offered to pay five hundred denari for any man to join up with Octavius and avenge their former general's death. The legions at Brundisium were Caesar's veterans. A dead tyrant meant more to them than a living consul. Tellingly they had never served under Antony ("the appeaser" – as some of the soldiers called him). Some of the senior officers had also met Octavius in Apollonia. Balbus appealed to both their honour and purses. Not even the Senate could rival the amount of money and false promises that were spread around during the night. Soldiers have spent so much time around whores over the years that they become like them – and offer themselves out to the highest bidder.

Antony's greatest enemy was himself, however, as he summoned his men before him the next day. Some shouted out for the general to join Octavius' cause. Some demanded that Antony match the bounty that Caesar's heir was offering. At the beginning of the year the legions had expected to be fighting in a glorious – and profitable – campaign in Parthia. But now they believed they were being coerced into fighting a civil war for a fraction of the reward. My agent also noted how, though Antony might be praised as a soldier and officer, he has no track record as an overall

117

commander. I can picture his snarling face and blood-shot eyes. Antony poured oil, rather than water, on the flames of discontent and mutiny. "You will obey orders!" he shrilly cried, his hand clasping his sword. Blank and dispirited faces looked back at him. Antony longs to be Caesar but thankfully he lacks Julius' charm and clemency. His charmless and cruel wife goaded him on (my agent reported that Fulvia was "as angry as the Medusa, with a withering stare to rival her"). Luckily Antony's better half, Enobarbus, was absent and couldn't advise caution. Antony set an example – the wrong one – and executed a number of popular officers and legionaries. Apparently Fulvia spat in the faces of the soldiers just before they were tortured and killed. Also, it was rumoured that during one centurion's execution blood splattered her chin and she licked it off like wine. I will duly turn such rumours into facts. Fulvia enjoyed herself all too much. Politics is vindictive and treacherous enough already without having women getting involved in proceedings as well. For every scream that sounded out across the camp Antony lost more and more men. Yet still he continued to dig his own grave and tried to instil loyalty through fear. Any man can make mistakes but only a fool persists in his folly. The legions he punished the most – the Fourth and Martia – were the ones which marched off to join Octavius. Antony did half of Balbus' job for him. One man's tragedy is another man's happy ending. When the trickle of legionaries deserting Antony turned into a deluge he saw the error of his ways. But he could not turn back the tide despite promising to match Octavius' bounty for each man. It was too little, too late.

So where does this leave us my friend? The Second and Thirty-Fifth legions are still due to join-up with Antony soon, along with a contingent of Moorish cavalry, but his army has been significantly diminished. Victory over Decimus Brutus, as Antony looks to take Ciscalpine Gaul, is not a foregone conclusion.

118

Decimus is up for the fight. He wrote to me the other week to say he would be the anvil onto which Antony could strike but that he would hold firm until the forces of the Republic could attack Antony's rear. "Put a real and metaphorical spear between his shoulder blades." Yet at present the army of the Republic would barely defeat a troupe of travelling players. The Senate, as ever, has been big on promises but short on delivery. Such is our war chest that Hirtius and Pansa may end up commanding an army full of eunuchs, greybeards and housewives. Still, it could be worse. At least it won't be an army full of Gauls. The first words they learn in Latin as children are, "I surrender".

We will need Octavius' forces to tip the balance in our favour. I can only hope that by championing him I can sway the Senate into forming an alliance. I believe I can control him, train the errant pup. He should be given praise, titles of distinction – and then be disposed of. What Octavius has been doing, in building a private army, is nothing short of villainy but the enemy of our enemy must be our friend. The ends justify the means. Or am I just telling myself what I want to hear? Perhaps this old advocate has told himself and others more lies over the years than the sum of the falsehoods that have come out of the mouths of the clients I have represented. But I must try to save the Republic. I may not be able to command legions but I can mobilise language and send it into battle.

It is getting late. Tiro has just stoked the fire but he has slyly taken away my basket of logs, to prompt me into going to bed. Even the stars in the sky seem heavy-lidded. They are seemingly closing their eyes rather than blinking.

I hope you are well. You must be missing Caecilia but if it's any consolation your loss has been my gain. She is a great comfort and great company. I was unsure whether she would take to the capital – Rome can prove too real (or unreal) at times – but she has an uncommon glow about her at present and there is a spring in her step. I joked to her yesterday that, if I didn't know any better, I would say that she was in love. She laughed and replied that she most definitely didn't have a suitor in the capital at the moment.

In regards to some other news which may be of interest Quintus Caepio died last week. All in all he was a half-decent advocate and half-decent man. He won or lost cases with an enlightened, enviable equanimity. "Just so long as I get paid," Quintus would say. His funeral was attended by Rome's biggest and best fraudsters and embezzlers – ones who he had represented over the years. Some brought their strapping young sons along and made a point of introducing them to the rich widow. I could ask, do they not have any shame? But, alas, we already know the answer to that question. Sentius Taurus, who duly attended the funeral, approached me recently about acting as his advocate in his imminent trial. He has been accused of accounting fraud, again. I turned him down flat. "Euclid would have to re-write the laws of mathematics to clear your name," I remarked. I half expected Sentius to then ask if I could provide him with Euclid's address or furnish an introduction.

The only defence I can muster for Sentius is that at least he is a colourful character. Our new breed of politicians/criminals are so dull that they don't even have any traits to satirise. They spend the half their lives working as clerks to senators and the remainder of their existence as senators themselves. It used to be that men went into office because of their wealth but more and more there is a professional class of politician who enter office in order to extort wealth from their position. In their culture of bribes (offering and receiving), cronyism and expense scandals they make Sentius look like an amateur. Yet these men, invariably of middle-class rank, strut around like patricians and possess an elitist contempt for the likes of soldiers, farmers and tradesmen. Too many consider me an irrelevance too, an antique from a bygone age. They joke or *snigger when I walk past. When I challenged one of these oily-haired bureaucrats the other day and said that Antony could well turn himself into another Catiline he looked at me blank-faced. Catiline was neither a memory nor lesson from history for the dullard. "To be ignorant of what occurred before you were born is to remain always a child," I stated.*

I feel like I may be the only thing standing between Antony and another dictatorship – a Roman Cassandra. But I have no desire to compose the Republic's funeral oration. I will not go gently into that good night. But it's late and I do need to get some sleep. I have impersonated Nestor for too long. I will write again soon and I look forward to your reply in regards to the latest turn of events.

Cicero

15

Rain pimpled the marble slabs from an earlier shower. The dapple-grey clouds augured further rain or a storm.

Octavius noticed his foot tapping in nervousness and impatience as he sat on a stone bench in his garden, waiting for Cicero. He put a stop to the movement, tucking his leg beneath the bench. He did not wish to display any anxieties to the statesman – or himself.

Octavius had received a message from Cicero a day after returning to the capital, having met with his newly expanded army. Firstly – and most importantly – Octavius had paid his new soldiers. He thanked them for their support as well.

"I will repay loyalty with loyalty just as I will repay blood with blood in terms of those who murdered my father. I am not a revolutionary, nor do I crave a senseless civil war. I just want to make sure that Caesar's reforms and promises are honoured. I must defend myself and Caesar's legacy."

Oppius also used the visit to set in place a training regime for officers and legionaries alike. The army would need to be battle-ready soon, whether it faced Antony or the forces of the Republic.

The statues of Caesar and Alexander the Great, which had previously resided in the corner of the garden, had been replaced by newly acquired sculptures of Cincinnatus and Aristotle. There was a slight chill in the air and Octavia, who had visited her brother that morning, insisted that he wear a red woollen cloak she had bought him, over his tunic. A small, polished bronze table sat in front of the bench with some of Cicero's favourite foods upon it.

Octavius rose to his feet when he heard the approaching footsteps as an attendant escorted the esteemed statesman out into the garden where his master was waiting. The two men, separated by decades, greeted each other warmly. "When you shake his hand do so as an equal," Balbus said, before the meeting. "There is no reason to defer to him. Remember, he requested to see you. Cicero needs you more than you need him. But do not underestimate him. An old fox is still a fox."

Cicero's usually round face seemed drawn. His brow was wrinkled in fatigue and worry. But there was still a stubborn vigour in his demeanour, his bright eyes were still intelligent as well as rheumy. The veteran politician smiled to himself as he noticed the new statues which had been introduced into the garden to make a subtle impression on him. No doubt the book, strategically placed on the bench, was one of his own. Cicero smiled because he had stage-managed such scenes before. Sometimes men can behave like women and flattery can get you everywhere (even when you know you're being flattered).

"Thank you for meeting with me at such short notice," Cicero remarked, after Octavius offered his guest a seat. The young man heard the old man's knees crack as he did so.

"I meant it when I said that I would always have time for you. I should even be thanking you. This meeting gave me a genuine excuse to cancel a lunch with Flaccus Vatinius."

"One is always full after dining with Vatinius. You feel like you don't want to eat for the rest of the day, or listen to his conversation for the rest of the year."

Octavius laughed. There was part of him which could barely believe that he was in the company of Cicero and trading witticisms with him. But he reined any feelings of admiration and deference in. "Where possible let him speak first," Balbus had advised.

"Is that a statue of Cincinnatus? I have a marble bust of him – a present from Atticus – in my study at my country villa. He had a cause – that of preserving the Republic – and the Senate then gave him an army. You are in a slightly different position, however. I will speak plainly. I neither have the time nor the will to deceive or play games. You now have an army, Octavius, but what I want to give you is a cause, akin to that of what Cincinnatus possessed. Save the Republic from the tyranny of Mark Antony. The enemy will soon be at the gates. When I first invited you to my house in Puteoli I remember talking with you privately in the garden. I posited that one cannot save one's soul – and Rome – in regards to choosing a life in politics. Not for the first time in my life, I was wrong. You now have the opportunity to save both at the same time. You would not believe me if I told you that Julius would have wanted you to act this way or that, nor would I expect you to. But I do see something of Caesar in you, Octavius. I also see something of myself in you. Yet even more so I'm hopeful that there is something of the Cincinnatus in your heart. Should you commit your legions to the defence of the Rome – and fulfil Caesar's legacy – will you not return to your studies? A man who gains power may be considered great but one who then freely relinquishes that power may be considered greater. The life of a soldier is far less precarious to that of a scholar, as much as certain academics have had their knives out for me over the years," Cicero said, believing that Octavius would never now give up his pursuit of power. *He's got the taste for it.*

Octavius smiled politely, as though he was being humoured rather than flattered. He offered his guest some wine and food before responding in earnest. Octavius wanted to convey that he wasn't in a rush to commit himself, either way. The young Caesar had time and an army on his side. *I can afford not to appear desperate – and appearances are reality.*

"I've heard the Senate call me a would-be Catiline or Sulla but never Cincinnatus. The majority of the senatorial elite treat me with, at best, indifference but, at worst, contempt. According to them I'm a stripling and the descendent of a commoner. Either because of pride, stupidity or tradition they view me as a threat or a figure to ridicule. Even if I had the will and means to do so how am I supposed to help a group of people that will not accept my help?"

"If the Senate are in the dark as to how perilous the situation is becoming I will soon make them see the light. We both know Antony is venturing north. Should he defeat Decimus Brutus and take command of his legions then his army in the north will hang over Rome like the Sword of Damocles. He could swoop down on the capital and play the tyrant and thief at will. If Antony gets what he wants then you will never get what you want. He will spend your inheritance faster than he will catch the pox and he will use the former to pay for the whores who'll cause the latter. It is not just a question of the Senate needing you. Equally, if not more so, you need the Senate. Antony is a mindless thug. The only virtue he has is that he's not his wife. Similarly the only virtue Fulvia possesses is that she's not her husband..."

"Antony is more the Senate's problem than mine."

"I received a letter from a friend of mine the other day. He has added a young poet of some promise to his retinue. I read one or two of his compositions. A line from one of the pieces sticks out in my mind at this moment and seems apt. *It is your concern when your neighbour's house is on fire.* I may prove to be first on Antony's proscription list but you will be second. Indeed it wouldn't surprise me if Antony was behind the attempt on your life during the ambush on the road to Rome all those months ago."

"You may be right. But it also wouldn't surprise me, given their hostility towards me, if the Senate have been behind the attempted assassination."

Octavius remained stone-faced but his inward eye replayed some of the bloody and terrifying scenes of the attack in his mind. He remembered the deaths of Tiro Casca, Roscius and Cleanthes.

Cicero breathed out, in exasperation. The statesman had hoped to flatter Octavius into an alliance. It seems he wouldn't be able to threaten or scare the youth into submitting to his will either. Yet there is more than one way to skin a cat, Cicero thought to himself.

"Shortly before Julius' death I had dinner with him. He joked that, after he was gone, plenty of people would come forward and attribute all sorts of sayings and legislation to him. 'I will doubtless come across as vain and contradictory, as a result,' he remarked. He also added – with a wink – that people may make things up and therefore he might be considered funnier and wiser that he was also. I mention this because I hope that, when I talk about Julius or quote him, you believe I'm being honest," Cicero stated, his brow wrinkled in earnestness. The philosopher had indeed been to dinner with Caesar before his murder but they had spoken about literature and politics.

"I know how fond Julius was of you. Even if you did somehow put words in his mouth he would probably be flattered that you were doing so," Octavius replied, before drinking some water and putting a honey-coated asparagus tip into his mouth.

"Julius may have considered the Senate as being his enemy sometimes but he still believed in its fundamental purpose. When he defeated Pompey at Pharsalus the Senate was treated with clemency rather than condemnation. Antony has no such respect for tradition, or the intelligence to recognise the Senate's central role in government. If you truly care about Caesar's legacy then you must care about the Senate too. If you truly care for the fate of Rome you should care about the Senate. Antony will not be as forgiving as Caesar if he wins a civil war. He will make the Senate disappear as easily as he can a jug of wine."

Cicero grew a little breathless. As an advocate, during a trial, he would pace up and down – fixing his eyes on the jury or defendant. He no longer had the strength to pace but he believed that he could

126

still make – and win – an argument. Yet Octavius appeared unmoved. Usually youth grew agitated and age bred calm but their roles were strangely reversed.

"The Senate isn't Rome. The Senate may judge Antony to be an enemy of the people. But history has shown that the Senate hasn't always been a friend to the people either. Just ask the Gracchi."

"We could debate the virtues – and crimes – of the Senate all day but the fact remains that sooner or later you – and your army – must choose a side."

I have. My own.

"The Senate must also decide whether it's on my side. Surely you do not expect me to just loan out my legions as if I were a pimp and they were my whores?"

"A fair point. But surely you do not expect the Senate to believe that, should your soldiers be similar whores, they will remain virginal? A man who buys a thoroughbred does not let it go to waste by keeping it in his stable."

"The Senate needs to understand that it's my thoroughbred though. Why should I allow Hirtius and Pansa to ride it? I must command my own army within any prospective alliance or coalition."

Cicero briefly looked up to the heavens for inspiration. He could not quite decide which would prove the more difficult task – convincing the Senate that Antony was their enemy or that Octavius was its ally.

But convince them I must.

*

An army camp, just outside of Mutina.

Smoke from campfires belched into the air. Ribald jokes were shared over lunches of various quality and freshness. The sound of drill masters, barracking new recruits, could be heard in the background. Talk was of the previous civil war or the impending one.

A group of soldiers formed a horseshoe around their general. The rapid frequency of sword clanging upon sword created one long metallic ring as Decimus Brutus fenced against two centurions. The legionaries applauded their haughty – but competent – commander's ability. The two centurions, who could have easily bested their general in a proper fight, would be given discreet bonuses. Caesar had put on similar exhibitions of military skill during his campaigns in Gaul, Decimus recalled.

Had he paid his men to lose too? Probably.

Decimus magnanimously thanked and praised his defeated opponents after the sparring session. He smoothed his oiled hair and called for a jug of water and some cheese and fruit (he would leave it to the likes of Antony to dull his wits with wine at midday – although as a youth he had been a drinking companion of his now enemy). The autumnal wind was bracing but tolerable. Brutus' pinched, aristocratic face appeared even more displeased when he saw rainclouds on the horizon.

After issuing orders to his senior officers – to provision his legions, levy more troops and schedule even more drills for his new recruits – Decimus was approached by a messenger. The rider seemed even more breathless than his mare as he handed over the three letters – which all contained the same central message: Antony was heading north.

Let him come. I started this. I'll end it.

Decimus had been the libertore who had persuaded Caesar to attend Pompey's Theatre on the day of his assassination. "Without me history would have been different," he regularly told those who would listen. "I played the great Caesar like a flute on the day. I was also the one who delivered the death blow when we stabbed him," he proudly boasted, correcting those who thought Cassius or his cousin Marcus Brutus had killed the tyrant. Unlike his cousin however, Decimus acted from more of a personal than political grievance. He had sided with Caesar during the civil war and been instrumental in capturing the key port of Massilia from Pompey's forces there. But Decimus felt he was sufficiently un-lauded and under rewarded when the war was over. Caesar had promoted others instead of him and rightly judged that he would bequeath the bulk of his estate to his undeserving great-nephew. He had to die. Justice had been done. And if Decimus could vanquish Caesar he could do the same with Antony.

I had no crisis of conscience then. I have even less of one now.

"The message confirms our suspicions. Antony is on his way," Decimus informed his lieutenant, Rufus Attus, who had served with him whilst he was fleet commander for Caesar against the Veneti.

The grizzled, taciturn veteran nodded in reply. "We must prepare for a defensive campaign until Hirtius and Pansa can be bothered to relieve us. We should begin fortifying the town immediately. Send out parties to scour the province for supplies. Our stomachs are more important than theirs. Military thinking dictates that an attacker needs a ratio of three to one to capture a fortified town. Antony will need twice those numbers. I would rather die than yield to that drunken letch. Hopefully Antony's army will catch a pox before it gets here, as doubtless he is taking the route which takes him past as many brothels as possible between Rome and Mutina."

Aye, let him come.

*

Cicero and Octavius talked long into the afternoon and not only because they were conscious of giving the good impression of not solely wishing to talk about politics. Both wished to convince the other that they were friends, or mentor and student, rather than reluctant allies. There were times where they convinced themselves too.

The pair retreated into the house when the rain started. Octavius had one of his slaves rush to the market to fetch a jar of his guest's favourite goat's milk and a fresh loaf of bread. While they were waiting Octavius, like a proud parent showing off his children, gave Cicero a tour of his library. His books were in some ways a reflection of his thoughts. He wanted Cicero to approve of his library – and him. He wanted to be the teacher's favourite pupil.

As much as Cicero judged that the young Caesar was friendly and engaging – ultimately one could never know what he was truly thinking. A wall of ice surrounded a fiery heart – or a wall of fire surrounded an icy heart. Such insularity could breed loneliness. And loneliness could mean vulnerability. Cicero briefly flirted with the idea of setting a honey-trap for Octavius, using Caecilia, but then he dismissed the idea immediately.

"Such is the smile on her face sometimes and her habit of mysteriously disappearing I could deduce that Caecilia is in love. She tells me that she is spending her days learning how to weave silk but she could just be spinning me a yarn," Cicero joked to Octavius as they sat on two couches facing one another in the triclinium. "Thankfully I believe she is far too sensible a girl to fall in love... But what about you? You are now old enough to have fallen in love. Is there a special someone in your heart?" Cicero was all too aware that the young Caesar was as fond of the fairer sex as his namesake and had even placed a mistress or two in his bed to tease out some information or weakness.

"As much as I may be Caesar's heir I am also, to some extent because of that, a penniless orphan. I'm too poor to have anyone fall in love with me," Octavius cynically joked.

I composed love poetry for Briseis. I told the wife of Blandus Savius that I loved her last week, in order to bed her. But no, I've never been in love. But could I ever fall in love? Maybe. With someone like Livia...

"Love is rare but it is also real. The same may be said of friendship and also a trustworthy politician."

"A trustworthy politician? I worry that someone has spiked your goat's milk. But I agree. I believe that my mother and Marcus Phillipus are happily married. He is also a trustworthy politician. But tell me, were you not happily married to Tertulla for a time?"

"It would have been a short time, if that. Imagine marriage – or love – as a block of wood. Life is the axe or whittling knife which slowly or rapidly diminishes it. The dawn of a marriage is always its brightest phase. Things are new, fresh and even interesting. But the night will always draw in and it's how you cope with the boredom and battle of wills. How do you keep the bed warm when lust's flame has died out? Petty disagreements, which should mean nothing, add up and come to mean everything. You may feel trapped or, conversely, give yourself the freedom to do anything to anyone. Men prove to be the cause of unhappiness and infidelity in marriage far more than women. As a philosopher I sometimes discuss the make-up of man – how he can be a paragon of virtue and yet there are occasions where he behaves with all the civility of a stray dog. And then I sometimes think upon women and posit that they are the real paragons of virtue. But then I think about Fulvia... Over the course of my career as an advocate I bested among others Hortensius, Catiline, Cato and even Caesar. But I cannot recall, over the course of my marriage, ever winning an argument with my wife."

"Tell me more about Cato and Catiline," Octavius asked, remembering how he used to question Cleanthes about Rome and its leading figures.

"When you thought that Cato was sober he was usually drunk but when you fancied him drunk his judgement was often sober. His hatred for Caesar was only rivalled by the love he had for the sound of his own voice. He was principled to the point of tediousness and few could live up to his high standards. But he sometimes did – which made him admirable. His death was a mixture of vanity and virtue, tied together in a Gordian Knot that not even I can wholly unpick... As for Catiline when he spoke people listened. When he took off his tunic women – and some men – swooned. He was fantastically handsome, charming and abhorrent. When Catiline failed to get what he wanted by legitimate means he then resorted to illegitimate tactics, without blinking an eyelid. He was a spoiled child, a brattish aristocrat claiming an affinity with the people for his own ambitions, who couldn't take no for an answer. The likes of Catiline and Antony have no appreciation or respect for the constitution. The governance of Rome can be compared to an orchestra playing a piece of music. The orchestra is made up of various constituencies or classes: the people, aristocracy, the army, consuls and others. Should just one instrument be absent from the group then the composition will sound like a chaotic din. For most of my life I have endeavoured to act as a kind of conductor to this orchestra, trying to make sure these separate classes act in harmony with one another. I believe that Caesar also attempted to fulfil this role," Cicero said with feeling, and lying. "Or permit me to bore you a little longer with the analogy that the different institutions and classes in Rome are all vital organs within the same body. Antony is stupid, arrogant and violent enough to think that he could remove one of these organs – such as the Senate or tribunate – and the patient will survive. I'm not sure how long I would survive for if someone cut my head off. Hopefully not even I could insult someone so much that they would want to decapitate me though."

Shortly afterwards Cicero excused himself and returned home to continue to compose his Philippics.

16.

Rivulets of piss ran down the cobblestones of the narrow, sloping streets. The sun was beginning to set. A couple of house fires glowed in the distance.

Oppius and Pollux had just left the tavern, *The Silver Trident*. Pollux had wanted his friend to check out a serving girl there. Oppius mentioned that his fellow centurion might want to have a doctor check her out too. From her bow-legs it seemed she spent more time working upstairs than serving drinks, he argued.

"If I don't fuck her, I may not fuck anyone again," Pollux had said, knowing he may well be leaving the capital to go off to war once more.

"If you do fuck her though, you may not be *able* to fuck again. She could be as dirty as one of Teucer's jokes," Oppius replied, thinking how he had almost lost as many men to diseases from brothels as he had from fighting the armies of Gaul. There is only one thing that a soldier unsheathes quicker than his sword …

The streets were largely deserted. Some had gone home after an afternoon of drinking. Some were getting ready to go out drinking for the night. The shops had closed so there was little reason for women to leave their residences. Oppius and Pollux had only had a couple of drinks and a light meal of ham and cheese before heading home.

Both men walked in silence but thought the same thought: *War is coming, again. A soldier's life can only end one way.*

So many people – Cleanthes, Tiro Casca, Fabius – had said the same thing to Oppius at some point. "You will die in battle." He could ignore one of them but not all of them. Oppius had been tempted to retire before and after Pharsalus. Caesar would have granted him an honourable discharge, albeit reluctantly. The centurion could have died content, knowing that Flavius Laco had been the last man he had killed. But the army had been his home for so long he didn't know anything different. Some men fear a military life but others fear a civilian one. *Soldiering is the only thing I'm good for.* Oppius felt that his life was somehow the payment of a debt to someone or something he was unaware of. To Caesar? To duty? But how had duty repaid him? He'd won plenty of battles but lost too many friends.

Cephas Pollux walked with his head bowed down in thought. The ghosts of fallen comrades buzzed around him too, like flies. He could wave his hand and shoo them away but sooner or later they would come back, as if to feed on his own carcass. The soldier thought about comrades who were still alive as well and what he would do should he encounter them on the battlefield. *Kill or be killed… If I kill Antony will it be the end of the war as well as him?* As to his fellow officers, who had chosen to fight alongside Antony, he would not seek them out. Except for perhaps Felix Calvinus. *He is always quick to buy someone a drink so he can whisper poison into their ears or manipulate them. So they will turn a blind eye to his corruption and depravity. I could never prove it but I swear he used to embezzle funds from the legions to pay his gambling dents. Aye, I'll seek out Calvinus and kill him. Because the self-serving bastard would do the same to you…*

As much as Oppius and Pollux shared the same thoughts they would remain unvoiced, even after a jug or two of wine. Rome could be a lonely place even with its one million inhabitants.

The streets were largely, but not wholly, deserted. A woman could be heard scolding her drunk husband in the background. A stray dog howled and then yelped as a sot launched an old sandal at it. Four men approached the officers as they strolled through a yard which served as a fish market during the day. Oppius also heard the sound of three men walking behind them.

"Remember me?" Carbo Vedius asked, his guttural voice rough with cheap wine and contempt. A gloating smile was cut into his features, like an open wound. Finally the baleful sailor had found – and cornered – his quarry. One of the men whom Oppius had bested in the tavern along with Vedius had spotted the centurion through the door of *The Silver Trident*. Knowing how much his friend was keen to find the soldier he quickly ran to the quayside inn Vedius was drinking in that afternoon. The navvy roused as many men as possible, as quickly as possible, to get his revenge. For too many sleepless nights, since his painful encounter with the centurion, hatred and humiliation had been his bedfellows.

Oppius calmly took in the menacing group of men standing in front of and behind him. Thankfully his attacker wanted to savour his moment. Although the centurion wouldn't want to stand in a shield war with the sailors Oppius could tell that they were all seasoned brawlers. Vedius stood in the middle, next to another man he recognised from their first encounter. Flanking them were a bald-headed veteran seaman who wore a long earring with a small anchor at its end. On the other side was a squat, compact brute with no discernible neck. He seemed to seethe rather than breathe, like a panting dog – or one which was about to attack. Oppius noticed the knife in his claw-like hand, its blade mottled with rust and blood. The centurion would have backed himself with four against two – Pollux would have fancied those odds too – but the three men behind them, carrying cudgels and knives, gave Oppius pause.

It only takes one knife in the back.

"I remember you – although you'd look even more familiar if laid out, whimpering on the floor," Oppius replied, unintimidated.

"You should be the one on the ground, on your knees – begging for your miserable life. I bet you didn't think that your last battlefield would be a stench-filled alcove in Rome. This yard though will now prove to be your graveyard."

Oppius heard a couple of the men behind him snigger. He could also smell wine on their breath. The wine would give them courage and enflame their anger but it also might dull their wits and reflexes.

"You seem as popular as ever Lucius," Pollux drily remarked. His knuckles cracked as he made a fist. His fingertips lightly brushed against the hilt of his sword on his other hand whilst he turned to half-face the trio of potential assailants behind Oppius.

"It could be worse. We could have bumped into my ex-wife," Oppius said.

"You can laugh. But your luck has finally run out."

"I thought that happened long ago, when I was introduced to my first wife. You were gambling with your money when I first met you. But now you're gambling with your life. Walk or, at best, limp away."

The smile fell from the centurion's features. Despite his apparent advantage it was the sailor who suddenly felt intimidated, though he dared not show it in front of his men. Vedius hoped that the soldiers were carrying full purses so he could honour his word and pay his drinking companions for their help.

Titus let out such a loud laugh that Teucer and Marcus Agrippa heard it from the rooftop they were perched on, which overlooked the yard. The training exercise was turning into something more real and interesting. Oppius had instructed Agrippa to shadow him for the day, as if he were a target or enemy agent. Teucer showed the young archer certain tricks of his trade, such as how to maintain line of sight and find the best vantage point to take his shot. The archers would now shoot more than just theoretical arrows however. Agrippa was keen to attack straightaway but Teucer said that they should wait for a signal, though the two men should nock their arrows just in case.

"Aim for the man in the middle, from the group standing behind them. I'll take out the one on the right. When the fighting starts aim for anyone attacking Pollux and I'll cover Oppius."

Agrippa nodded in reply. His mouth was dry. His heart was beating fast, not from the anxiety over taking a life but because he feared he might miss and one of his friends would die as a consequence. He wondered how much of the forthcoming episode he should share with Caecilia. *I want her to think me brave but not violent.*

Teucer received his signal from Vedius, rather than Oppius, as the sailor gave a telling nod to one of the cudgel-wielding men standing behind the centurions. As much as Vedius had thought about delivering the killing blow to the soldier – slipping his knife in between his ribs and twisting the blade as he looked him triumphantly in the eye – he had no wish to attack the dangerous combatant first.

Instead of Vedius hearing the dull thud of a cudgel striking his antagonist's skull the air was filled with a dog-like yelp and howl as an arrow pierced the base of the sailor's spine. Agrippa also felled his man as the missile punctured his lungs through his back. The soon-to-be corpse gasped rather than screamed. Oppius and Pollux moved with more speed and purpose than their opponents, knowing that Teucer and Agrippa were poised to attack. At the same time as drawing his gladius Pollux moved forward and kicked the man nearest to him in the groin. He then stabbed his enemy through the neck. He later joked to Teucer how his opponent didn't scream in agony because he had "kicked the bastard's balls so far upwards they got stuck in his throat".

Oppius drew his sword and in the same sweeping movement sliced off the fingers of the short but muscular sailor coming towards him with a rusty blade. The knife fell to the floor, as did its wielder as Oppius punched the point of his gladius into his navel. Blood and his intestines splashed onto the ground, mingling with the smell of garum and fish guts produced by the market earlier in the day. Oppius dropped his sword, however, as the bald-headed veteran soldier struck him on the forearm with a short club, studded with nails. The centurion let out a curse but rather than retreat or aim to retrieve his gladius he moved forwards and grabbed his attacker's long earring, yanking it downwards. The bottom of his ear landed on the floor, like a large gob of red phlegm. The side of the sailor's head and shoulder was quickly drenched in blood. He howled in pain. Agrippa put him out of his misery with an arrow through the chest. Teucer killed the man next to him, shooting him in the back as he looked to run away. His last thought was a desire to have his day over again and not walk past the tavern and report on seeing the centurion.

Terror and prudence fired Carbo Vedius' retreat. He could not bring his friends back from the dead. Confusion reigned too. His intention had been to ambush his enemy rather than be ambushed himself. Questions would be asked if he went back to the tavern without his shipmates. More questions would be asked when they discovered that his friends had been murdered. A ship was not the best place for a distrusted or despised man.

17

The Temple of Concord.

The breeze blew away what few clouds hung over Rome as if the gods had commanded the four winds to provide a clear view of the Senate. Attendance was higher than usual, partly thanks to the clement weather. Cicero, not usually one to pray, had offered up a smattering of a prayer the night before so that it wouldn't rain.

"More than bribes, election rigging or false accounting of votes the climate has influenced voting and legislature over the years," the veteran statesman had commented to Tiro that morning. "Rain can put such a dampener on democracy."

In order to generate as great an audience as possible for his return to the Senate Cicero and Tiro had also informed certain senators and gossips that he would be giving a daring, historic, speech.

Tiro had laid out a freshly-laundered toga that morning. He had also arranged for Rome's finest barber to trim what little hair his master had left and shave him. He was back where he belonged. *Centre stage.* His name was on people's lips again. The statesman felt more emboldened than anxious that morning as the two men ironed out the final creases in the speech.

"I know I can save the Republic, Tiro, because I have saved it before."

Cicero sat on the stone steps which circled the temple as it began to fill up with senators. He soaked up the atmosphere and appreciated the irony – smiling to himself. *I'm about to declare war in the Temple of Concord… It was also here, all those years ago, when you ordered the state to take up arms against Catiline.*

The aged statesman surveyed his audience, judging who would be for him, who against him and how many he could win over. Many senators had their slaves provide cushions for them when sitting on the cold, hard steps. Few had been part of the Senate all those years ago, when he had denounced Catiline. *You've survived them all: Pompey, Lucullus, Caesar, Crassus, Cato. Your ideals have also survived them. Let us hope that those ideals can survive you.*

Cicero sighed inwardly, however, as took in some of his fellow statesmen.

There's Marcellus Faunos. If only his reputation was as spotless as his gold braided tunic... Domitius Gallus has also deigned to show his red-nosed face. His wine merchant must be out of the capital today... And there's our youngest member, Eprius Minatus. Has your brother forgiven you yet for buying votes from the gilds and rigging the election in your favour, consigning him to be an even greater non-entity in history than yourself? Are you still affecting a more plebeian accent in order to align yourself with the people?... And let the gods be praised it's Mucios Sardus, with his chin resting on his hand, projecting an air of thoughtfulness. I wonder, are you thinking about your latest mistress or which lobbyist has paid you the most this month to propose certain legislation? And the Senate wouldn't be the Senate without the Metellii sitting in a row. Even though you're occupying the lower tier you're still managing to look down on everyone... And I mustn't forget you, Rufus Drusus, mumbling beneath your breath – rehearsing a witticism which you'll do your best with to make it seem like it's a spontaneous comment... Ah, and Antonius Blandus has just arrived. Tiro said that you have recently gained a business partner in Tarius Curio, the sword manufacturer. I wonder whether it'll be this month that you propose we award a government contract to your new company. Or you may show some decorum and integrity and bring the subject up next month... Alfenus Petro. I'm about as pleased to see you as a leper, as you are me I imagine. Though you must surely be looking forward to

140

voting against me. Will you be disagreeing with me out of personal animosity or just habit today?... And in the absence of Antony we have the second most respected scoundrel in the Senate, Dolabella. My rapacious, corrupted, corrupting, philandering former son-in-law. I know how disapproving you are of your disapproving father-in-law. But how much are you truly a friend to your co-consul? He purchased your loyalty through paying off your debts but because of that shame and humiliation you may quietly be cheering me on today. Antony will not blame you for what comes out of my mouth ... I have a mountain to climb converting such folly into virtue. My hammer may break in work-hardening such mettle, or a lack of. But the greater the difficulty, the greater the glory...

Dolabella, after various formal announcements, was neutral in his tone as he introduced the venerable proconsul. Cicero stood and paused – waiting for quiet. *Silence is one of the great arts of conversation.* He asked for a cup of water. He puffed out what little chest he had and felt twenty years younger. Purposeful. He scanned around the temple, appearing to look everyone in the eye. Undaunted. Unbowed.

Liberty or death.

"I come not to praise Antony but to bury him. And he will be buried in a grave of his own making. And into his grave I intend to dispose of his tyranny and grand larceny. Fear can silence me – us – no longer. Our former Master of the Horse has befouled rather than cleaned the Augean stables. I here declare that Mark Antony is a despot – an enemy of the state. He must be challenged and defeated, else *we* will soon be challenged and defeated. The Senate and Antony cannot co-exist. It must be one or the other. He has more respect for his entourage of whores, clowns and drunkards than he does this august body of men. He poses a greater threat to Rome than Sulla or Caesar ever did. Should Antony vanquish the forces of Decimus Brutus then he will use his army of the north to

141

garrison and enslave the capital. Even our noblest families will not be free from his ire and avarice. I offer up a simple syllogism. The Clodii and Metelli represent our finest traditions and virtues. Antony has no respect for tradition and virtue. Therefore Antony will have no respect for the Clodii and Metelli. You may well argue with me but you cannot argue with logic. Antony will only remember and admire your names when it comes to him drafting his proscription lists, as he remembers and admires your villas and farmlands."

Cicero deliberately paused and let his grim words hang in the air. *If they will not be moved by duty then let them be moved by fear – a survival instinct.*

"As the Senate once reverberated with the words of Cato the Elder – 'Carthage must be destroyed' – so too must we now exclaim, 'Antony must be destroyed'. For in his actions, if not words, has Antony not pronounced a death sentence on us? Some will argue that the price of war is too high but I say that the prices of despotism, subjugation and poverty are too high. Antony once sent a group of his slaves to my house to vandalise my property and humiliate me because I had dared to criticise him. I would you now send out an army to humiliate him.

"But 'ah, Cicero,' you might declaim, 'are your words and actions not borne from a personal grievance? Should we go to war over someone slandering you?' But – and some of you might disbelieve your ears when I say this – you should ignore me. I do not matter. Antony has dishonoured this institution far more than he has slighted me. The public grievance far outweighs any personal one I might feel. The sot and villain has made a mockery of our sacred constitution and due process. He makes up laws like one of his actress-mistresses would make-up a line when forgetting the words to a play. If one of his friends has gambling debts then he proclaims all debts to be null and void. The idea of the rule of law will soon be considered a myth.

"Antony expropriates land for himself from greed or, worse, seemingly on a whim. He moved into Pompey the Great's villa like a squatter. In this once great man's house there are now brothels in place of bedrooms, cheap eateries in place of dining rooms. In the past few months he has been more a minter of coins than consul. Someone should inform him that there is a wide gap between gain and glory, however. I hear that his accountants no longer count his money but merely weigh it. Money has ever been despised by great men. Antony seems to gorge on it. Was ever Charybdis so ravenous? Power and wine have gone to his head. Our consul possesses henchmen rather than attendants, the wickedest of all is his wife. As we have seen from her behaviour at Brundisium the dog's bite is worse than her bark. Antony's philosophy appears to be that of a villain in a play, 'Let them hate me so long as they fear me'. Should the uncultured, uncouth dolt be bothered not to fall asleep when attending the theatre he would realise that such villains get their comeuppance and meet nasty – but justified – ends."

Cicero inserted another strategic pause. Over the rim of his cup of water he was pleased to see senators nodding their heads in agreement with him. They were becoming more animated – and angry. Someone was finally giving voice to Antony's crimes.

"Recently though Antony has given speeches and instigated insidious and cowardly whispering campaigns against myself – positing that I am a villain who should meet a nasty end. He accuses me of being an enemy of the state?! Perhaps he is a figure from comedy rather than tragedy after all! He accuses me of instigating the civil war, pouring poison into Pompey's ear to break with Caesar. I cannot allow such poison from Antony to infect the truth. When I sensed that a malign war was threatening our native land I never ceased to advocate peace. You all know what I said to my late friend: 'Gnaeus Pompey, if only you had never gone into partnership with Julius Caesar – or never dissolved it! The first course would have befitted you as a man of principle, the second as a man of prudence.'

"Our deluded consul has also recently implied that I was somehow behind the plot to murder Caesar, despite a lack of evidence and witnesses to substantiate such a ludicrous claim. Such is my dedication to fairness and truth that I will not pettily give credence to the rumours that you yourself were involved in the conspiracy. Perhaps people are implicating you because, when trying to find the culprit of a crime, an advocate would ask, 'Who benefits' And have not you benefitted the most since your friend's death, grasping power and using Caesar's estate to pay off your debts? But I will exonerate you. No one would ever believe that you could be party to such a noble action of freeing Rome from a tyrant. Service to the Republic isn't quite your style. I posit that you secretly celebrated Caesar's death but that you were not one of the authors of it. Yet I cannot exonerate you from the charge of instigating the civil war. It was you, who in stirring up trouble as a tribune, gave Caesar his pretext for crossing the Rubicon. You were supposed to be an envoy of peace but, either through wickedness or ineptitude, you unsheathed the civil war. You were the cause of the Senate having to desert Rome. The blood of Roman citizens and soldiers is on your hands. We still mourn our losses from that disastrous conflict which sometimes pitted brother against brother. Lives were lost. Antony took them. The authority of this institution was shattered. Antony shattered it. Indeed all the calamities we have seen since the start of the civil war – and what calamity have we not witnessed? – we can ascribe to one man, Mark Antony. As Helen was to the Trojans, so this wretched man is to the Republic – the cause of its ruin."

As if on cue a few close supporters of Cicero cheered their mentor on and damned Antony. The mood was becoming more heated. In the space of a few moments a senator could laugh at a witticism but then grow indignant at Antony's transgressions.

"The enemy will soon near the gates of Mutina. If he is not stopped he will then stand at the gates of Rome. We may be waiting for the First of January for Hirtius and Pansa's tenure in office to validate our course of action but this date holds no significance to Antony. The noble Decimus Brutus has decided to stand up to the tyrant. He vows to keep his province in the hands of the Senate and the people of Rome. Brutus is a true servant of the Republic, conscious of his namesake, following in the footsteps of his celebrated ancestor who vanquished Tarquin the Proud. He has given us the lead. Let us follow him in order that we can continue to lead ourselves. He cannot and should not stand alone. I have vowed to protect the Republic too. I defended it when I was young and now I am old I will not abandon it. We must all be libertores now. Will men put up with you, Antony, when they did not put up with Caesar? In your lust for despotic power I can compare you with him but in all other respects there is no comparison. You are not fit to either wear or wash his toga. Antony must not be allowed to return to the capital unfettered. What some appeasers might call peace with honour I call servitude. Do you want the Senate enslaved to a drunk and letch?"

*

Brutus' sandals slapped against the flagstones on the veranda and distracted Horace from his quietude and enjoyment of the view. The valley was marbled with rock and littered with thorny shrubs and skeletal trees but there was still an air of warmth and beauty to the scene, the would-be poet fancied. Horace had never known his commander to pace about so much or project a mood of fretfulness. He likened him to a husband outside his wife's chamber, expecting the delivery of their first child. Brutus was ruminating on the delivery of Cicero's speech in the Senate. Today was the day. Brutus was not just invested in his friend's key address because he had a hand in naming the series of speeches Cicero was intending to give (it had been Brutus who had named them the Philippics, after Demosthenes' attacks on Philip of Macedon). Cicero's speech could well decide the fate of Rome and whether the Republic defied or submitted to Antony's monarchical reign.

Remember your own advice to me about oratory, all those years ago. "Rhetoric is one great art composed of five divisions: invention, arrangement, style, memory and delivery." Do not just go for the cheap laugh. There's too much at stake. Do not make it all about yourself either.

His noble brow was furrowed, his beard was streaked with grey. Horace noticed that a jug of wine was seldom further than an arm's length from his general at night, yet to his credit Brutus was never drunk in front of his soldiers. He was seldom sober in front of his wife, however. Brutus glanced at the sundial again, judging that Cicero would still be addressing the Senate back in Rome. He wished he could be back there too.

"How do you think Cicero's speech will be received?" Brutus had shown the young officer a letter from Cicero, outlining his line of attack.

"Caesar filled the Senate with lots of new blood before his demise. They will not have loyalty to Antony, nor he them I imagine. Antony has made little attempt to court the patrician families of Rome either, who still possess a bedrock of wealth and influence. But Antony may be wiser than we think. He has concentrated on building an army rather than building factional support in the capital. Who needs a hundred senators on your side when you have ten thousand soldiers? Curule chairs are won by money and swords," Horace argued.

146

But who knows what will happen? Time will bring to light whatever is hidden and will cover up and conceal whatever is now shining in splendour.

Brutus was about to disagree and laud the ideals of the Republic – and cite the golden age of Athenian democracy – but he remembered that he would only be able to return to Rome and win back his honour with an army at his back. Horace continued: "But if we consider that the Senate has now been cornered by Antony – cornered animals will often fight back. Cicero may shame or frighten the Senate into action."

Brutus remained inexpressive. The Senate and people of Rome had disappointed him too much for him to put his faith in them. Should Cicero succeed though it would mean that generals, as opposed to politicians, would decide the fate of Rome. Decimus needed to hold out for reinforcements. Antony could defeat his enemies' armies separately but not as a whole.

An attendant disturbed both men's thoughts as he came out into the garden and handed his master a message. At first Horace thought it was a letter from Cassius. Brutus was in regular correspondence with his co-conspirator and, although their characters and motives might be diametrically opposed, their fates were inexplicably linked to one another. It appeared that it was good news as a hint of a smile fractured his general's stoical features.

"It seems that we will soon be having a visitor Quintus. An old friend, Matius Varro, will be coming to the province. I will invite him to stay with us. Like yourself he is an officer that prefers the library to the parade ground."

Brutus was about to add that Matius was one of the few soldiers Porcia enjoyed the company of, but he thought better of it. Not only might it highlight that she did not enjoy the company of Horace but the general was in no mood to talk about his wife or even mention her name.

*

Cicero allowed an increasing number of pauses during his speech, for fellow senators to applaud and agree with his arguments. They also cursed their unrighteous consul and offered up further examples of his heinous crimes against themselves personally or the state. Cicero did not yield the floor too much though. The rest of the Senate were his chorus. He remained the conductor. Feeling that he had done enough to damn Antony as a public enemy the statesman turned his attention to casting Octavius in the role of a potential saviour.

"But there is another noble Roman who feels the same as I do – who would lay down his life for the Republic. Octavius Caesar has, in effect, already saved Rome once. While his forces were posted close by to us Antony was unable to attack and occupy the city, as I believe he still intends to. Octavius desires to enter public life in order to strengthen it instead of, like Antony, usurp it. I have spoken with Octavius on numerous occasions. He is well read – and not just because his shelves are filled with volumes of books by yours truly! At the centre of his garden stands, pride of place, a statue of Cincinnatus. Many of you have met Octavius. Is there a greater example of a traditional, conservative, morality in our younger generation? Antony may try to scorn him as being low-born but his natural father would have been elected consul had he lived. Octavius only wishes to enter the course of honours early whilst Antony wishes to do away with the authority of the Senate and course of honours altogether. We should allow this noble young man to have his wish; it is nothing compared to everything that is at stake. Octavius wants to bend the law, compared to Antony who habitually breaks it. We must give a formal command to the young Caesar. The people and soldiers will rally to his

148

standard yet Octavius will serve under our command and, like Cincinnatus, become a citizen once more when he is no longer needed as a general. Any personal vendetta he harbours will be put aside for the good of Rome. He values the Republic, respects nothing more than the authority of the Senate and desires the fall of Antony over his own elevation.

"I give you my guarantee, my vow, my pledge, that Octavius will always be the man that he is today. Oh what is there in Antony save lust, wickedness, crapulence and ambition! He has plundered our treasury and private lands, taxed us into poverty. He turned Caesar's funeral into a riot, created legislation for personal gain or to punish his enemies. At Brundisium he slaughtered centurions and legionaries, heroes of the Republic. And now, along with his equally despicable brother Lucius, he leads his army north towards Mutina. Reports are already coming in that he is emptying barns and slaughtering cattle as he burns his way through our countryside. Soldiers feast while citizens starve. Fathers and sons are being conscripted into his army. Mothers and daughters are being taken too – may the gods protect them. Despite his vices and treason there may be some among you tempted to send envoys of peace to our second Catiline. The name of peace is sweet, the reality even sweeter; but there is a world of difference between peace and subjugation. Antony desires the latter. Although I can understand such a will to try and find a diplomatic solution it will ultimately prove to be a waste of time – and perhaps a waste of life in regards to those who are sent. Do you believe Antony is marching north with his army because he enjoys the mountain air or the aesthetics of the scenery? Sending envoys will be tantamount to sending two blind men to put out a forest fire or sending a surgeon to revive a corpse. Antony is intent on war. He is intent on our destruction.

"Yet where there is life there is hope. As Octavius' army defends Rome Decimus Brutus defends Gaul. To the military might already at our disposal we will soon be able to add armies commanded by Hirtius and Pansa. Both consuls are familiar with the heat of battle and fruits of victory. They will lead – and Octavius will follow them. The time is ripe. With one voice we must declare Antony an enemy of the state. The people stand with us too. You have seen the crowds in the Forum, crying out for a return of liberty and prosperity. They know what we in our hearts know. Nothing is more abominable than shame, nothing is uglier than servitude. Romans are born for honour and freedom; let us either retain those birth rights or die with dignity. Let us defeat tyranny and Antony together, for they are one and the same."

The cheers for Cicero reached a crescendo and sang out into the air surrounding the temple. Jeers too sounded out, for their despotic consul. Old men rose to their feet (or some merely stamped them) and applauded the great orator who had given voice to opinions whispered in dark corners, among trusted friends. Even Alfenus Petro applauded the man he had labelled "a relic" than morning. The statesman's words had started a fire upon which many wanted to sacrifice Mark Antony. Those who were not persuaded by Cicero's rhetoric and passion nevertheless appreciated his appeals to logic and necessity. Antony needed to be deposed else they would be. To achieve their aim they would need Octavius' legions.

There was a fire burning inside Cicero too. His heart thumped with pride and triumph. He felt thirty years younger, free from ailment or fear. History would record that he saved the Republic, twice – he gloried. Three generations of Romans rallied around him and clapped the proconsul on the shoulder, lauding his words and virtues. He had even converted some politicians he had judged as being beyond redemption. Cicero reacted with due modesty and quiet dignity to all, however. More than any compliment, or suggestion of a reward to be conferred upon him, Cicero took to heart the brief smile and nod of approval Tiro offered him after his speech.

The vermillion sun shone, illuminating and warming the great temple, as if also approving of the historic moment, Cicero thought. He wondered what Octavius would think of his speech. Cicero had advised Balbus to forewarn the boy that he would occasionally be critical of Julius. Cicero explained to Balbus that he did not want to seem too much on the Caesarian party's side, in the eyes of the Senate. In truth he had meant every word of his condemnation of the dictator. History would be his judge, not Octavius.

The die was cast.

18.

The hour was late. It had been a long day for the recently installed propraetor. Octavius had woken to Lucius Oppius standing outside his door. The no-nonsense centurion had worked him hard that morning, helping to strengthen and condition his body for the campaign ahead. He couldn't be seen to be frail. Oppius also gave the young Caesar refresher lessons in swordsmanship. Although Octavius would never be a great soldier he still needed to be proficient in defending himself, both on foot and on horseback. During the afternoon Octavius had a meeting with several senior senators as well as Hirtius and Pansa. They informed him that Dolabella had left the city during the previous night. Cicero remarked that he was as much "fearing the expropriation of his stolen wealth as he was losing his tawdry life". They also spoke about the imminent conflict. Afterwards Octavius visited his mother and Marcus Phillipus. For the rest of the afternoon he had locked himself away to catch up on various correspondence. Work even took precedence over seeing his latest mistress, Valeria. His ardour was cooling for her regardless. "She talks too much – about herself. I'm not sure which she complains about the most, her aged husband or the cost of Chinese silk for her dresses. Thankfully she has duties to perform in bed which prevent her from talking too much. I dare say Valeria has been the cause of her husband's decline and ageing though. She's slowly boring him to death," Octavius half-jokingly reported to his friends.

Octavius sat by the fire with Agrippa. They had, along with Oppius and Balbus, just finished having a light supper. The centurion and political agent had retired to go home. It was a custom of the two young friends to talk late into the night, for at least one evening a week, to catch up on events and share their thoughts. Octavius noticed how Agrippa had shaved off his burgeoning beard. Had he done so out of sympathy for him? Octavius had tried and failed to grow a beard. He had hoped that it would make him look older and more distinguished. Agrippa had shaved off his beard however because Caecilia had said she preferred him without one. It scratched her face when she kissed him.

"They do not trust me, which is apt because I do not trust them," Octavius remarked, in reference to his meeting that afternoon. "The supposed good and the great of Rome spoke to me as if I were an unwelcome smell today. They hinted as much as they could, without being direct, that I was too young and low-born to have earned my new-found position. Ateius Metellus paused and sneered when he said that, 'This is not Velitrae, but Rome'. Although I am the one coming to their aid they acted like I was the one who should be eternally grateful. I bit my tongue so much during the lecture that I thought it was lunchtime. I suffered the glorified bunch of thugs and they suffered me. They have the airs of princes but morals of snakes. Cicero was present and did his best to grease the wheels but the atmosphere was strained. Cicero apologised for the behaviour of some afterwards but I dare say he then went back into the chamber and argued that they had nothing to apologise for. Hirtius and Pansa seemed genuinely gracious though. They skirted over my lack of experience and talked to me as an equal. They both spoke fondly of Julius and we even discussed literature and history – although Hirtius spoke more about the history of certain types of food... But I showed due deference to all. Balbus is right. If I appear to submit to their authority then they may grant me more freedom, believing that they'll be able to rein me in at any moment. I will even allow Hirtius to take temporary command of one of my legions when we march north. I will be sure to remain its paymaster however."

Agrippa nodded his head in agreement but was more distracted by his thoughts concerning his own encounter that day with Caecilia. They had lunched together, as usual. They went to their "love nest" as they called it. Their love making lacked their usual passion and consideration though. Both had been thinking about what was being left unsaid.

Finally, after getting dressed, Caecilia had broached the subject of Agrippa leaving to go to war.

"I have to say it. I owe it to me and to you, Marcus. I do not want you to leave. I would rather you were an architect than soldier," she had said. Her hands had begun to shake a little as she fastened her silver pin into her hair.

"Can't I be both? You fell in love with both. Octavius needs me," Agrippa had replied, trying to be reasonable.

"I need you too. We could leave, together, today. Run away. I have money. I could get more from my father." Her voice had faltered with emotion. She was upset with Agrippa for leaving her but also because he appeared to be so reasonable and calm. Love should defy reason.

"I want to change the world – not run away from it."

"The world will change as it sees fit to do without us. But *our* worlds will change if you go. I can't sleep, I can't eat properly, thinking that I might never see you again."

"We will see each other again, I give you my word."

"But how can you make that promise?"

"Because I'm a better soldier than I am an architect. And you've given me something to live for."

Caecilia had returned not his conciliatory smile.

"Even if Octavius comes back, having been victorious, he will lose in the end. He has too many enemies. Even Cicero remarked to my father in a letter the other day that Octavius should be praised, used and then disposed of. It's folly, rather than heroic, to fight for a lost cause."

From the beginning they had promised each other that the world of Roman politics would not intrude upon their relationship. They would be on the same side even if Octavius and her father were not. Caecilia had broken that promise and something had shattered as a result. Both wished that she could take back what had just been said.

The smile had fallen from Agrippa's face as though a little piece of him had died. Dejection had stabbed at his heart as he realised she did not believe in him and his cause. He also knew he would have to keep what Caecilia had said from Octavius in case his friend enquired where the intelligence had come from. Octavius would then ask him to forsake her or, worse, use her to extract more information about their enemies. Yet at the same time Agrippa needed to warn Octavius of Cicero and the Senate's intentions – although he told himself that things could wait. Octavius was already aware that he could, or would, be betrayed by the Senate. He didn't want to burden his already overburdened friend.

Caecilia had seen that she had hurt him but didn't apologise. Her pretty features, flushed with anger, had grown pale with sorrow. Yet her pride still overruled her love.

But love had overruled Agrippa's pride. He didn't want to argue. He wanted to remain hopeful – for both of them.

"The war may be over with one decisive battle. Once we can mobilise all our forces we will outnumber Antony."

"You cannot believe that. Even if you defeat Antony then the armies of the Republic will turn on you. And if, somehow, Octavius survives that encounter then Brutus and Cassius' armies will return to give battle. I just do not want to see you shackled to Octavius when he eventually falls. Stay here, with me. If Octavius truly respects you as much as he says then he will respect your decision to choose a different path. You should not think that the name of Caesar is synonymous with glory. Consider the beaches of Britannia, the forests of Gaul, the plains of Pharsalus and his own death. The name of Caesar is synonymous with blood," Caecilia had argued, quoting her father, trying to scare or shame Agrippa into staying. "Why do you have to go?"

"Because I'm a soldier," Agrippa replied – quoting Lucius Oppius, when he overheard someone ask him the same question. Agrippa had answered with a sense of duty in his voice but he recalled how Oppius had spoken with remorse or resignation. For months, since meeting the centurion, the young soldier had wanted to be like him – but not at that moment. The grief on Oppius' face as he spoke had given Agrippa pause.

A silence had swollen up between them. Caecilia had been ready to leave – but couldn't. She wanted to say a thousand things – both words that she had rehearsed in her head and ones that would come at the spur of the moment. In her nightmares and waking dreams she pictured him falling in battle. Tears moistened her eyes as if she were already mourning him.

Agrippa had gazed out of the window. He could see the grand, gleaming properties in the plutocratic district of the *Keels*, named after certain extravagant houses there designed in the shape of a keel.

She comes from that world. A different world. From old money. She comes from those same patrician families who scorn and wish to destroy Octavius. Who wish to undo Julius Caesar's land reforms and the opportunities he provided for the poor to better themselves. They want to return to a Rome found in the history books. But it's a fiction. She may be from the past but I want her to be part of my future.

Agrippa didn't doubt that Caecilia loved him but he did doubt that her father would ever consent to his daughter marrying him.

Unless, shackled to Octavius, my star can burn bright enough.

They had each made a promise to write to one other every day. They kissed each other, one last time. They embraced, one last time. The room had immediately felt colder and emptier when she left, Agrippa thought to himself. He had noticed that the plants she had bought, when he had originally rented the apartment, were dying. Love nests sometimes only last a season.

The flames continued to flick upwards in the fireplace. Octavius continued to talk and Agrippa continued to vaguely listen.

"I said my goodbyes to my mother and Marcus Phillipus this afternoon. More tears burst forth from her eyes than water gushed from the statue-fountain of Salacia in the garden."

"Have you said goodbye to Octavia also?"

Octavius paused before answering, transfixed by the dancing flames. "I will write to her."

Octavia understood her brother's need to go to war but that did not mean she approved of it. Octavius furrowed his brow as he briefly thought of her husband. He had just discovered that Marcellus was having an affair and, despite his own infidelities with married women, felt no contradiction in condemning his brother-in-law's behaviour. The propraetor would arrange for them to divorce when he returned to Rome. As much as Octavius believed that his sister was too good for most men he wanted to marry Octavia off in order to cement a political alliance. He needed supporters amongst the populares and optimates alike. Lepidus was a candidate. Despite or because of Rome's great families looking down on him he needed to form alliances with them too. Though the Clodii and Metellii claimed to be principled – and would only breed with certain bloodlines – they were pragmatic too. If Octavius proved victorious in the north one of the families could decide to form an alliance with him. Octavius needed to increase his powerbase. Like Caesar he had no desire to disband the Senate but ultimately it needed to be directed and overruled occasionally.

"Sometimes saying goodbye in person can be too awkward or painful," Octavius added.

Agrippa nodded and stared philosophically into the fire.

19.

Dear Atticus,

As you may have heard I have continued to deliver my Philippics. Some of my more dove-like colleagues have complained about my scathing tone but I would argue that I have not been scathing enough where Antony is concerned. I caught wind of a rumour that, after hearing about my speeches, he put me on a proscription list featuring just my own name. Antony thinks he can take everything from me – little realising that at my age I have nothing to lose. He will be sorely disappointed that I have converted my wine cellar into a library for Tiro and there are no suitable outfits in my closet that he can pass onto his harem. I've little doubt that the wretch will take pleasure in burning my books though, in order for one of his bestial orgies to run on longer into the night.

Unfortunately, despite my vigorous efforts, Antony still has supporters in the Senate. Someone raised a proposal yesterday. Instead of declaring that we were in a state of war he wanted us to say that we were merely experiencing "a public emergency". This is what happens when we allow advocates to become politicians. Statecraft becomes a matter of semantics.

Pansa has just marched north with his recently levied army. With both of Rome's consuls now absent it has been suggested that I be declared a temporary dictator. I have refused the honour – although if anyone else wishes to fill the dreaded role I will challenge them and accept the position. My aim in politics, as you know, has always been to strengthen the constitution rather than strengthen my own personal political power. My crowning glory is to make sure no one wears a crown. And that includes Octavius. He is devoted to me and has even taken to calling me "father" in his letters. I have indulged and obliged him by sometimes calling him "Caesar" in return. I hope that the boy will not feel too betrayed if I have to betray him.

More than a chink of light begins to shine over Rome – and that light comes from Macedonia. Brutus has ousted Antony's other deplorable brother – Gaius – from the province. Brutus has won battles on the ground and in hearts and minds. He has defeated soldiers and won them over to our cause at the same time. The tide is definitely turning.

Cassius too has plunged another dagger into the heart of tyranny. Antony's partner in crime, Dolabella, mustered an army and travelled to Smyrna. Under the banner of friendship he entered the city but then promptly tortured and murdered its governor, Gaius Trebonius. Cassius was in the area however and not without men and a cause. He hunted the dog down. I was glad when I no longer called Dolabella my son-in-law. I am even gladder to pronounce him dead. Despite Cassius' noble act however the Senate has been slow, cowardly or inept in not awarding him greater powers and resources. They have blocked my proposal to grant Cassius an official command in Asia. Suffice to say I have written to our friend to encourage him to take command unofficially. Brutus may be the better statesman but Cassius is the better general. They complement each other. Hirtius and Pansa are merely keeping the seats of the curule chairs warm for them.

In short, Antony no longer has forces to call upon in Macedonia and Syria. The noose is slowly tightening around his neck. Let us leave space however for his shrewish wife's head. Fulvia either applauds his crimes or instigates them. Some women should be seen and not heard. But she should be neither seen nor heard.

In terms of a woman I have been pleased to see and hear more from Caecilia has been spending an increased amount of time at the house. Perhaps she has grown tired of Rome and shopping. She certainly seems distracted or listless. I asked her if she would *prefer to go back to my country villa – or to venture home to you – but she answered that she would like to stay in the capital. She has taken a surprisingly strange interest in events in the north – asking me for daily updates about the military and political situation. There is little change day to day but winter is turning into spring and as soon as the final snows melt in the north blood will seep into the ground. Decimus continues to defy Antony at Mutina. Antony has surrounded the town but Decimus' resolve and his defences remain strong. Shortly before Antony's army arrived Decimus slaughtered his baggage animals and salted the meat, in preparation for the siege. Antony will not be able to starve him out. Perhaps we should have taken note of Decimus more when he carped on about how he should have been given more credit for Caesar's victories. Despite his heroism however he will be glad of reinforcements and sharing in the glory of defeating our pernicious enemy. The veteran legions, commanded by Hirtius and Octavius, should be within striking distance soon. Once Pansa's army arrives they will be able to surround Antony and the besieger will become the besieged... I do so hope that Antony decides to fight to the death.*

   Cicero

20.

Dusk glowed, brazier-like, on the horizon. Wisps of cloud encircled the jagged mountaintops in the distance. The heat of battle, or rather a skirmish, filled the air. Oppius stood in the rear line in order to assess the progression of the attack. Also no one in the front line would dare try to retreat past him. Other skirmishes had broken out over recent days between the two armies, camped close to one another. Some had been due to accidental manoeuvres or over-zealous junior commanders attempting to prove their mettle. Some were planned offensives in order to probe the enemy and gain intelligence about the strength and morale of the opposition.

The fighting was more chaotic than coordinated as the two cohorts clashed within a forest, which bordered a river. On the far side of the river stood the fortified town of Mutina. The woods had been eerily quiet an hour ago, save for the plaintive sound of birdsong and the wind blowing through the vernal trees. Blood now began to splatter against bark, ferns and the mulched-up ground. The unnatural roars and high-pitched screams were depressingly familiar to the veteran centurion. A faint smell of sulphur filled his nostrils from the gaseous nearby marshes. Oppius had his sword and shield at the ready and gave nods of encouragement to the young legionaries around him. Armour glinted through trees in the fading light. Too many of the new recruits would wear as much armour as they could, thinking that it would make them invulnerable, Oppius thought. But every armour has its weak point. Every army has its weak point too. Many thought that his own side's weak point would be Octavius, who would act rashly or naively – sending soldiers to their death in the name of glory. But the young Caesar seldom suffered a rush of blood. Oppius was impressed by the way he listened, deferred to the more experienced Hirtius and (prompted by himself and Agrippa) was concerned with logistics and his legions being equipped and provisioned correctly.

The screams grew louder as did the clanging of arms. The advance line had orders to fall back if they met too much resistance. The fresh, rear line could then counter-attack. Due to the terrain there was little method to the enemy's advance and similarly there was little method to the cohort's retreat. Yet over the sound of everything else Oppius could still hear the reassuring voices of Pollux and Milo issuing commands and holding the line.

The retreat shouldn't turn into a rout.

*

Enobarbus had been out on a routine inspection of sentries and the camp's defences when the enemy had attacked. He gave orders for the focal point of the offensive to be reinforced by legionaries further up the river bank. They would neither be broken here nor break through to the enemy. Enobarbus observed the fighting from a watchtower in the vicinity. Night was drawing in. Neither side would want to fight in the darkness nor commit too many men to the pointless clash, Enobarbus thought to himself. Neither side wanted a war of attrition. He was pleased, however, that the legion, filled with new recruits and veterans alike, was pushing the enemy back. He would instruct the quartermaster to give the combatants an extra ration of wine for the night.

*

Pollux' arms ached. His voice was hoarse. His bearded face was smeared with grime and gore. His men were starting to be overrun. He suddenly punched his shield forward, knocking his hare-lipped opponent back into a tree. At the same time he stabbed his gladius forward, piercing the leather breastplate of another enemy. The centurion quickly withdrew his blade and turned around,

163

attempting to parry a spear thrust from a feral looking legionary. But the spearhead wasn't deflected totally and it sliced through his thigh. Blood gushed from the artery and Pollux fell to one knee. By now the enemy that had been knocked into the tree had recovered. He too, his sword at the ready, stood over the formidable – but wounded – centurion. The prospective victors grinned, savouring the moment. They were hyenas, bringing down a lion. Pollux pursed his lips in resignation. Both men were about to deliver killing blows. He could try to parry one but he could not avoid both. The centurion didn't think that he would die in such a way but every soldier who dies on the battlefield probably thinks that.

A shield flew through the air and crashed into the feral-looking infantryman's chest. Oppius slashed his sword downwards, cutting open the hare-lipped legionary's neck and chest.

The tide of Antony's forces crashed against the advancing second line of Oppius' cohort and was buffeted back. Fresh screams and battle cries curdled the air. There was a stand-off, however, among some combatants as they stood, weapons drawn, refraining from engaging with their enemy. Some were too fatigued or too cowardly to fight. Some remembered their conversations over campfires that "Romans shouldn't fight Romans" and that Caesar's veterans shouldn't fight each other either.

Oppius gave the order and had his junior offices pass it along the line that they should retrieve any wounded and form an orderly withdrawal. Enobarbus passed on an order that the second line should be ready to beat back any enemy advance but that it was not to move forward itself. Enough blood had been spilled – wasted.

*

Night descended. Agrippa and Teucer stealthily crept through the forest, wearing dark brown tunics. Their faces were blackened. The line of enemy sentries downstream had thinned as reinforcements had been called in to deal with Oppius' attack. Six men had now become two standing on the riverbank next to a beacon, which was due to be lit if any enemies were spotted.

The heavy rain in the morning had softened the ground, muffling their footsteps. The archers reached the treeline. Their mission was to eliminate the sentries and swim across to the town in order to deliver a message to Decimus Brutus. Hirtius had lit his own fires in the camp over the past week to indicate to Brutus that reinforcements had arrived but neither army could be sure if it was aware of one another. Oppius had come up with the plan of creating a diversion and having the messengers swim across the river. Teucer volunteered for the mission. Decimus would recognise and trust the archer – and Octavius offered him a healthy bonus. After hearing the Briton had signed up Agrippa decided to join his friend on the near suicide mission. "I'm your second best archer and one of the strongest swimmers in legion," Agrippa had argued, after Octavius had tried to dissuade his friend from taking part.

As Teucer whispered instructions as to which sentry Agrippa should target the young officer began to doubt whether he should have volunteered for the dangerous mission. He could be killed whilst trying to take out the sentries. The current could be too strong and he could drown in his attempt to swim across the river. Decimus' men might mistake him for a spy or enemy combatant and fire upon him. And should he succeed in delivering his message to the general then he could well perish during the swim back.

Teucer, observing the doubt and anxiety in his friend's face, offered some words of encouragement.

"Don't worry lad, we'll be alright. I'm not fated to die tonight. I intend to die an old man, in bed, lying next to my wife – or better still a mistress half my age."

Arrows thudded into the sternums of the sentries. The two nimble archers quickly rushed out from the treeline and, using their small, freshly sharpened daggers, slit the throats of their enemy. Agrippa briefly wondered if either of the two dead men had a wife or intended waiting for them back home. After his debriefing about his mission Agrippa had written a letter, which he gave to Oppius for safekeeping and asked him to open and deliver should he not come back. Agrippa had had tears in his eyes when writing the heartfelt missive.

...I never knew what I was capable of until I met you. I never knew what, or who, I wanted until I met you. I never made love to anyone until I met you... I should have married you but I hope that in the eyes of the gods – and in your heart – we are married... But if you are reading this then I am gone and I want you to consider yourself free to marry. Love again... As much as time seemed to beautifully stand still when we were in our apartment together, as if we were two figures captured in a painting, I do not want you to live in the past and mourn me too much. You've got too much to give the world... Please do not let the memory of when we were last together be the abiding memory you have of me...

The cold water suddenly concentrated Agrippa's mind back onto his mission. But rather than thinking of the woman he loved as a distraction Caecilia was his goal – the reason why the soldier would be able to swim across and reach the other side of the river.

*

Octavius appeared thoughtful on the outside but worried about his friend. *Should I have ordered him not to volunteer for the mission? All this will be for nothing if I gain wealth and power and have no one to share them with. Talent and loyalty should be rewarded. Marcus, Oppius, Octavia. They're more important – real – than trinkets and honours.*

Octavius sat around a rectangular dining table in a large tent, accompanied by Hirtius and Oppius. His small plate of ham, cheese and asparagus tips was half eaten. He had barely touched his wine either. His co-commander shared not his austere appetite. He sat with various full – and empty – plates in front of him. Aulus Hirtius was a general, statesman, scholar and gourmet. A crop of black hair, streaked with grey, sat upon a round, plump face. Buried in his soft, pink features was a flat nose, thick lips and a small set of hazel eyes which shone with intelligence and amiableness. Despite his girth Hirtius still managed to be able to ride and fight as well as the next man. He had also consciously trained harder over the past six months, knowing that he would likely have to resume military service. The folds of his tunic hung over his low hanging belt. Although Octavius did not entirely trust the consul, whose first loyalty was to the Senate (or himself), he enjoyed his company. "Hirtius is as well read as he is well fed," the propraetor had reported to Cicero in a letter. Octavius and Hirtius had, on more than one occasion, spoken long into the night with one another over dinner. He praised the consul on his ability to mimic Caesar's writing style when finishing off his commentaries. He listened, enraptured, as if he were a boy again, as Hirtius spoke of his time on campaign with Caesar. "I can remember the start of one battle. Julius was worried that, due to our superior numbers, some of the mounted officers might retreat at the first sign of difficulties. So he duly ordered that all officers should relinquish their horses and fight side by side with their men. Suffice to say Julius was the first one to hand the reins of his charger over, to be sent away… Julius was a man of extraordinary abilities. He strengthened the Republic." Suffice to say, when in the company of Cicero and other leading senators, Hirtius had argued that Caesar had weakened the Republic.

Although Hirtius was not entirely pleased or comfortable with being saddled with the youth as a co-commander the experienced soldier never patronised or criticised his junior. Hirtius was also genuinely impressed with the mature manner and sharp intellect of Caesar's heir.

The consul smiled and licked his lips as an attendant brought out a large oval plate, filled with lamprey and red mullet swimming in a mushroom sauce. The general had instructed his scouts and messengers to bring back his favourite foods whenever they could. In order to preserve his produce it was often heavily salted, which led Hirtius to drink even more wine that he was accustomed to. No matter how much food or wine Hirtius consumed, however, he never appeared satiated or drunk. Such was the amount of food and drink at one end of the table, compared to the other, Oppius fancied that it might collapse.

"They will have made it across by now," the centurion remarked, sensing that Octavius was thinking about the mission and his friend. "Decimus will have given instructions to his men to capture rather than execute anyone they find."

"And do you believe that he will remember your archer from his days campaigning in Gaul?" Hirtius asked, seemingly more interested in removing his fish from its bone than he was concerned with a key military operation.

"Teucer is thankfully far too an annoying character to forget. Also, Decimus would have sat in on various archery tournaments over the years amongst the legions which Teucer would have won. He will know and trust him."

"They are also laden with official, sealed letters from me," the consul replied, trying to reassure himself as much as others.

"Not only will we be swimming with the weight of expectation on our back but we'll now be crossing the river with a lead pipe strapped to us," Teucer had half-jokingly complained, when he heard about the messages he would be carrying.

Oppius had commented, before they marched north, that Decimus was a more than competent general – which was high praise indeed from the centurion. His flaws included arrogance and self-regard, however. He believed himself Caesar's equal – and superior to everyone else. Decimus judged that he was entitled to a consulship; Caesar owed him the honour due to his martial achievements and family name. "Without Caesar I cannot be consul but without me Caesar could never have become a dictator," the general had commented, when Mark Antony was promoted over him.

As well as being a slave to his pride Octavius condemned Brutus as a traitor. As well as breaking his oath, having sworn to protect Caesar, Decimus had been the one who had manipulated his friend into attending the Senate meeting on the morning of his assassination. Octavius even caught wind of a rumour that the libertore had boasted about "outwitting the wily general and statesman."

During his meeting with Agrippa, just before he left for his mission, Octavius had been tempted to alter his lieutenant's brief and order him to kill Brutus when he reached Mutina. But circumstances dictated Octavius needed to rescue his enemy rather than damn him for now. Caesar had even given instructions in his will for Decimus to act as Octavius' guardian. *Yet I must come to his rescue. Life has a black sense of humour. Principles have to be sacrificed for pragmatism. Life has thrown up the irony too that Gaius Trebonius has been slain by the ally of my enemy. I'm glad he's dead but I feel deficient for not having held the dagger or given the order myself...*

Octavius' soul burned – certainly his stomach turned and he was unable to eat – when he thought about how he was not honouring the promise he made to himself and his supporters: that he would avenge Caesar's death. *They must die.* "A man who forsakes a vow forsakes his honour," Julius had told his great-nephew many years ago. He had taken Octavius aside after his grandmother's funeral;

the boy had impressed his great-uncle in composing and delivering the funeral oration. "You have brought honour to your family today, Octavius. More than martial glory, material gain or political success – family and friends matter. Compassion is as great a virtue as courage. The power of a stylus is greater than that of a dagger. Read Cicero as well as the latest dispatches about my campaigns…"

Caesar and his legacy matter. Decimus, Mark Antony, Cassius, Brutus. I must destroy them all else they'll destroy me and Caesar's legacy.

"We should attack as soon as Pansa arrives. The latest communication has him arriving at midday, the day after tomorrow. Antony still seems to be obsessed with capturing the city, perhaps out of pride. Or he wants Mutina as a base of operations. But he will not be able to starve them out or assault the walls within the next few days. We can and will attack Antony from three sides. We have him right where we want him," Hirtius said, staring with delight at a spiced radish on his fork and popping it into his mouth.

Or Antony has us where he wants, Lucius Oppius thought to himself.

21.

Insects buzzed around oil lamps hanging from the ceiling of the tent. Four wine cups, with varying amounts of Massic left in them, pinned down the map which was spread across the table. Antony gazed at the plan of the nearby town, Forum Gallorum. He thoughtfully stroked his beard and nodded in satisfaction. The general could not think of a better location in the surrounding area, or province even, in which to set his trap.

Antony was joined in his command tent by his brother Lucius, Domitius Enobarbus and his highest ranking centurions – Gratian Bibulus, Felix Calvinus and Marius Sura. Although the latter trio of officers looked pensive as they stared at the large map of the battlefield for tomorrow, their minds were on other things. Bibulus mulled over which gods he should make offerings to tonight. Manius Sura at the smooth-faced serving boy who he had just ordered to top up his wine cup (having not volunteered it to help flatten out the map). Felix Calvinus' mind turned back to the game of dice he had been playing before being summoned to Antony's war council. He hoped that the break from the table wouldn't ruin his run of good luck.

Enobarbus looked at the three centurions. Each face told a story – a war story. *They may all have their vices but they possess the right virtues as soldiers.*

"Domitius, can you would update us on how our ruse is progressing?" Antony asked, his tone more business-like than usual.

"Our messenger, carrying intelligence that we mean to continue to besiege Mutina, has been captured. The message is in code but our enemy will be able to decipher it. As for the plans this evening the men have been instructed to leave their tents up and let their campfires continue to burn as if they were still sitting around them. Should a scout from Hirtius' army reconnoitre the camp he will conclude that the bulk of our forces are still present. We will march out under the cover of darkness. The men have been told to carry only their weapons and a day's rations."

"Excellent. Thankfully Hirtius will believe that I am arrogant enough to remain in one place and have my enemies come to me … Bibulus, you will take your cohorts and conceal yourselves in these woods on the right flank. I can also provide you with cavalry and archers. When you appear from out of the treeline march your forces double time towards the enemy but there will be no need to break formation or have the men charge and sap their strength and momentum on the soft ground. Manius, you too will conceal yourself just over this reverse slope here."

Antony was tempted to make a joke that the centurion would enjoy lying with his men, but desisted.

"Enobarbus, Calvinus and I will hide the majority of our forces within the town itself. Lucius, you will be our lure. You will be accompanied by nearly a full legion. We will need to make the prize tempting enough for Pansa to give chase and have him pursue you into our ambush. I have little doubt that he will take the bait. Despite Pansa's close friendship with Hirtius he will be eager to cover himself in glory over that of his co-commander. But Pansa is not his friend's equal on the battlefield. I have campaigned with both soldiers over the years. Pansa's victories often came as a result of his veterans carrying him rather than from Pansa leading them. Once he has taken the bait, Lucius, you will lead him here." Antony pointed to a space on the map just south-east of Forum Gallorum. "The area is partly marshland. Pansa will be trapped like a fly in honey. Once his forces are bogged down you will turn on your pursuer. At the same time we will attack. The enemy will either rout or perish. You may well have thought, as I have done, that there is a chance that you will face former comrades in battle tomorrow. They will be thinking the same sad thought – but not when their swords are unsheathed. I will be willing to show clemency to our friends after the battle but not during it. Should the opportunity arise to cut off the head of the opposing army then do not hesitate to take it. The body of men around it will soon falter without its direction. The quicker we gain victory the more men we will inherit from the defeated army. Many will swap sides and believe our cause is just once they see that our money is good. If we can just subsume a third of Pansa's army then we should obtain a numerical superiority over Hirtius' and the whelp's forces. As to the latter I will pay a substantial bounty for anyone who can capture or kill him. Let his first battle be his last. I know the boy. He will run away at the first sign of trouble or not even turn up to fight, feigning illness." Antony thought to himself that, no matter what may occur, he would spread the rumour that Octavius hid in his tent while his army went off to fight. *He's no Caesar.*

Antony ordered his attendant to bring out another jug of Massic. They would drink to each other and the battle ahead. Morale had returned in the camp. His army was well paid and well provisioned for. The memory of Brundisium was just that, a memory. After leaving Fulvia behind Antony had spent more time with his officers and legionaries alike. He shared jokes and old war stories with them over jugs of wine around the campfire. Fulvia had encouraged a culture of harsh discipline (often doing so behind her husband's back) but Antony – like Caesar before him – believed in rewarding soldiers and treating them like men as opposed to children.

Antony went through the plan once more and then dismissed his senior officers. They had to ready their legions and also attend to their vices. The general asked his lieutenant to remain a little while longer, however.

"Do we know if Decimus is aware that his allies are close by and ready to relieve him?" the general asked, conscious that, out of all the opposing commanders he would face, Decimus was the most experienced and dangerous.

"I'm afraid that we cannot be sure either way. But if our ruse works and we defeat Pansa's army quickly then there will be little that Decimus will be able to do. Both he and Hirtius will fail to come to Pansa's aid in time."

Again Antony stroked his beard and nodded in satisfaction. His strategy of dividing and conquering would work.

"And what of events in Macedonia? Is our agent in place? It's poetic justice that Marcus Brutus should die by an assassin's blade, don't you think?" Antony said, permitting himself a sly smile.

"He is in place."

22

There are two sides to him.

Horace had spent the day in the company of Matius Varro. The centurion had arrived the evening before and, after having dinner with the lady of the house (Porcia had made a point not to invite Horace), had retired to his room before the young officer could meet him. Brutus was absent, attending to the imprisonment of Gaius Antony. He spent the following morning in town, sitting for a sculpture which some of his supporters in Athens had commissioned and intended to display alongside statues of Greek heroes who had fought for liberty. The irony wasn't lost on Horace that Brutus was spending the night arranging for the illegal detainment of an official, and the morning being honoured as a champion of political freedom.

Brutus had asked his adjutant to look after his friend while he was away. Horace had heard a number of rumours before meeting the enigmatic centurion. From his dusky features – thin lips, narrow eyes and slender face – some thought Varro was Spanish, Sicilian or Greek. More questions were raised, rather than answered, about his origins when people found out the soldier could speak five different languages fluently. When asked about his homeland Varro would often reply, "Well where do you think I'm from? If that's what you think then that's where I'm from…" Varro looked good for his forty plus years, handsome despite the rigours of military service and well-conditioned because of them. During his career the accomplished officer had fought under both Pompey and Caesar and, as well as commanding troops, had served as an envoy to the Senate. Indeed some judged Varro to be a spy as opposed to a soldier. Such was his rapid rise through the ranks at a young age it was rumoured that Varro must have had some form of a patron looking out for him, and at various points of his career it was whispered that he was the bastard son of Pompey, Lucullus or Sulla.

Varro was as well read as any student at the Academy and he would often put his education to use by drafting wills for his men or helping them find the words to write to loved ones. Such was his knowledge of literature and philosophy Horace was unsure whether to admire or resent his fellow scholar. When Varro was caught in a private moment he would appear thoughtful or brooding, but no one would ever be able to guess what the soldier was thinking or brooding about. "He is a closed book, but one worth reading," Brutus had told Horace.

Varro was well liked and possessed plenty of friends – but no close friends. If Horace had to classify the two sides of the centurion he would cite the Varro who was sober (who, even more than thoughtful, seemed troubled) and the Varro who liked to drink. Suffice to say everyone preferred the latter – including Varro himself, Horace sensed. The young poet judged that there were different types of drinkers, or drunks, in the world. Ones who were angry, ones who were sad and ones who were dull. Matius Varro was rare, however. He was a happy drunk. He neither became garrulous or excitable – just contented. "Drink lubricates the soul," the centurion had confessed during the afternoon, wearing a wry, satisfied smile on his face. But he wasn't a slave to wine like other soldiers – and men in general – Horace had encountered over the years. *Subdue your passion or it will subdue you.*

The two men spent the day walking along the valley. They wore plain tunics, rather than their uniforms, but still carried their swords and daggers. The weather was pleasant, as was the scenery. Pinkish clouds, which had clumped themselves together like frightened sheep, began to separate and shafts of amber sunlight shot through the gaps as if the gods were firing arrows made of gold. Craggy trees had started to blossom again. Moss and flowers softened and brightened up the rocky terrain.

Sometimes the men discussed philosophy and literature, but they also knew the virtue of silence and enjoying their own thoughts. As they set off that morning Horace was keen to hear about the latest news from Rome and the civil war.

"Has the fighting commenced in earnest yet? Has the civil war started?" Horace asked. If Antony was defeated then he could think about returning to his studies and poetry.

"In some regards the civil war started as soon as Caesar was assassinated. Or you could say it never ended. We are still fighting the same fight which Marius and Sulla fought and Pompey and Caesar continued. Rome is in a permanent state of war. Periods of peace are like brief intermissions between acts in a play – a tragedy rather than a comedy."

"War may be in Rome's make-up. You may drive out nature with a pitchfork but she'll constantly come running back," Horace replied.

Varro was impressed by the young soldier. *Brutus is right to speak well of him.*

"How do I know that we are in a state of war? Because the Senate has asked me to travel to Athens in order to assure its politicians and populace that we are not at war. Brutus tells me that you wish to be a poet, not a soldier. Maybe the latter will furnish you with the material to be the former after this is all over. A battlefield can be a crucible of extremes but it's the job of a poet – or perhaps more so a philosopher – to chart the extremes of the soul, so that he can steer his readers through a middle course. Homer sailed between Charybdis and Scylla so others didn't have to, though, ironically, he inspired many to do so. But cultivate the golden mean and you will avoid the poverty of a hovel and the envy of a palace," Varro said. Drink had already started to lubricate his soul.

"You could have been a poet yourself it seems."

"Unfortunately I would have been, at best, a second-rate poet. Which would, of course, have made me a first-rate songwriter."

Horace laughed. *There are two sides to him. I like one. I'm just not sure if I trust the other.*

*

Brutus returned that evening in uncommonly good spirits. He announced that he would be throwing a party the following day, which would include a troupe of actors performing a play in the evening. He hoped that Varro could stay another night to attend.

A burden had been lifted. After months of ambushes, skirmishes and political manoeuvring Brutus had subdued the province. Cassius held similar sovereignty in the east. As their armies grew so did their influence. Balbus had recently composed some propaganda stating that the two republicans were now "living like kings".

Matius Varro sat at his host's marble dining table. The room dripped with expensive mosaics, ornaments, paintings and sculptures alike. Porcia had spared little expense buying rich silk curtains, Persian rugs and couches worthy of Cleopatra. Although Brutus did not give his wife much of his time he did give her plenty of pin money in compensation. Shopping took her mind off things. Winter had passed but there was still a hoarfrost between husband and wife.

Whereas Brutus and Cassius would argue that they were receiving "donations" for their cause Matius knew that, in some cases, they were being financed through extortion money. Brutus had also returned to his former enterprise of charging extortionate rates of interests on loans he gave out.

"A toast, gentleman. To good friends and good conversation," Brutus exclaimed, holding his cup of Falernian aloft, smiling at his companions, Varro and Horace. "We may also be inadvertently drinking to victory at Mutina tonight if the battle is over and justice has prevailed. I received a letter from Cicero to say that Lepidus, who is encamped with his legions on the other side of the mountains in Long-Haired Gaul, has refused to declare for Antony. I should also say that the snake has failed to commit his legions to the army of the Republic. He will doubtless be the first to congratulate and pledge allegiance to the victor however."

"Like his wife, he'll get into bed with anyone," Matius joked.

Brutus let out a burst of laughter, not knowing the last time he had done so.

The wine and conversation continued to flow throughout the evening. A fire was lit. Laughter and wit crackled along with the burning logs. After dessert Brutus retrieved his bound copy of Homer and the three men played a game of Homeric lots, where each man took a turn to open the book at random and read a line. The line was supposed to represent the fate of its reader, either defining his character or prophesising his future.

Horace volunteered to go first. Many a time had the boy-poet snuck into his father's study and played the game on his own. Such was his intimacy of Homer he need only be given a first line to then quote the rest of the passage from heart. Horace had forgotten the amount of times his mother had called him into the room to perform his party trick in front of her friends. Horace, to dramatically heighten his submission to fate, solemnly closed his eyes as he opened the book. When he opened them the intoxicating phrases were like silk to the aspiring poet. Horace read out his line, smiling a little both before and afterwards. He would heed the words and he hoped that Brutus would take the poet's wisdom to heart too.

"Curb thou the high spirit in thy breast, for gentle ways are best, and keep aloof from sharp contentions."

Matius nodded in sympathy. Brutus' expression remained unchanged. Horace passed the book back to his host who, after draining his cup and nodding to a slave to re-fill it, turned his attention to divining his fate. Brutus had always preferred philosophy to poetry – and Roman authors to Greek – during his youth but he was familiar with Homer, if not as enamoured with him as his companions. Brutus didn't appreciate the constant interventions of the gods in the story, believing that man forged his own path in the world and was responsible for his actions. But his hands were still clammy and his heart beat that little bit faster. It was just a game, he told himself. The general opened the book. He read over the lines first in his head, from a passage which he had put a mark next to previously: *There is nothing nobler or more admirable than when two people who see eye to eye keep house as man and wife, confounding their enemies and delighting their friends.*

Either because of the lump in his throat or the awkwardness he would feel in saying the words Brutus recalled another line from Homer and offered it up to his friends, hoping that they would not see through his act.

"Without a sign the brave man draws his sword and asks no omen but his country's cause."

Brutus puffed out his chest as he spoke but Matius wasn't convinced by his performance. Horace's eyes blazed as brightly as the fire, believing in his commander, Homer and the fact that he may well be taking part in a moment of history. Drink was lubricating his soul.

Brutus took another swig of barely watered down wine and passed the book along, relieved to be rid of it.

Like Horace, Matius Varro had grown up with Homer. He could still vividly recall being seven years old and hearing a grey-bearded actor in the market perform *The Iliad*. Each day he would recite a different book and each day Matius would place a small coin in his hat, along with others, as payment. He read *The Odyssey* a week afterwards, devouring yet savouring each line. Every word was a jewel – precious, eternal. Homer fired a spark and other authors fuelled the flame. The boy worshipped Socrates, Aristotle, Thucydides and Plautus more than any god. Literature represented another world – a better world – to escape to. And philosophy helped pull back the veil covering the sometimes noble – sometimes ugly – face of the real world.

The centurion cradled the tome in his hands as if it were holy book. A breeze whistled through some shutters on the other side of the room. The book creaked open and Varro sucked in the words on the page – compelled and condemned to read the line which most thrummed upon his soul. The soldier's voice was clear, calm and yet sorrowful: "Hateful to me as the gates of Hades is that man who hides one thing in his heart and speaks another."

23.

Rain freckled Lucius Antony's face and armour. Sweat glazed his forehead and also streaked the flanks of his coal-black mare. He harried his commanders to harry his men – riding at the front, rear and alongside his forces at differing points. He hoped that some of his soldiers would take note of his courage and leadership and praise him over their campfires at night. The ground shook from Pansa's pursuing army. He had used his cavalry and archers to slow the enemy's advance, but he didn't want to slow them too much. The plan was working and the trap would soon be sprung.

Lucius Antony had gritted his teeth during his brother's war council. Lucius believed that he should have been allowed to command a wing of the army, rather than just acting as a lure. Had he not proven himself? Had he not been behind the procurement parties who had raided the north in order to feed his brother's army? Did the legions not look upon him as someone above the rank of centurion? He refrained from speaking out though, knowing that his brother would use the incident as an excuse to belittle him. Lucius felt like he had lived in the shadow of his older brother all his life. People had befriended him, both in his youth and now, in order to get closer to his brother. People smirked whenever Lucius mentioned being a descendent of Hercules. One could see the family resemblance when the two men stood side by side but Lucius' features were leaner – more hawkish – no one had ever deemed Lucius to be as handsome as his brother. No woman ever chose him over his brother, indeed the older brother often slept with the younger brother's mistresses (one of which Lucius had been genuinely fond of and thought he might marry). But one woman might choose him over his brother soon.

Fulvia… She pretends she doesn't care about his infidelities with younger women. But she does. She is only human after all as much as some might call her inhuman for her coldness and cruelty… She has already given me the eye… I could have had her already. But the time isn't right. It will be. Revenge will be sweet for both of us. Sleeping with Fulvia will more than make up for him sleeping with a dozen of my former mistresses… Her beauty may have faded but her powerbase hasn't. She has the political and financial connections I will need. But I have the name – and support of the army – that she needs… No matter what the outcome here today I will advance my cause. If my brother proves victorious then he will give me a province to govern, where I can grow my own war chest and army, or I will be the First Man of Rome and Italy whilst he attends to Brutus and Cassius in the east. But should he be defeated the faction will still need a leader. I will be able to challenge the boy Octavius and win over Caesarian support from his faction too. But let's just take one battle at a time.

*

The gods are on our side.

Gaius Vibius Pansa did not hesitate when the breathless scouting party returned and reported that they had located a sizeable enemy force travelling towards them on the Via Aemilia.

The commander galloped at the head of his army. His freshly dyed cloak billowed in the wind. His polished armour and helmet gleamed in the midday sun. Pansa was of average build. Cicero described the consul as being "a modest man, with a lot to be modest about." He had spent his career being proficient at carrying out orders given by other people. But now he had a chance to lead instead of follow.

We must engage the enemy before they reach the town.

Pansa heard cheers behind him as his men sensed that they could swallow up the inferior force with ease. He also heard them jeer, taunting the retreating soldiers. The general grinned, wolfishly, at the cavalry officer next to him.

Lambs to the slaughter.

Pansa knew that, behind his back, senators and senior officers judged that he was not his co-consul's equal in military prowess. But he would prove them wrong. The general issued orders for his cavalry to outflank and encircle the fleeing enemy, curving around them like the horns of a bull. It was a manoeuvre worthy of Hannibal, Pansa thought to himself. Perhaps he would be able to persuade Hirtius to write up the commentary for the battle as he had for many of Caesar's campaigns.

The enemy seemed to be suicidally heading towards the open ground instead of the relative sanctuary of the forest or town. Their retreat would be slowing due to the soft, boggy soil, Pansa judged. The general watched with satisfaction as his cavalry commenced to draw their swords – the blades freshly sharpened from the night before.

The noise was not that of the wind moving through the trees, but men. Soldiers. Thousands of them. The town became a hive of activity but Pansa realised quickly that the men he could see advancing towards him were not townsfolk. The sunlight bouncing off helmets, from legionaries marching over the ridge, also caught the stunned general's eye. Two wings of enemy cavalry poured out from the woods and Forum Gallorum. Their intention was to outflank and encircle Pansa's forces. The Republic's army would be gouged upon the horns of the bull. Antony ordered his cavalry to ride around the rear of his enemy in order to prevent it retreating. The blood drained from Pansa's face and he felt like a hand had gripped his heart. His throat became dry and he croaked out an order for his legions to form up in defensive formation.

Antony grinned. All was going according to plan. Not even Caesar could have planned and executed things more effectively.

184

Thankfully his men had retained their discipline whilst occupying the town, despite the temptation to loot and rape. Lucius had done well. The general would take his brother aside afterwards and personally thank and praise him. Although he would not laud Lucius in public and feed his vanity and ambition, Mark Antony thought to himself.

You can either surrender or die, Gaius. I will be fair and present the same offer to Hirtius, when I encounter him. Lambs to the slaughter...

*

The weight of evidence was against Antony splitting his army and attacking Pansa, Hirtius argued that morning. Oppius replied that most of the evidence could have been supplied by Antony. Caesar had employed similar ruses and false intelligence before too.

"I am not asking you to trust me, but to trust Oppius," Octavius added, not wishing to force the consul into thinking that he was ordering him to do anything.

"If I am wrong then the only harm done will be that of a few sore feet. But if I am right and Antony is planning to intercept Pansa on the Via Aemilia then we will need to converge our armies immediately," Oppius calmly, but firmly, stated.

Hirtius at first appeared unmoved but then he breathed out. *What harm could it do*? Caesar had trusted Oppius in military matters, all those years ago. And Hirtius trusted Caesar, when it came to his military judgement. The general had provided the centurion with two cavalry squadrons and two infantry cohorts. Hirtius also allowed Octavius to grant Oppius the use of the propraetor's Praetorian Guard.

"Will today be the day?" Octavius asked the veteran officer shortly afterwards, when they were alone. The anxious look on the youth's face made him appear ten years older.

"Hope for the best, plan for the worst," Oppius answered, unsure if he was putting the boy at ease.

"Should I ride out with you or remain here?"

The centurion believed that Octavius wanted him to answer the latter. He remembered the ambush on the road to Rome a year ago. Octavius had hid beneath a wagon as two of their friends were slain trying to protect him. Physical courage is a strange animal though, Oppius mused. He had seen some soldiers fight like lions in one battle only to whimper and run when next lining up in a shield wall.

Fear can be as great a spur for heroic actions as bravery. The heat of battle enflames hearts in different ways.

Octavius pictured the wild, contorted expressions on the faces of men who fought. He recalled the barbaric battle cries. He believed he was unable to lose control in such a way – become inhuman. *Or perhaps a man fighting for his life is the true face of humanity. But what will the men think of me if I choose not to stand with them and share their fate? History says that, to succeed in politics, one must garner martial glory too. History doesn't have to always repeat itself though. Wars are not just won on the battlefield.* Octavius also remembered something Caesar had once said to him: "The successful commander is sometimes the one who doesn't have to fight." Octavius didn't want to be labelled a coward but he also didn't want fail on the battlefield and let people see behind the mask. The propraetor tried to show that he was torn and disappointed when Oppius recommended that he remain at the camp. Octavius wanted to say to the soldier that he wanted Oppius to be proud of him – but didn't. Oppius wanted to say to Octavius how proud he was of him and that Caesar would be proud of him as well – but didn't. The two men merely gave each other a cursory nod.

Although he felt it prudent to leave Octavius behind at the camp Oppius elected to recruit Agrippa to his small force, who had successfully returned to the camp from his mission to Mutina. He asked Pollux and Teucer to accompany him too.

The quartet sat on their horses next to each other on the ridge of a hilltop which looked down over Forum Gallorum, the Via Amelia and the battle. Flat grey clouds marked the gloomy sky, like lesions. Oppius cursed Antony beneath his breath but he also begrudgingly gave him credit. He had skilfully deceived Hirtius and manoeuvred most of his army during the dead of night. Similarly his army was now moving with method and purpose as it converged around Pansa's legions. *Should I leave Pansa to his fate?*

Oppius' cavalry squadrons and cohorts wouldn't be able to tip the balance in Pansa's favour but they may just be able to help the defenders hang on long enough until Hirtius' army could arrive. The centurion knew that he would be sending countless soldiers to the deaths if they joined the battle – but more men would eventually die if he did nothing.

Agrippa observed the officer's face in profile. Worry and age coloured his expression. Somehow the veteran soldier could look both careworn and determined at the same time.

"Teucer, Agrippa – head back to camp and inform Hirtius of the situation. He needs to mobilise as many legions as possible, as quickly as possible. Tell him if Antony wins here today – either defeating or recruiting Pansa's army – then all will be lost for the rest of us."

A part of the Briton wanted to try and talk his old friend out of his decision to stay and fight but he knew Oppius well enough to know that his mind was made up. A brief nod and forced smile from the centurion said enough. A month beforehand Oppius had handed the archer several letters and briefed him on his affairs. The letters were to go to Octavius, Agrippa and Livia – should Teucer ever be able to locate her.

187

A lump rose up in Agrippa's throat. He wanted to say something to the centurion – to thank him, praise him – but couldn't. Agrippa felt a presentiment, churning in his stomach like hunger, that he would never see his friend and mentor again. Oppius, witnessing the anxiety on the young soldier's face, did his best to put him at ease (despite feeling ill at ease himself).

"Don't worry lad. I know it may seem like a suicide mission but I've been through worse. Sometimes it's not about advancing or retreating, sometimes you've just got to hold the line."

24.

The afternoon sun gave an extra sheen to the marble colonnades the slaves had polished that morning. Local dignitaries, merchants and scholars all paid court to Brutus as if he were royalty. Perfume, the smell of shellfish and bouquets of wine infused the air. Musicians played in the background. For the entertainment, later on in the evening, Brutus had organised for a troupe of players to perform a comedy.

The host and his wife smiled in unison as they greeted their guests. Brutus' arm ached from shaking hands. He received endless compliments as well as pledges of political and – more importantly – financial support. Porcia lied as much as she smiled, telling people how much she preferred Athens to Rome. She gazed at her husband, with affection and admiration, and duly charmed their attentive audience.

"I knew your father. He was unique – a keeper of the flame of the soul of Rome," Voluscius Caepio remarked to Porcia, in reference to Cato. Brutus took in the portentous local administrator. His hair and skin were as oily as his manner. He bowed to Brutus that little bit lower when he shook his hand, but the host was also aware of his guest's reputation for haughtiness and cruelty towards his slaves. Brutus wryly smiled to himself as he recalled how Voluscius had uttered the same words about Cato to him, many years ago, when talking about Caesar.

Brutus had smiled little that morning, however, as he read through a letter from his mother, Servilia. He had thought that, by putting distance between them, she might prove less overbearing. But he was wrong. As usual the letter was a litany of complaints and demands.

"Cicero believes he is solely responsible for galvanising the Republic – although that may be true in that everybody is now bored with his speeches and self-aggrandisement... Remember to think of Decimus and Cassius as rivals as well as allies. If they were willing to stab Julius in the back they will not balk at doing the same to you. Make sure you have more funds and legions at your disposal than them. Bleed Athens dry if you have to, in order to save Rome."

Servilia apportioned most of her letter though, either subtly or overtly, towards Porcia. The two women had never been fond of each other despite their family connection through Cato. Cicero had once quipped to Caesar over dinner that the two women were dogs, fighting over the bone of Brutus' spare time. Servilia deemed Porcia too prim, proud and obsessed with her dead father. Porcia judged her mother-in-law in return to be licentious, manipulative and obsessed with Caesar. From her knowing about the recent discord between husband and wife Brutus realised Servilia had planted at least one spy within his household.

"I have heard gossips in Rome argue that you were motivated to murder Caesar out of a devotion to your wife – and her devotion to Cato and will to avenge his death. You must be seen to be motivated from principle and a love of Rome. A wife must stand by her husband no matter what. And she must realise that she is the wife of a general, not just a praetor, now. Porcia's sensitive character is not suited to the climate or the challenging times ahead. You must save the Republic, even at the expense of saving your marriage. You will need to forge an alliance with one of the Metellii or Claudii to strengthen your influence in the Senate. Many women in their clans are coming of age. As much as I loved Cato dearly he is of no use to our cause now. I know that you will do the right thing. Porcia herself, if she still loves you, will understand..."

Brutus tossed the letter into the fire after reading it. As much as he had inwardly criticised his wife of late he resented anyone else openly speaking out against her. They didn't understand or appreciate her in the way he did. *I still love her. I think.* Brutus was all too aware of the friction between his mother and wife. Servilia had neither liked nor approved of Porcia from the start. She wasn't good enough for her son – but perhaps no one was. Servilia grew jealous of Porcia's influence over Brutus, little realising that, by her desire to direct and hold her son close, she had driven him away.

The hurt of losing her son to Porcia was compounded by the hurt of losing Caesar to an array of mistresses – although Caesar's love affair with himself held an even greater sway over his actions. As much as Caesar had gifted to Servilia a giant black pearl, worth more than all the jewels he had given other women combined, it was not enough for her. Julius had once told Servilia, with seeming genuine affection, that she would always have a place in his heart, but he could not give her all his heart. She tried to take a more active role in politics, to be of greater value to Caesar so he would spend more time with her. She even offered her daughter, Tertia, to the dictator as a mistress so she could spend more time with him – try to influence him – that way. But Caesar was his own man and she realised she could never be Calpurnia or Cleopatra (who had given the dictator that which Servilia had wanted so desperately to give him over the years – a son). Some days she woke up and would try to devote herself to Caesar and win him back and other days she would brief against him and curse his name. She took other lovers but life proved a shadow of what it once had been after being Caesar's favoured mistress. And eventually age withered her. Servilia no longer turned the heads of those in power. Other – younger – women captured their eye. She increasingly drank to dull the ache and emptiness in her heart. She sometimes behaved inappropriately in a bid to be the centre of attention again, like she had been in the glory of her youth. She often wore more make-up to appear younger but, as Cicero cruelly joked, "she is unable to paint over all the cracks."

Sometimes Brutus was ashamed of his mother. Sometimes he resented her. But he also felt sorry for her. Rightly or wrongly she blamed Caesar for her unhappiness. Did Brutus blame him too?

Although she had not plunged a dagger into him Servilia had been an integral part of the conspiracy to assassinate Caesar. She had encouraged her son to meet with Cassius. The conspirators had also met at her house to plan the deed.

For all of your criticisms of Porcia did you not act from personal rather than political motives in wanting Caesar dead? But in my pride, jealousy and out of revenge for hurting you did I not kill him for selfish reasons too?

Brutus glared long into the fire that morning, hoping to find answers. But he just found more questions and sorrow.

*

Horace began to feel exhausted from all the pleasantries and small talk. He told himself that the party was good practise for when he would have to seek a patron as a poet. He laughed at terrible jokes and agreed with ill thought out comments as if playing a game with himself.

The adjutant had spent the morning double checking the latest accounts for his general. The numbers for income and outgoings had become dizzying compared to just a few months previous. Soon Brutus and Cassius' forces would eclipse those of the Republic's. Brutus had recently arranged a recruitment drive for men and capital. He and his agents had travelled to various towns and instructed them to pay a donation so that the army could defend them against Antony and his tyranny. Brutus called it "protection money".

Horace allowed one of the slaves to fill up his cup again, although he was conscious of diluting his wine more than usual. The party would go on into the evening and he wanted to have a reasonably clear head when watching the play, considering that he been allowed to compose a few extra lines and scenes for the production. Brutus had kindly put the suggestion to Ovidius Cinna, the lead actor and manager of the group of players. Cinna was aged around forty though he seemed to have the energy of a twenty year old. When Brutus had heard that Cinna was in the area he invited the troupe to perform at the party.

"Our host tells me that you are a budding writer, Horace. My advice would be don't give up the day job though – and I'm not saying that because I do not want any rivals. I remember when I started out as a poet, many years ago. I would wake up in poverty one day and, in the next, merely be more debt-ridden," Cinna exclaimed, laughing at his own joke and warmly clasping the young officer on the shoulder. "Less is more. Never write two or three words when you can write just one. Although you will need to win over the husband for a patron it is often the case than his wife will control the purse strings. So win over her as well. Have a wealth of compliments to draw from when conversing. Employ different ones for different ages. Different vintages have different tastes. Similarly your patron may want you to do more than just sing for your supper. Shut your eyes and tell yourself it's all for the art or, if it proves to be of greater consolation, think of the money."

Horace attempted to dip his toe in the waters of complimenting wives of possible patrons during the party but his shyness – and ineptitude – caused him to fail. The women thought him of too lowly a rank or not handsome enough.

If they only knew that I was a poet, that I could immortalise them in verse. Poetry can be as lasting as marble or rust like iron. I could fill their ears with music. There's certainly plenty of space between the ears of most of them. Most of the women here seem fit for satire and epigrams as opposed to love poetry though … Some of the dresses are so tight that I may need to call on the army surgeon to cut them out of their clothing, although in some cases I suspect that there will be plenty of civilian volunteers who'll be up for the task. At some point I will need to play my part and attract a patron or a patron's wife. But as much money as it takes to enter society I need to one day be wealthy enough to be free of it. Live the quiet life in the country. This is what I pray for. A plot of land – not so very large, with a garden and, near the house, a spring that never fails and a bit of woodland to round it all off. Aye, we all must play our part to get what we wish for. Just look at the performance being played out between Brutus and Porcia. But am I not already playing a part in telling myself that I'm destined to become a great poet. Cinna may be the only honest man here, for at least he admits that he's an actor.

Horace wended his way through the ever increasing throng and headed out to the garden at the back of the house. The breeze immediately cooled his flushed face and refreshed his thoughts. A few other guests had commenced to congregate outside and could be seen whispering – and canoodling – in corners. The lone figure, standing at the foot of the garden, attracted his attention. Although it seemed that Matius Varro was desiring privacy Horace approached the centurion. He was still a slight riddle, which the poet had still to unravel the meaning of.

Matius gazed, or glowered, out across the valley rather than back at the house. Campfires dotted the plains and reminded the soldier of Pharsalus, the days before the battle. *So many died then and for what? Caesar, Pompey, Antony, Brutus and Cassius. All charming, brilliant and mad. Perhaps Caesar was different though. He knew his life was being played out on a stage and that life is a joke played on man. The best thing you can do is just laugh along with it.*

Matius appeared to be in no laughing mood, however. As much as he stared off into the distance the centurion appeared to have something at the forefront of his mind.

"I hope that I'm not disturbing you, Matius."

"No, it's fine. I needed a break from the party. I was just collecting what few thoughts I have left rattling around inside my mind," he replied. A smile lightened the darker expression which had previously shaped his features. There had been a storm on his brow – murder on his mind. The centurion sighed, gently, relieved at being freed from his reverie.

"I hear that you will be leaving us later, after the play. You are packed and ready to go."

"Duty calls," Matius replied, unconsciously clasping his sword as he spoke.

"Brutus will be sad to see you leave, not least because he has yet to try and recruit you to his cause."

"Brutus is doing a more than adequate job of creating and training a grand army without my help. The question is, Horace, which you are wise enough to have asked yourself, will Marcus be as equally adept at disbanding his army when the war is over? I hope that, in his cause to become a great man, our friend does not forget how to be a good one. It may prove to be the death of him."

"He may, like Caesar, become a god," Horace half-joked. But Varro still wasn't in a laughing mood. He looked grim. The centurion's voice was mournful, prophetic, as he shook his head and replied: "Nobody lives forever."

25

The gods are on our side.

Antony surveyed the battlefield. Pansa's army was all but surrounded, he surmised. The enemy had yet to rout or surrender – with the veterans bravely fighting on and propping up the new recruits – but the day would be his. A few cavalry skirmishes around the main fight had proved inconclusive but the general couldn't help but notice the bodies – of men and horses alike – littering the ground, stuck in the mud, like macabre statues. The marshland had aided Antony in deterring the enemy from making a quick retreat but it also now hampered his forces from attacking as efficiently as they could.

As usual the battle would be won by the infantry. Cohorts formed up in their shield walls and crashed against each other, butting like rams. Swords stabbed outwards between interlocked shields and soldiers fought each other furiously for a quarter of an hour before the second rank replaced the first, to carry on the fight. They were like two boxers, standing toe to toe. Antony judged he would win because he had greater reserves to call on.

Unlike other battlefields which Antony had fought on there were pockets of open land spread over the plains where the ground was too soft to occupy. Despite the discipline of some of the officers and cohorts the fighting broke up and became chaotic in places, where small clusters of men – or individuals – fought one another.

Pansa, it seemed, was trying to lead from the front, Antony observed.

He's either brave, mad or foolish. At least he's showing some character for once though.

Antony gave orders for Calvinus and his cohort to engage Pansa and the men surrounding him – to break through and kill the consul.

If their commander fell there would be little motivation for his legions to fight on. Antony preferred to spill as little Roman blood as possible. The more lives spared today, the greater force he would have to attack Hirtius, Decimus and Octavius with in the coming days. Antony dreamed of being able to face the latter in single combat. He would embarrass the stripling and then kill him, skewer him on his long cavalry sword like a piece of meat.

I'll swat him like a gadfly.

*

Their horses churned and spat up mud as Agrippa and Teucer galloped back towards their camp. The tamp of their hooves seemed calm compared to the beating of Agrippa's heart. The fate of Rome was potentially in his hands. If he couldn't deliver his message then Hirtius would not reinforce Pansa. If Pansa wasn't reinforced then Antony would defeat him and possess the momentum and men to defeat Octavius.

They were being pursued by half a dozen enemy cavalry. The patrol had spotted the two archers and were closing quickly. Their mounts were stronger, swifter and fresher.

"Ride on, I'll deal with these bastards behind us," Teucer breathlessly remarked to his comrade.

Agrippa was going to argue that they should stick together but he knew that one of them needed to deliver their crucial message. Teucer was the better aim and Agrippa was the better horseman. The young soldier merely gave a nod of acknowledgment and appreciation.

"Go on, fuck off. If I get misty eyed it'll ruin my aim. And don't look back," Teucer added.

Agrippa kicked his heels into the flanks of his mount and, despite the temptation to do so, didn't look back.

The field they were riding through was on a slight slope. Once Teucer reached the top he slowed his horse and wheeled it around to face the oncoming enemy. Sweat trickled down his back. He took two deep breaths and then nocked his first arrow. For the first time in his life Teucer recited the Legionary's Prayer: "Jupiter, Greatest and Best, protect this legion, soldiers every one. May my act bring good fortune to us all."

It brought the soldier comfort that he had left instructions for Oppius to send his money back to his tribe in Britannia – should he die.

If Oppius perishes too than Octavius will honour his promise to look after my people. The future of Rome is in good hands. The lad and Agrippa have got something about them. I've drunk enough, whored enough and killed enough. It's time to let the next generation make the same mistakes as the old – and come up with some new ones too.

The first arrow sang through the air and thudded into the chest of the lead decurion, knocking him back off his newly purchased black colt. The impressive shot didn't deter the rest of the patrol however, indeed it seemed to spur them on to cut down the archer before he could fire on anyone else. They barked orders into the ears of their mounts and the horses snorted and rode on harder in reply. Javelins were readied. Teucer and the enemy knew that there would not be time to fire on all six before they reached the top of the slope. It was a suicide mission. The Briton could and would still try to defeat them all though. Teucer was able to fire off three more arrows – and kill three more of the enemy – before the horsemen were in range of their target. Even the thought of his imminent death didn't distract the archer from his aim. The thought of attempting to retreat was similarly dismissed. *I won't show my back to the bastards.*

Teucer was able to fire off one last arrow – and fell his enemy – just before the spear punctured his lung. He prayed that Agrippa would now be safe. Teucer's last thoughts were that he hoped he would soon see Roscius and Fabius again, in the afterlife, and share a drink with them. The Briton slumped forward on his horse and died. His death, however, did not prevent the remaining enemy combatant from stabbing the archer several times with his javelin out of a frenzied sense of revenge for murdering his comrades. The cavalryman, once he had regained his composure, thought twice about pursuing the second archer – just in case he was as remotely accomplished a shot as the first.

*

Squelching sounds could increasingly be heard across the battlefield as rain filled the air and the glutinous ground grew even softer. Mud and blood smeared the armour and faces of all. The first wave of men to die began to add a fetid stench to the proceedings.

The veteran legionaries surrounding their consul recognised the prospective threat and duly closed ranks and reinforced their numbers. Bibulus had ordered his cohort into a wedge formation. They had moved through their own lines and then broken part of the first rank of the enemy's shield wall. The officer had arranged for his best spearman to be at the vanguard of his force and once in range of their target he gave the order for them to launch their volley. The superstitious centurion offered up all manner of prayers, to all manner of gods, that he would succeed in his task.

The consul, who had fought valiantly throughout the day, saw the swarm of spears arc towards him. But it was too late. His eyes were stapled wide in surprise as a javelin pierced the side of Pansa's armour and ribs. His eyes only half-closed as he fell to the ground, however. Their commander was still alive and the senior officers around him bellowed out orders to continue to fight. A member of the consul's bodyguard, Libo, cradled Pansa in his arms. The commander tried to speak but a trickle of blood issued forth from his mouth, as opposed to words. A legionary, with tears in his eyes for his commander, cut the spearhead from its shaft so they could move him. The plan was to now get their general to a physician. The army of the Republic would fight on and await for his return and orders. Libo gave the order for a squadron of cavalry to accompany him. Thankfully Antony's forces hadn't entirely surrounded them. They rode free from the battlefield towards Bononia, where a surgeon could attend to the general.

*

Their lines were thinning. Determination alone cannot win battles. When some of the Republic's soldiers were not fighting for their lives they had time and space to think about surrendering. The tang of blood was in the air, as was the prospect of defeat – or a massacre. Too many corpses were already sticking out of the ground. Curses, grunting and an incessant metallic clash of arms rattled the air.

Mark Antony had at first been jubilant at hearing the news that Pansa had been seriously wounded and conveyed from the field of battle. But then he gloomily thought how one man could no longer give the order to surrender.

And if he dies I will not have the opportunity to humiliate him and the Republic. Pansa has swapped sides once. He could do so again.

Antony admired and pitied the great mass of men, knee deep in mud and gore, fighting a losing battle. A survival extinct or savagery compelled them to struggle on, he judged. Years of training or a devotion to a cause motivated others. Experience had taught the general that most men would be fighting for the friends alongside them too. But many of their comrades had fallen. There would soon be no one to fight on for.

They must now surely be questioning whether they should continue to fight…

Arms ached. Armour was knocked out of shape. Sweat soaked the felt lining of their helmets. Skin and chips of bone flecked the muddy ground. Some must have questioned whether they would last the day. Others questioned whether they would get paid. Antony noticed that there were plenty of soldiers with their heads now hanging down, bowing to defeat.

But then, as if the sun had come out from behind the clouds, heads rose back up. A small relief force had arrived, marching northwards along the Via Aemilia. Oppius gave command of one of the cavalry squadrons and cohorts to Pollux while he took command of the remaining units, including the force of praetorian guards. A vague hope spread throughout the ranks of Pansa's forces. Hirtius' army was on the way. Some also recognised Oppius, believing that the *Sword of Rome* was worth another two cohorts.

Calvinus and Sura gave orders for half their soldiers to disengage and manoeuvre themselves to face the oncoming enemy.

Pollux's wounded leg began to throb but he was itching to fight still. His old friend, Aulus Milo, rode next to him.

"How's the leg?"

"Hurts like a bastard. Thankfully I won't lack for enemies to take my frustration out on," Pollux replied, thinking the thought that his friend now voiced.

"Do you think they made it back to the camp?" Milo remarked, in reference to Teucer and Agrippa being able pass on Oppius' message to Hirtius.

"I checked the map. There were no taverns or brothels on the way for Teucer to stop off in. So yes."

The grizzled veterans laughed, hoping that it wouldn't be the last time they would do so. The two centurions soon after dismounted, drew their swords and marched alongside their men.

Mark Antony briefly coloured the air with curses. All was not now going according to plan. Although but a dot in the distance he was sure that Oppius was leading the small force which was about to attack him. Antony still felt a shard of betrayal when he thought about his old friend.

You can't win today, Oppius. All you can do is die trying. You picked the wrong side. Should you somehow survive then your name will be one of the first I'll put on a proscription list, even though you've probably not got a pot to piss in or any property to speak of.

Antony summoned a messenger. He instructed the rider to give orders to Bibulus that Oppius was a priority target.

Oppius took personal command of the praetorian guards. Many faces before him were familiar, veterans from Gaul and Pharsalus. None of them, whether from professional pride or habit, would show their back to the enemy. He could hear a mass of soldiers behind him as Antony's cohorts marched towards them. But the centurion was happy for the enemy to sap their strength, trudging through the mud. His sweaty palms tightened around the ox-hide straps of his shield. His head felt like an oven within his helmet but Oppius, like the stone-faced praetorians before him, didn't display any discomfort.

Pansa's army had fought well to survive this long, the centurion judged.

We just need to do the same. Hold out until Hirtius arrives. The longer we can endure the more hope they'll be. And where there's hope there's life.

Before an unnerving silence could take root the centurion addressed his troops: "The walls protecting Rome begin here. We are its first and last line of defence. I could say do Caesar proud today. Many of you fought for him as he fought for you. But more so do yourself proud today. Be all you can be. There's iron in your hands and iron in your hearts. And they'll be gold in our purses if we see out the day. Reinforcements are on the way but let's not give them too much work to do, eh?"

Laughter broke out and the tension in the air – and in the soldier's expressions – was eased.

"We have but one task to do today: hold the line. Rome expects that every man will do his duty."

The centurion had to nigh on bellow this last order lest his words be drowned out by the roar of the enemy as they attacked Pollux and his men across the way.

The attack was diminished, although not defeated, as a volley of javelins scythed down the front ranks of the advancing legionaries. Men behind them lost their momentum and formation as they stumbled over their fallen comrades.

Oppius and Pollux had deliberately positioned their forces on the firmest ground they could find. They also bolstered the ranks of new recruits by inserting veterans to fight alongside them. They would hold the line against the first offensive. The question was though, how many subsequent offensives could they endure?

*

Antony gripped the hilt of his sword, making a fist. He was tempted to enter the fighting himself in order to take his mind off things and feel like he was making a difference. He still possessed the greater reserves although they were unfortunately positioned on the wrong side of the battlefield, unable to wipe Oppius and his cohorts off the map. Antony's forces also still surrounded the bulk of Pansa's army. The mass of his legions still remained on the battlefield, like a giant block of ice. But his forces were chipping away at it and it was melting from the heat of battle. But the general had expected to be triumphant by now. Antony was tempted to use some of his forces to fortify his position but then he dismissed the idea, believing that he was on the cusp of a complete victory.

Would his ruse still last? Or would Hirtius and his army arrive in time? Should he send a message to Enobarbus, back at the camp near Mutina, to order the remainder of his forces to join the battle? Antony began to have more questions than he had answers to.

*

The fighting continued on numerous fronts. Endless wars had created veterans and veterans prolonged battles. Whilst some shield walls held their ground others broke and the fighting became more frayed and disparate. Despite Antony's numerical superiority, of infantry and cavalry alike, he was still unable to outflank and rout his enemy. At the beginning of the day the general had been willing to offer Pansa's army clemency and the opportunity to be recruited to his cause. But now he was willing to put them all to the sword. They were an obstacle, which he still annoyingly needed to remove.

The corpses and wounded began to pile up on both sides. The chilling high-pitched screams of the injured and traumatised could be heard over rasping battle-cries. Mud caked upon armour and could be found in hair, ears and mouths. Sometimes the ground was more red than brown, however, with pools and rivulets of blood.

*

Lucius Antony's cavalry attack, which he had ordered so as to break through the enemy cohort's flank, proved ineffective. The veterans kept their shape and Pollux called upon his own cavalry – and a smattering of archers – to drive the horsemen away.

Pollux continued to growl and bark orders at the newer recruits. He felt a trickle of blood wend its way down his leg from where one of the sutures in his wound had broken. He seethed in both anger and pain. His gladius was awash with blood and sinew as he relentlessly stabbed at the enemy shield wall and pushed it back.

Where the cavalry had failed Calvinus hoped that his infantry would succeed. Calvinus wanted to kill Pollux out of personal spite and for strategic reasons. The tough, veteran officer was the keystone. If he could remove him from the formation then the whole edifice might collapse around him. Both centurions had never seen eye to eye. Calvinus resented Pollux for being promoted before him and Pollux believed Calvinus had accepted bribes over the years and, through working with the quartermasters, embezzled funds from the legion.

Calvinus wanted his enemy to come out from behind the shield wall, so he could isolate him. He soon got his wish when Pollux saw him in the opposing ranks. Pollux went for him, like a red rag to a bull, ducking his head behind his scutum and charging forward. The handsome yet battle-hardened officer was startled by his enemy but not afraid of him.

"Calvinus," Pollux exclaimed, pointing his sword at the opposing centurion. "We know how treacherous you are. But at least try not to be spineless." The former drill master's voice out-sounded everything going on around him, to the point that the two shield walls ceased fighting.

With his blood also now up – and not wanting to lose face in front of his men – Calvinus moved forward. His sword crashed against Pollux's shield. Such was the force of the attack that Pollux's wounded leg nearly buckled. The two centurions traded blows and curses. Hatred fuelled their reserves of strength. Pollux suddenly forced his opponent back. The lines of Calvinus' shield wall opened to allow the combatants to fight on but then closed again, swallowing them up.

Calvinus snarled-cum-grinned. He was confident that he could defeat his wounded enemy but he now didn't want to leave the result to chance.

"I never liked you Pollux," the centurion breathlessly remarked. "Someone do me a favour and kill this bastard."

The more honourable veterans in the circle of soldiers around Pollux didn't move but a number of the more bloodthirsty new recruits looked to impress their officer. Pollux killed one legionary and wounded another but, like Caesar trying to fight off his assassins, he was outnumbered. They stabbed him like a piece of meat. Pollux' blood freckled Calvinus' face as he stood over the centurion's butchered corpse. He sniffed, drew some phlegm up into his mouth and then spat on his fallen opponent. The vainglorious officer was about to add some derogatory remarks but, rather than words sticking in his throat, Aulus Milo's javelin did. The hulking centurion had led a few veterans into the belly of the beast of the enemy's ranks. Milo slaughtered a number of the legionaries who had murdered his friend, his sword slashing open necks and faces. There were tears in his eyes as he realised he couldn't save his fellow centurion yet Milo and his comrades fought courageously and retrieved the body of his friend so he could be buried with full honours.

*

Despite the stamina, bravery and skill of the praetorian guards their lines were thinning. Oppius found himself plugging the gaps with fresh-faced youths who were more used to handling a hoe and shovel than sword and shield. The centurion took a rare rest to catch his breath before he would again return to the front rank. His body ached and felt like one giant bruise. His armour had been battered out of shape.

Either the fighting's got harder or I've got older… At least we've given all given Antony more than just a bloody nose. He might now not have the numbers to overwhelm Hirtius.

Oppius offered up a prayer that Octavius and Agrippa would live through the coming week. He thought it would be too much to ask the gods that he could do so too. The veteran stared down at the sword in his calloused hand. The hilt had been worn down. The blade was chipped.

You haven't lived a bad life. I would have liked to have had a son or daughter though. I would have liked to have seen Livia again too.

Lucius Oppius sighed. The old soldier soughed like the wind, expelling any last regrets or sorrows and walked towards where the fighting was at its most intense.

"Just hold the line," he wearily uttered, unsure this time if he possessed the strength or luck to do so.

*

One side seemed to collectively gasp in relief and the other in horror. Death had ploughed through their ranks but many now in Pansa's army believed the gods were on their side. Prayers of salvation turned to ones of thanks.

Despite the need for haste Hirtius gave some consideration to his offensive. Like Antony he ordered his legions to attack at different points – from over the sloping plain and through the woods and town. Trumpets sounded, alerting Pansa's forces that reinforcements had arrived. Endless polished helmets gleamed in the late afternoon sun. An ocean of men descended upon the battlefield, come to wash away their enemies. Their mail armour rhythmically clinked as cohort upon cohort came into view. The sky even seemed to brighten for the almost defeated soldiers. As with Pansa's hardened troops many of Antony's veterans decided to fight on instead of surrender. They were either too proud or too fatigued to move off the ground they had gained. Death still had some furrows to plough.

Antony's horse became skittish but the general tried to remain calm. He gave orders for his legions to form up in defensive formation. If they had not already been fighting all day Antony's forces may have had a chance. If Antony had fortified his position they may have survived.

*

"Hold the line," Agrippa called out, with authority, from his sweat-strewn mount. "Reinforcements have arrived."

His words, which rang out across the line, boosted the spirits of the defenders and diminished those of the attackers. Agrippa rode at the vanguard of a squadron of cavalry which had skirted the woodlands and come out on the southern end of the Via Aemilia. The legions, which were marching behind him, kicked up a cloud of dust behind the trees.

The line had held not across the way, however, as part of the shield wall collapsed. Even Aulus Milo could not hold back the tide. A fair part of the cohort began to rout. Neither side were aware of the imminent reinforcements. Manius Sura led the attackers and his eyes soon became fixed on the prize of an enemy standard. The centurion picked up a stray javelin from the ground and skewered the retreating aquilifer.

I'll cover myself in glory today even if everyone else doesn't.

As Sura bent down to clasp the standard he felt the ground ominously shake beneath him. Several enemy horses galloped in a row. The centurion raised his hands, in surrender, but Octavius' cavalry blade was already moving through the air.

Octavius, along with Agrippa, volunteered to lead the first party of soldiers off towards the battlefield. Hirtius sketched out a plan of attack. He addressed his senior officers, warning them of the situation: "By the time we reach Forum Gollorum Pansa's army may have already been defeated. It may be the case that we are outnumbered."

As co-commander Octavius also addressed the men: "I would not have a single man more than I do; for these I have here with me are

Rome's finest. The chefs alone can remain back at this camp, in order to prepare our victory feast…"

Octavius would share the fate of his army. He would also do all that he could to come to the aid of his friend, Oppius, who was willing to sacrifice his life for his commander's cause. More than one centurion commentated that Octavius' speech was "Caesar-like".

*

Antony's granite-hard veterans fought on bravely. Few of them had ever surrendered before and they had no desire to experience defeat now. But Hirtius' influx of fresh troops tipped the balance. The weight of numbers told and the dam eventually burst. The bulk of Antony's forces scattered. Some put down their arms and asked for clemency. Some retreated into the woods. Some collapsed and drowned in the marshes. Antony made his escape too just after hearing the news that Decimus Brutus had broken the siege and attacked his camp, outside Mutina. Like Pompey, after Pharsalus, Antony blamed everyone but himself for the defeat. He prayed that he would be able to evade capture and that Enobarbus would survive the day too, giving little thought for his brother as he did so. The plan, if defeated, was to rendezvous at the foot of a pass leading into the Alps.

*

Carbo Vedius was half-buried in the mud but still very much alive. Unable to return to his ship he ventured north and signed on with Antony's army. He winced when he first put on the uniform of a legionary but the food and money compensated the sailor for his unease. Vedius had at first pretended to be dead in order to live but he continued his ruse and lay like a snake in the grass upon seeing the centurion come ever closer towards him. Every dog has its day.

The centurion had haunted his dreams and plagued his waking thoughts ever since their last encounter in Rome. Vedius vowed to kill Oppius to avenge his friends – as well as satisfy his own animus. He had imagined encountering the soldier again but never thought it possible.

It's fate… The gods are on my side…

Vedius planned to wait for his enemy to pass by him. He would then stab him in the back. As tempted as he was to want to look the centurion in the eye when he died, he did not want to give his dangerous opponent an opportunity to defend himself.

Oppius, whether out of habit or a conscious choice to continue to lead his men, was one of the men furthest forward as Antony's army routed. His forearm, as well as his blade, was covered in blood and sinew. He felt light-headed. His throat was dry. He needed a drink, water or wine.

Vedius slowly rose up from out of the mud, a creature more than man. His eyes narrowed. His mouth widened too, into a vicious grin. He could almost taste a sense of vengeance.

It will only take just one knife in the back.

Oppius shook his head at the all too familiar scene of carnage and a waste of life before him. Too many fathers would be among the dead, leaving their children orphaned. And conversely too many fathers would soon be mourning sons who had fallen. Flies began to dance around and settle on bloodied, contorted bodies. A clash of arms still rang in the background.

The war won't end here. But this will be my last battle…

The sharpened iron point entered and punctured a lung. A soldier's life can only end one way. There was an agonising stabbing pain and a sense of shock. But then there was nothing.

26.

The guests departed. Most of the staff had gone to bed, their limbs aching as much as the party goers' heads. Some of the audience had enjoyed the production of Terence more than others. Horace was gripped from the start, enjoying everything for differing reasons. He leaned forward on his seat throughout and mouthed the words to the lines he had contributed to the text.

Pale Death knocks equally upon the poor man's gate as at the palaces of kings... The greatest lesson in life is to know that even fools are right sometimes... It is of no consequence of what parents a man is born to, so long as he is a man of merit...

In contrast Matius Varro politely applauded at the end but for the most part sat with his chin buried in his chest. Again it seemed as if the weight of the world was on his shoulders. He was a man staring into the abyss with his reflection looking mournfully back. Others in the audience bowed their heads during the production because they had fallen asleep. Porcia thought that the calibre of acting did not equal that to be found in Rome.

His accent is from no place in the known world. They think they are all being profound but really they're pretentious. He gesticulates more than a Jew. If he saws the air with his hand any more he may get a splinter...

Before taking his leave Cinna asked Brutus if he could introduce a couple of his stagehands to his host.

"They admire you greatly."

Although somewhat fatigued from a long day Brutus mustered the energy to accept a few more compliments before he retired to bed. He said that Cinna should fetch the men and he would see them all in his study shortly. The general entered his study, looking forward to having a few moments alone where he could breathe out and collect his thoughts. But Brutus was not alone. Matius Varro was waiting for him.

The once austere study was now opulent. Expensive paintings and statues decorated the room. A small bust of Diogenes sat on a table next to a bust of Cato the Elder. Silk inlaid drapes covered the door leading out onto the balcony. The room shone with polished bronze and gold fixtures and fittings. The floor had been recently re-tiled and gleamed beneath the ornate oil lamps which hung from the ceiling. A newly enlarged hearth also housed a recently stoked fire.

The centurion stood sentry-like next to Brutus' desk in the half light. He had changed into his uniform and his sword hung from his hip too. The general was at first startled – but then pleased to see his friend.

"Have you re-considered and are staying the night? I had hoped that you could stay with us even longer, Matius. Porcia will be sad to see you go, as will I."

"As late as it is I should really leave tonight. Duty calls," the soldier replied, creasing his brow either apologetically or in resignation. *I must kill him.*

"Well I must insist that you come and visit us again when your mission is over. We may know by then the outcome of the impending battle between Hirtius and Antony. Should Antony prove victorious I will endeavour to recruit you, Matius. I have the funds to pay you well and I also have scope to grant you a senior position. Although my army has recently expanded I am in need of experienced officers to command the legions."

"And what if Hirtius proves victorious? Would you then disband your army?" the centurion asked. He raised his black eyebrow in scepticism as if already doubting the honesty of Brutus' prospective reply.

"I would, providing I was confident Rome was secure and protected."

And who is going to protect Rome from you? "I'm unsure at the moment as to when I'll be coming back this way."

"Rome needs you, Matius. You served under Antony did you not? You also served with his lieutenant, Domitius Enobarbus. You are familiar with the enemy's strengths and weaknesses. Although I warrant that Antony's weaknesses can be summed up in two words – wine and women."

"Antony might argue that they are the source of his strength and motivation," Matius replied. Brutus was unsure if the dry-witted soldier was joking or not.

"I have a brief meeting to attend to, any moment now. But please let me say goodbye in earnest to you afterwards."

The centurion looked a little uncomfortable, as if he had his own business to attend to but couldn't reveal what it was, but nevertheless nodded. Matius decided to wait outside, on the balcony, before saying goodbye to his friend.

Clouds blotted out the stars. A chill wind numbed his features but the soldier had suffered far harsher weather over the years. A wistfulness shaped his heart and expression as Matius gazed out across the void. The darkness consumed all.

He's changed. But do we not all change? He's proved that there is a little Caesar in us all in terms of pride, ambition and conceit... Unfortunately the blood on your hands from Julius' death was just the start. You're ankle deep in it now. Soon you will be knee deep in it. And eventually you'll be covered in blood, head to toe, like Coriolanus – a hero and villain in equal measure, like Caesar.

Cinna entered the room with a wide smile on his still made-up face. Brutus wondered whether the grin stemmed from his natural disposition or from the fact that he was about to be paid. He was flanked by two of his stagehands. They didn't necessarily have the air of men who were lovers of the theatre or Brutus' cause. They were rough-hewn. Stubble dusted the faces of both men. Both had flat, broken noses. Both possessed pot-bellies but were still powerfully built. They looked more like soldiers than stagehands. The man on Cinna's left, Strabo, had a star-shaped scar on his cheek. He closed the door behind him. The man to his right, Menas, smiled amiably, revealing a set of chipped front teeth as he approached his host.

"I suppose you will want paying, Cinna," Brutus remarked, half hoping that the actor would be happy with the reward of having performed for him.

Cinna continued to smile and then nodded to Menas, who stood next to the general. The brawny ex-soldier moved quickly for his size, positioning himself behind Brutus and restraining him.

"This is villainy."

Confusion and indignation fuelled Brutus' tone before he was silenced by Menas placing his large hand over his mouth. His eyes were stapled wide in terror and hatred.

Cinna possessed an air of calm and authority about him. His smile widened, reptilian-like. The stagehand standing beside him similarly smirked. There was malice in his eyes and an ivory-handled dagger in his palm. Strabo had killed before and was looking forward to killing again.

"You will be paying a price today, Brutus, but not in gold. You will be paying for your treachery in murdering Caesar," Cinna announced, with a sneer, as he walked over towards the general's desk and picked up the dagger which Brutus had used to assassinate Caesar. His host had proudly shown him the weapon whilst on a tour of the house earlier.

Whilst a young actor and playwright Caesar had recruited Cinna as an agent in Rome. Cinna had seduced patrons and their wives – and pillow talk bred indiscretion. Knowledge is power. Due to his

214

loyalty to Caesar – and the handsome fees he paid – Cinna also occasionally served as an assassin. When Enobarbus offered the actor the opportunity to avenge Caesar – and to be paid for the deed – Cinna accepted.

"Enobarbus said that you would be keen to invite me to your house when you heard that I would be in the area. Your wife is a great lover of the theatre, although not so great an actress that she couldn't disguise her haughty disdain for us during parts of the performance. It seems you have kept this blade polished and sharpened as though you knew it would be used again at some point. I am a playwright, I am used to dealing with irony and poetic justice. Is it not ironic and just that you should be murdered with the same weapon with which you killed your enemy and friend?"

The smell of acetum on Menas' breath and the cheese on his hand made Brutus feel nauseated. What sickened him more though was the playwright's villainy and duplicity – and the fact that he had been so completely fooled. Brutus struggled in vain to free himself from his captor.

"You thought you were freeing Rome by murdering Caesar but really you were damning it. Antony will now bring order back to the capital. I may well receive the greatest applause of my career when people find out that I avenged Julius' death – and that the people will no longer have to suffer one of your long, pious speeches." Cinna laughed a little at his own joke. An actor wouldn't be an actor unless he enjoyed the sound of his own voice. "I may leave it to fate as to whether your wife survives the night or not. I have promised my men that they can take her jewellery. Should they be in her room when she wakes up then her fate will be sealed. Maybe I should allow them the use of this dagger on her, to cut open her dress first and then her heart. I could also instruct Strabo here to pluck out her eyes. At least then she will be unable to look down on everyone."

Again Cinna sniggered at his own witticism and again Brutus struggled to release himself from the stagehand's clutches. He was more worried for his wife than himself. He loved her. Brutus cursed the playwright but the words merely sounded like muffled moans. He also wanted to beg the assassin to punish him but not his wife. She should not suffer for his sins. He would give up all his wealth to save her. But Brutus recognised the look in his enemy's eyes; the agent would honour his promise to Enobarbus and Antony.

Cinna walked across the room purposefully. He looked his victim up and down, wondering upon which part of his body to plunge the dagger into. He was tempted to strike his enemy twenty-three times so as to match the number of stab wounds Caesar had endured. But the agent wanted a clean kill. The staff would find their master's corpse in the morning, by which time he would have made his escape.

Cinna had nothing more to say. But Matius Varro did.

"Not content with murdering a play by Terence, you now want to murder your host. Even a dog, or a Gaul, has better manners than that," the centurion remarked as he came in from outside.

Alarm struck Cinna's face at seeing the soldier, but then he relaxed once he realised the centurion was alone. His men had easily bested legionaries – and centurions – before.

"There are heroes in drama my friend but in the real world there are only villains."

Cinna nodded his head at Strabo. The stagehand sheathed his dagger and then drew out a sword strapped to his thigh, concealed beneath his long-skirted grey tunic. Matius Varro drew his gladius in reply. Strabo was confident that he could best his opponent. In his experience most senior officers in the army knew plenty about fencing but little about real combat. But for all of the centurion's reading of philosophy and literature Tiro Casca, the veteran legionary, had tutored him in fighting – and winning – ugly.

Matius scooped up the marble bust of Diogenes from the table and launched it at the advancing assailant. Strabo lifted his hand to defend his head and the bust struck his forearm. The bone cracked. The stagehand let out a howl. Strabo lost his momentum and it was the soldier's turn to attack. The stagehand swung his sword wildly to try and drive the centurion back. Matius ducked under the blade but rather than retreating the officer stabbed his gladius downwards and impaled it into his opponent's foot. The howl was this time cut short from the centurion slicing the tip of his blade across his enemy's throat.

Menas slightly lessened his grip on Brutus, distracted as he was by the fate of his friend. Brutus used the distraction to his advantage. He lowered and then whipped his head back quickly, smashing it into the stagehand's face. His nose broke (again) and the blow knocked out one of the assassin's chipped front teeth. Brutus broke free. His anger eclipsed the pain he felt on the back of his head. Menas also shook off the impact of the attack. He roared and raised his dagger but as he did so the general grabbed the nearest weapon to hand – a bronze poker – and stabbed his opponent through the stomach.

Horace had been reading in the library, along the corridor from his general's study, when he first heard Strabo scream in pain. The adjutant instinctively put down the scroll he was reading, drew his dagger and ran towards the sound.

Cinna seethed at the turn of events. His instinct was to flee rather than fight. But the pale-faced adjutant stood in his way by the door. Ironically Horace had been the one person in the household the assassin had been willing to spare that night, when planning his attack. But not now. Horace appeared stunned, with either fear or confusion, as he faced the dagger-wielding playwright. Cinna was less indecisive however. He thrust his arm forward. The urbane actor bared his teeth in a savage snarl as he did so. Horace was unable to parry the attack – but fortunately he didn't have to. Matius, recognising the peril his young friend was in, threw his sword across the room and brought down the agent. No matter how many times the actor had been killed on stage it seemed to come as a shock to Cinna that he could die in real life.

Epilogue

It was as if he had been stabbed. Agrippa told Octavius that Cicero had said he would use and then dispose of him. The two men spoke in the garden of a house in Mutina, the day after the battle. The garden – with its manicured lawn, dazzling flowerbeds and murmuring fountain – was a world away from the charnel house of the previous day's fighting. Exhaustion and grief had tempered any sense of triumph. The surgeon, Glyco, had endeavoured to save Pansa but to no avail. Hirtius had also died during the fighting. The general had wanted to prove that he was as courageous as Caesar. Octavius immediately gave due praise to his co-commanders, although he mentioned in private that both men had died before they had a chance to turn on him.

Despite Octavius' fortitude Agrippa knew more than anyone how much the news concerning Cicero would hurt his friend. But Agrippa felt he had a duty to tell him – as much as he asked that he be allowed to keep his source for the information secret.

"I wish I could say that I'm surprised. But Caesar must be Caesar, and Cicero must be Cicero," Octavius remarked, his expression half shaded beneath his sunhat. His tone remained wilfully neutral but resentment and remorse churned his stomach. He felt sick. Octavius' faith was shaken in himself as well as in the philosopher. There was a hole in his soul where Cicero, or virtue, once resided.

If my mentor is willing to betray me then my enemies will doubtless do so as well. But standing armies have more power than sitting senators.

"The Senate will order you to hand over command of the legions to Decimus Brutus. Reports have been confirmed that Decimus is pursuing Antony across the Alps. I suspect that Antony intends to join up with Lepidus in Hispania."

"The Senate will have more chance of ordering me to hand over the Golden Fleece. I will use and then dispose of them. When will they learn that Rome was not created for the good of the Senate but that the Senate was created for the good of Rome? Let Decimus pursue Antony. We shall neither aid nor hinder him. Our priority should be to further bind the legions to us. We must honour the dead, tend to the wounded and pay any bonuses. With just a handful of legions I was able to demand the rank of praetor. With the eight I now command I can be consul."

During the afternoon Octavius visited the legions. Many banged their shields and called out his name, "Caesar, Caesar..." This time Octavius knew that they were honouring him as opposed to his great-uncle. He smiled, thanked the soldiers for their service and waved his hand. An outward show of gratitude and triumph masked a deeper sorrow however.

Caesar would be proud of me. But Cleanthes wouldn't.

He had won a great battle and saved the Republic. On a personal level he had proven his mettle too. Yet in the cold light of day Octavius realised how reckless he had been, riding into the fray with little thought for his own security. He experienced a rush of blood either to save or avenge Oppius. But he would have ice in his veins from now on. He had little desire to see a field of battle again and witness the aftermath of a sea of corpses. His bath had taken twice as long the previous night as his servants looked to wash all the grime and blood from his body. Others could fight his battles for him. It was safer and they were more qualified to do so.

There is little glory and honour in being struck down by a stray arrow or being trampled to death by a horse.

When Octavius had a window of time later that evening he began to write a series of letters to a number of families of the fallen. Not only was it the honourable thing to do but it was an effective way of maintaining support. Caesar had composed similar letters of condolence out of both sympathy and self-interest. Octavius also wrote letters to his mother and sister. He was tempted to write a letter to Livia too. He closed his eyes and pictured her smile, heard her laugh and breathed in her expensive perfume. They had stolen glances through crowded rooms. Despite or because of the number of lovers he took Octavius couldn't stop thinking about her.

Does she think about me too?

*

Brutus slept surprisingly well after the attempt on his life. He slept in the arms of his wife. He told Porcia that he loved her. He apologised for his behaviour towards her and Porcia even apologised to him in return. The general realised his wife was a source of strength to him, not weakness.

The following day Brutus tried one last time to petition Matius Varro to stay. They spoke in the general's study. The servants had just finished scrubbing the blood from the walls and tiled floor.

"Can your mission not wait?"

"It has waited too long already in some respects. Every day which passes, having not done my duty, is a day wasted – one that gnaws at my soul. I have not altogether been honest with you, Marcus. I am travelling east not in the name of Rome but for my own selfish purpose. Many years ago my father, who served as a diplomat, was sent to Egypt to gauge the character and intentions of Ptolemy XIII. The civil war was still in the balance then, before Caesar tipped the scales in Cleopatra's favour. Both my mother and father were murdered, however, before they reached Alexandria. But I have recently found out who killed them. A man named Apollodorus, a Sicilian. He now serves as a bodyguard to the Egyptian queen. I must kill him. It's the only way I will find peace and lift the

221

burden," the determined centurion declared, although he felt the burden lift slightly for having told his friend the truth.

"Your intentions are noble, Matius. But let me now make an argument for my selfish purpose as well as for Rome. As much as you have a cause, how much of a plan do you have to see your cause through? How will you get close to the queen and Apollodorus? How can you be assured of success, especially as you will be acting alone? A sense of duty and vengeance have not clouded your judgement so much that you will disregard logic, I hope. To travel so far and come so close – and then to fail – will further the tragedy of the death of your parents. I owe you my life, Matius, and I am in no position to ask anything of you. But grant me two years of service and your cause will become my cause. Cleopatra herself will not be able to deny you your revenge."

Matius Varro stared ahead of him, a picture of solemnity – seemingly unmoved either way after having heard Brutus' offer. He noticed the bust of Diogenes – its nose and cheek chipped from being thrown across the room the previous night. The scholarly officer thought about Alexander the Great's encounter with the philosopher. Alexander had granted Diogenes any wish. Diogenes, lying in the sun at the time, merely asked Alexander if he could get out of his light. Matius thought how, if Alexander could have granted him any wish, he would have asked for the opportunity to kill Apollodorus. In some ways Brutus was now granting him his wish. The fires of revenge can consume all, stripping away everything else from a man's existence. His father would have wanted him to avenge his death but not at the expense of his entire life.

I must kill him – in two years from now.

Brutus promised the centurion a senior rank and enough gold for Matius to buy his own army to defeat Apollodorus.

"If nothing else Horace will be pleased that you'll be on staff. He will need a drinking companion now that I've promised Porcia I'm giving up the late nights," Brutus said to his friend.

Matius smiled to himself. *People can change.*

*

Tiro had woken his master despite the late hour. The news was important. The messenger had ridden non-stop, changing horses several times, so that Cicero could be one of the first to know about the outcome of the battle. Knowledge is power. The secretary had entered the statesman's bedroom. Wax tablets littered the bed. Tiro wasn't quite sure if the musty smell filling his nostrils emanated from the room or the man. He lit a brace of oil lamps and woke the proconsul.

Cicero sat up in bed. His joints ached in other seasons as well as winter now. He squinted as his eyes adjusted to the light. He then squinted in disbelief as he took in the words of the message. Some of the news was good, some of it unwelcome and some of it unexpected.

The wax tablet felt as heavy in his hands as a tombstone. Hirtius and Pansa were dead. *Where there is life there is despair.* His agent mentioned that Glyco, Pansa's physician, was being detained on suspicion of poisoning the consul. Octavius was the prime candidate for ordering the physician to assassinate Pansa. But Cicero knew the character of Glyco and he would prove innocent in being involved in any conspiracy. Would he let an innocent man be executed though, if it meant Octavius could be found guilty – and eliminated?

Cicero handed the tablet to Tiro, who read over the message with speed and care.

Antony had thankfully been defeated. The Republic was saved. Decimus Brutus was pursuing the enemy of the state over the Alps. "Hopefully Decimus knows to bring Antony back in a coffin rather than chains," Cicero commented. But victory had come at a price. The young Caesar was now in sole command of a great army.

"I must write to Octavius immediately. We should praise and honour him – whilst at the same time relieving him of his rank and legions. Give with one hand and take with the other. We must act quickly before he gets any ideas into his head – or Balbus puts them there. Octavius will listen to me. He will not want to disappoint me. And I am doing this, believe it or not, to save his soul as well as the Republic. I still have a part to play, before I leave the stage, Tiro."

The secretary nodded in agreement whilst believing that Octavius was now the lead actor in the drama being played out. The youth had accumulated more power within just one year than others had accumulated over a lifetime. *It seems that Octavius has inherited Caesar's divine luck as well as his name.*

Tiro instructed a servant to provide Cicero with a cup of barley water and some cereal with honey. He then left the statesman to his stratagems and correspondence. Tiro was tempted to wake Caecilia and tell her the latest news from the north. She had taken an uncommon interest in military matters of late.

*

The terrain was as unwelcome as some of the grim expressions on the retreating soldiers' faces. Although huddled around campfires men still shivered, some in terror, at reliving the gruesome battle. The remnants of Antony's army had, with leaden steps, trudged through the snow and mountain passes. There were equally as many upwards and downwards slopes but their legs felt like they had to endure more of the former. Some died from their wounds. Some died from fatigue. Progress was slow but steady. Food was hard to come by but no one would thankfully starve to death – yet. But no matter what they ate the bitter taste of defeat spoiled their appetites.

Most of the men remained loyal to their commander and only complained beneath their foggy breath. Antony had led by example after the battle and offered his horses to the wounded – ordering his cavalry officers to do so too.

The first time the general had smiled, since the defeat, had been when he had seen his lieutenant at the rendezvous point. Enobarbus was wounded but alive, having escaped from the camp before Decimus' forces could overrun it.

The two old friends had sat around a fire. Logs crackled and cinders, like petals, swirled upwards into the night. Antony had donated the remainder of his vintages to his men. He had drunk acetum before and he would doubtless do so again.

"It was a near run thing, Domitius," Antony ruefully remarked, staring into his half-empty wine cup, dwelling upon again how close he had come to securing a great victory.

Enobarbus wryly smiled to himself, recalling how he had overheard a legionary say the same thing but in relation to how close he had believed Antony's forces had come to being completely wiped out. The lieutenant, despite private criticisms of his leadership, still had faith in his commander.

"Have you sent a message ahead to Lepidus, so he can prepare for our arrival?"

"Aye," Antony replied, still undecided as to whether he should beg or bully the general into furnishing him with the legions under his command.

"And what about Fulvia? Have you been able send off a message to her too?"

"I dare not tell her where I'll be just in case the harpy decides to join me," Antony said.

Enobarbus looked at his general by the light of the writhing fire. His beard was no longer trimmed. His once chiselled features appeared sunken. His armour was battered and besmirched. Antony had not so long ago looked like a marble statue of a demigod. But cracks were now appearing in the stone.

"Maybe it wouldn't be so bad if the harpy did join us. In befouling our food she may improve the flavour."

Both soldiers let out a small laugh. Enobarbus winced in pain slightly as he did so, from the wound in his leg.

"How's the injury?"

"I've suffered worse. Thankfully the cold is helping to numb the pain."

"You will recover, my friend, as we will recover. I will rebuild our army, as much as for those brave souls out there as for myself. All is not lost," Antony declared and gripped his sword.

"Let us hope that Cinna has succeeded in his mission."

"Aye. It is a shame that Cassius isn't a lover of the theatre, as much as the snake is inclined to put on an act for people. Cinna could have ensnared him also. But sooner or later we will see the heads of Brutus and Cassius liberated from their necks. The whelp too shall suffer. His luck will run out, as will his money. There's still everything to play for. We may have lost the battle, Domitius, but we have not lost the war."

*

The dead of night.

More than he had ever craved a drink, more than he wanted to win the archery tournament or even have sex – Agrippa just wanted to see Caecilia's smiling face again. He pictured how her silken hair hung down and framed her elated features as she straddled him whilst making love. He wanted to hear her voice as she hummed in pleasure whilst kissing him or recited passages of Thucydides. He gazed up at the clear night sky. Cleopatra, Fulvia and Servilia combined did not possess the diamonds equal to the celestial scene above as stars beamed upon an expansive sea of black silk. He wondered if Caecilia was staring up at the same sight. *I'll wait for you and I hope if I fall behind you will wait for me.*

Agrippa was exhausted yet still unable to sleep. He sat out on the balcony, flanked by two glowing braziers. Plumes of smoke spiralled upwards across the city. Bakeries and taverns were open once more. He heard the sound of distant celebrations as the recently besieged town enjoyed the taste of freedom and wine. The inhabitants gave thanks to Caesar as much as to Decimus Brutus.

It was as much a time of grief as triumphalism though for the young soldier. He felt little pride in inheriting the title of the best archer in the legion.

Already he missed the Briton.

"Teucer would have regretted not being here, now that the brothels are open again," Aulus Milo had mentioned to Agrippa. "We had a bet. I said that he wouldn't be able to bed all the women in one whorehouse between dusk and dawn. Teucer replied that it was a bet he would happily accept – win, lose or draw."

Agrippa was distracted by the sound of footsteps behind him. Octavius had been unable to fall asleep either. He thought about the savagery of the battle and the vomit inducing smell of corpses. But more than anything else thoughts of Cicero – and his betrayal – disturbed Octavius' peace. There are some wounds and scars which remain unseen. *I thought you were different, better, than the rest. You tried to raise the Senate up but ultimately it dragged you down to its level.* His friend had become another enemy. In cutting Cicero out of his life, a little piece of him had died.

But enough blood has been spilled. Cicero will lose my ear. I do not want him to lose his life. But I will not put my faith in him – or anyone else – again. I will also never give away my heart. But how can you give away something which doesn't exist?

Ice – and bitterness – ran through his veins. His soul was as bright and cold as a diamond or a star in the sky.

227

"Evening. I will soon be saying 'Good morning' I imagine," Octavius said, as he grabbed a chair and sat next to his friend. "Remember when we used to stay up late into the night and talk about the future? Neither of us came close to guessing what would occur."

"I blame the copious amounts of wine we drunk. It dulled our wits and imaginations. I also remember how Salvidienus used to join us occasionally. He would gabber on about becoming an aedile. I must make sure to write and tell him how you're about to become a consul," Agrippa replied, thinking how he would write another letter to Caecilia first.

"A lot has happened in the past year, since those days in Apollonia. As far as we've come though, Marcus, we still have far to travel. But I couldn't ask for a better travelling companion. You've learned your trade as a soldier it seems. I now need you to learn your trade as a general. It's you and me against the rest of the world."

"I can live with those odds. But let's take on the rest of the world in the morning. Tonight we should toast fallen comrades."

"Aye," Lucius Oppius said, appearing out of nowhere like a ghost. Grief and determination infused his heart. The centurion came out onto the balcony carrying a large jug of Massic and three cups. He gave the first to Agrippa, the man whose sharpened iron arrowhead had punctured the lung of Vedius, just before the navvy-turned-legionary had tried to stab the veteran soldier.

Although Octavius duly honoured Teucer and Cephas Pollux there was a streak of selfishness in him, or pragmatism as he called it, which meant that half his thoughts were focused on his own concerns. He recalled a scene from the previous morning, whilst Joseph shaved him. Octavius asked what Caesar had done, after winning a great battle.

The aged Jew had lowered his razor. There had been a fleeting moment of indecision in his expression as he toyed with lying to his new master. But his shoulders dropped, he sighed and told the truth.

"He started planning for the next one."

As Octavius raised his cup to his fallen friends he looked up at the glittering night sky. Had Caesar's soul ascended to the heavens and been marked by a star?

My star will burn brighter.

End Note

Augustus: Son of Caesar is a work of fiction. Although inspired and informed by history I have, in many instances, made stuff up. The keen historians among you will have noticed how I conflated Cicero's *Philippics* into just one key speech. Similarly, I merged the two battles which decided the outcome at Mutina into one. I will leave it to the reader to unpick and separate the rest of the fact from the fiction.

I recommended a number of books and authors in the end note of *Augustus: Son of Rome*, should you be interested in reading more on the period and its leading figures. Since the publication of that book a couple of notable titles have also been released, Adrian Goldsworthy's biography of Augustus (which is the best biography of I have read in regards to the second half of his life) and Lindsay Powell's biography of Marcus Agrippa.

Thank you for all your support and emails. They're much appreciated. Please do get in touch if you have enjoyed *Augustus: Son of Caesar* (as well as the *Sword of Rome* and *Sword of Empire* books). I can be reached on twitter @rforemanauthor and via richardforemanauthor.com

Octavius and Agrippa will return.
Richard Foreman.

23626686R00141

Made in the USA
San Bernardino, CA
28 January 2019